VOLUME 2 | 2021

MONKEY

T0166616

EDITORS
Ted Goossen
Motoyuki Shibata

MANAGING EDITOR
Meg Taylor

CONTRIBUTING EDITOR
Roland Kelts

MARKETING MANAGER
Tiff Ferentini

ART DIRECTION & DESIGN
The Office of Gilbert Li

DIGITAL PRODUCTION
Bookmobile

WEBSITE
Kaori Drome

COVER
© Taiyō Matsumoto

INSIDE FRONT COVER
Map of Kyoto (1863)
by Kahei Takebara

© MONKEY New Writing from Japan
2021, Volume 2
All Rights Reserved

ISSN: 2693-9126 (print)
ISSN: 2693-9134 (ebook)
ISBN: 978-0-9972480-8-1
ISBN: 978-4-88418-568-8 (Japan)

Published annually by
MONKEY New Writing from Japan,
a nonprofit corporation.

MONKEY New Writing from Japan
422 East End Ave.
Pittsburgh, PA 15221 USA

Distributed by Consortium in the U.S.
and Kinokuniya in Japan.

Printed in Japan by Shinano.

MONKEY New Writing from Japan
benefits from close collaboration with
MONKEY, a Japanese literary journal
published by Switch Publishing.

We gratefully acknowledge the
generous support of Tadashi Yanai.

Subscribe, shop online, and
sign up for our newsletter at
monkeymagazine.org

THE MONKEY SPEAKS

Japanese literature is on a roll. Four of the *New York Times* 100 Notable Books of 2020 were novels from Japan, while two of *Time* magazine's 10 Best Fiction Books of 2020 were written (and translated) by *MONKEY* regulars: Mieko Kawakami's *Breasts and Eggs* (David Boyd and Sam Bett) and Aoko Matsuda's *Where the Wild Ladies Are* (Polly Barton). So now the secret is out, and our authors and translators are getting the attention they deserve.

In this issue, you'll find a selection of Japan's new writing, by both household names and newcomers, with some modern classics and contributions from our friends in English-speaking countries. We are excited to welcome the translator Morgan Giles, and also the indomitable Rose Bundy, who entrusted us with one of her fine translations of Yūko Tsushima before she passed away earlier this year.

The 2021 volume of *MONKEY New Writing from Japan* celebrates travel in "A Monkey's Dozen." Since the pandemic began, physical travel has become something we remember, not something we actually do. We may "Zoom" with our colleagues and friends, but we cannot share a meal with them, nor can we set out to experience new landscapes and the pleasures and vicissitudes of life on the road. Instead, we travel within our imaginations. It is our hope that the stories, essays, poems, and artwork in this travel issue will transport you to curious, hilarious, and moving places, where you will be intro-duced to people you have never met before—from a small band of Buddhist pilgrims who set off by ship for the holy sites of ancient India to the crowds that, even today, are drawn to the "thorn-pulling" Jizō of Sugamo in Tokyo.

To all our readers, we say: Happy Travels!

Ted Goossen
Motoyuki Shibata
Meg Taylor

VOLUME 2 | 2021

MONKEY

Travel: A Monkey's Dozen

Amabie is a mermaid-like spirit
who protects against pandemics
© 2021 Asako Tabata

Hiromi Kawakami

Sea Horse

translated by Ted Goossen

IT HAS BEEN AGES since I left the sea.

Now I live in Tokyo, on the fringes of Setagaya. In front of the train station are two rundown video rental stores, and beside them an old tofu store and a pastry shop selling cakes and, as of five years ago, fresh-baked bread. Across the tracks, a supermarket. Its doors stay open until 10 pm. A local market used to be there, but it was torn down some years ago and the supermarket put in its place.

My husband is a transport company executive. His office is in downtown Tokyo. The company's headquarters are in Hiroshima. He always comes home late.

How long has it been since I was handed over to my current husband? Thirty years? I can't remember exactly.

We have four children.

The oldest boy has a job in Aichi, doing computer-related work. The next two are twins: one lives in a university dormitory in Tohoku while the other works at part-time jobs, crashing at his friends' homes or, sometimes, here. The fourth child, our only daughter, dropped out of high school and now works nights in one of those video stores (the one closer to the tracks).

The fourth child can't wake up in the morning. I took her to the hospital for a checkup, but all I got from the doctor was that she was suffering from orthostatic something or other. Is that the name of a disease, I asked? No, he said. My daughter and I trudged home carrying a mountain of vitamins and blood-strengthening medicines. Neither of us said a word.

This husband comes home late. The one before worked at home. He was a painter. I modeled for him a number of times. He saw something wild and untamed in my body, so he always made me pose naked. "Clothes don't suit you," he would say. "You put them to shame." As I recall, one of his portraits of me won some sort of prize. No one talks about him anymore, though. He is totally forgotten. He had been feeding me for about twenty years when he announced he had tired of me and handed me over to my current husband.

Apparently, the artist passed away not long after that. I can't read very well, and TV exhausts me, so I never learned exactly when or how. It was more than ten years later when, quite out of the blue, my current husband let it drop that he had died a long time ago. "Is that so?" I asked. "Yes," he answered. And that was that.

The husband before the artist was a university professor, and the one prior to that was a rich merchant who owned a lot of land. I have only a vague recollection of my husbands before the war. I think a tycoon of some sort and a viscount from some place or other are mixed in there somewhere, but I can't be certain.

So many husbands, yet until I was handed over to this one, only one child. It was born when I was with the merchant landowner, but it lived less than three years. I suppose half-human children don't have the staying power that others do. In fact, I regarded its survival to that point as a kind of miracle.

That baby's grave is there even now, in the cemetery at Zōshigaya. I go there occasionally to offer incense. After my daughter dropped out of school, she and I began visiting the grave from time to time during our outings. On the way back, we stop by a dessert cafe in Ikebukuro, where she orders *shiruko* sweet red bean soup and I have the *mitsumame* gelatin cubes in syrup. Then we catch the Yamanote Line to Shinjuku and transfer to the private railroad that takes us home.

TEMPTATION LURED ME from the sea.

It was night. The air was warm and carried the fullness of spring. I had raised myself half out the water to breathe it all in when another, more powerful aroma wafted from the shore.

I have but a dim image of my other husbands, but my memory of the first is as clear as can be.

The man had a strong odor. He was brimming with an inner fierceness. I could search the oceans, I thought, and never find another man like this one. That inner force moved throughout his body, heating his blood. His physical presence was compelling.

I swam to shore, leapt up on land and made a beeline for him. I couldn't hold back, not even for a second.

I rushed up to him. He looked a little surprised, but his hesitation quickly vanished.

We spent the next few months together. His home was a rough shack on the water. The winds sometimes blew the roof away, and when the waves were high the floor was swamped.

He was a fisherman, but he was better suited to trolling for women than trolling for fish. Even after my arrival he continued playing around. Sometimes he would bring a woman back to the shack. I would sit there in the dark and watch intently as they copulated.

When they had finished, the man would always chase the woman away. Not that any of them needed much encouragement. The man's reputation in the village was far from savory. As soon as the woman left, the man and I would waste no time setting to it ourselves. Warm breezes blew through the walls as the lapping tides slowly soaked the shack.

After six months of this, I was passed on to the boss of the village, the man the fishermen relied on. My own man was flat broke.

This new man gave off the fragrance of incense. His skin was very fair. I immediately tried to return to the sea, but to no avail. He placed a metal ring around my neck and linked it to a long chain bolted to a stake. I could move only as far as the chain allowed, which meant I couldn't leave the room.

The furnishings of the room were luxurious, the bedding always sheathed in fine silk. In the corner was a painted screen decorated with images of beautiful kimono, and tucked behind it a fancy ceramic chamber pot for me to use.

I was angry, though, and refused to squat over that thing. But every time I made a mess, my husband thrashed me. I howled bloody murder each time that happened. He may have smelled strangely sweet, and his skin may have been fair, but he was still awfully strong.

For years, I lived chained up like that. When I shed tears of longing for the sea, the waves rose in response. Violent storms increased, and young people moved away, so the village fell on hard times.

The fishermen's boss passed me on to my next husband. He lived in the mountains, far from the sea.

MY CURRENT HUSBAND says our fourth child is my spitting image.

She's a strapping young woman, that's for sure. Once, back when she was still in high school, she brought her classmates over to visit. They were all compactly built with skin darkened by the sun. They talked and laughed incessantly.

My daughter sat among them, quiet as a mouse. She seemed at a loss what to do with her body, so big and soft and white among all her tanned friends.

My first three children are all boys. Some resemble my husband, others don't. Not one of them looks like me. Only my daughter does.

The days when I would rail against my husbands, weeping and mourning my loss of the sea, ended decades ago. I came to feel almost completely human, especially after my children were born. It reached the point that, most of the time, I myself forgot that I was different.

Although my first child was sickly and died before the age of three, my four children with my current husband haven't been sick a day in their life. They may be half-human, but they developed very much like human children. In body and in character too, they leave a distinctly human impression.

There were signs, though, that the fourth child would turn out differently. She somehow stood out from the human crowd. It wasn't that noticeable when she was young, but as she got older it became more evident. By the time she started high school I could see how much her spirit diverged from that of the other students. It wasn't just that she was bigger; there was also something vast and boundless about her. While years and years of training had tamed my spirit, hers was like mine had once been. Looking at her, I felt as though my original self had been reborn.

It seems that my daughter was picking up boys at her job in the video rental shop. Or maybe she was the one being picked up. She would go to their rooms, but according to her they never had sex or even fooled around. Really? I asked. Then what do you do?

We just hang out, she replied. Playing games, watching videos, sending emails.

You play games?

Yeah, one of us plays while the other talks on the cellphone.

My fourth child told me all this in snatches, with stretches of silence sandwiched between. She doesn't volunteer much, but she'll answer when I ask. Her father finds it hard to deal with her, so he's stopped trying. He comes home later and later now that the other three kids aren't around so much.

Why don't you have sex? I asked her.

Because I don't feel like it.

Have you ever done it?

No.

You could give it a try.

I will eventually.

My fourth child almost never misses work at the video shop. Even on her off days, she's always willing to fill in for her colleagues if asked. The shop at night relaxes her, she says. It feels like the night sea.

I sometimes think back on the sea at night. It has been an eternity since I left.

MOST OF MY HUSBANDS have treated me well.

They have kept me well fed and clean in beautiful rooms, and decked me out in nice clothes. I am always at their beck and call, like a well-maintained car in their garage.

I wanted to return to the sea as soon as possible. That awful ring around my neck was eventually removed, yet the sea grew more and more distant as I was passed from husband to husband. To reach the coast, I would have had to change trains, and I didn't know how. I tried to escape a number of times, but I always failed. They quickly caught me and brought me back. Then they thrashed me. Once I had been cleaned up and beautifully clothed again, they abused me however they pleased.

As long as I didn't try to escape, each of them was kind to me. Yet behind that kindness was an absence of any real concern, as if they were dealing with a small animal. A chilliness.

Was it something in me—that part of me that humans lacked, perhaps—that made my husbands behave in such a way? After coming up on land, I tried so hard for so many years to fit in with my husbands, with people in general. Yet, in the end, I failed.

I came to accept my lot. As long as they treated me well, I was satisfied. My memories of the sea grew ever fainter. It was so remote. I hadn't laid my eyes on it in such a long time. It felt like forever.

There seems to be a verbal agreement that passes between my husbands each time I am handed from one to the next. This is the injunction: "Never let her near the ocean."

Yes, this is their motto. She who comes from the sea must be kept from the sea. Otherwise, she will return.

All my husbands have followed this dictum. Now I am living in the Setagaya neighborhood in Tokyo. I could reach the ocean, I suppose, if I changed trains several times. But I have already forgotten what it's like. And trying to remember that which one has forgotten is terribly painful. It's like searching for the eye of a tiny needle at the bottom of a deep hole, only worse.

I am not human. Yet now I live completely surrounded by human beings. Having children made it that way. I no longer weep for my beloved ocean. My current husband seems not to be taking the injunction too seriously. Our children have been to the sea on several occasions. My husband is the one who took them. I always stayed at home, the excuse being that I was under the weather. The first three children embraced the sea. Only the fourth refused to go near the water. According to my husband, she wouldn't budge an inch, stiffening her body and wailing, her face a bright red.

That fourth child has a name. I told her what it was on the occasion of her first period. It is not to be rashly spoken aloud. It can be used only when absolutely necessary.

My first child has no name. Neither does the second or the third. They have human names of course, but not real names. Only the fourth child's name was given to me. It threaded its way through the night sea and the chilly air to where I lay. I had just given birth.

My legs were still spread when they took the baby and placed it on my chest to be nursed. It took to the breast with great enthusiasm, though it had just come into the world. At first the milk just oozed, but the baby sucked so hard that before long it was gushing out. Thick, rich milk dribbled from the corners of the baby's mouth. One by one, the drops landed on my skin.

I have a real name too. None of my husbands has heard it. Not even the first. I have spoken it aloud only rarely, even back when I was living in the ocean, and to do that I had to swim to the farthest northern reaches where no one lives and whisper it behind the rocks on the seabed.

Drawn to my voice, the shrimp and starfish left their hiding places and swam to me. Transparent jellyfish leisurely wove their way through my long, trailing hair. Although I was living in the ocean, I had never really taken to it. I didn't mix much with those like me, but chose to roam the northern waters alone. I told no one my name, and no one told me theirs. On and on I swam through the frigid sea, silently mingling with its creatures.

My fourth child stands behind the counter of the video rental store, so large and pale and out of place. I sometimes walk down to the station at night just to get a glimpse of her. I don't go inside, but stand a bit away in a spot that affords a view of the brightly lit interior. A woman coming home from work passes through the station wicket and is sucked into the store. A young man on a bicycle emerges from the dark streets and is sucked in as well. My fourth child barely notices them passing before the counter, as if gazing over an interminable landscape.

I quietly call her name as I watch her from the darkness. Bathed in the fluorescent lights, she has no idea I am there. Their brightness makes her form blurry, indistinct. There in the cold light, she seems to be melting away.

After a while I head home. My husband isn't back yet. He seldom catches even the last train these days. Sometimes I am awakened by the closing of a taxi door, but by three in the morning, the hour of the Ox, I am fast asleep. A few hours later, my fourth child comes home after her shift. Our house is used to these late-night comings and goings. Small night creatures squeeze in through the tiny holes in the wall. Little by little, the trapped air of day escapes into the great outdoors through the cracks in the windows. In my bed, I sense past husbands riding the night air to reach me. They spin about me in circles, gather on the ceiling. When morning comes, they will go back to where they came from. In my dreams, I try to picture their faces. But they are all so vague. Like the firefly squid of the northern sea, they flash on and off, off and on, always eluding my grasp.

My own name is half-forgotten. It has been so very long since I tried to remember it.

I HAVE BEEN CLOSE TO THE SEA only once in all these years.

My husband at the time was a strange man. He was seldom home. Instead, he lived on the road, seeking out the heart of the mountains and the ends of the sea. Whatever he brought back he crammed into his house, his private citadel. Marble busts of women and men. Fabrics of all colors. Roots of trees. Stuffed animals, examples of the taxidermist's art. Rattan baskets with lids. Old leather-bound books. Atlases.

He was not at home when I was passed on to him. One month elapsed, then two, and still he had not appeared. I staved off starvation by drinking lots of tap water. When there is no food, I am quite able to subsist on water alone.

Then one day the taps went dry. Apparently, my husband hadn't paid his water bill. There was a river nearby, so I went out to soak in it. We were in a city, though, so it was encased in concrete and had wire fencing strung along its banks. I had to wait until night, when no one was around. I climbed over the fence, shed my clothes, and hopped in. The river was shallow. Water weeds longer than my hair twined about my arms and legs. Large wild carp poked my sides as I drank. The water tasted awful.

The river grew wider and deeper as I floated downstream. I passed schools of large and small carp. They stayed in a single place, while I was moving.

How long did I drift like this before I realized I was nearing the ocean? Several days, perhaps. I could smell it on the air, and I grew worried. No, a voice inside me was whispering. You shouldn't return to the ocean yet. It was autumn. Rows of soft clouds ranged high above me, a mackerel sky. As I floated along on my back, I thought no, the time to go back has not yet come. The ocean was tempting me, though. Just as my first husband had. My body was being pulled in its direction. But my heart stood opposed. This clash continued for some time.

Finally, I turned around and began to swim upstream.

Slowly at first, then more rapidly. Schools of small fish made way for me as my streamlined form cut through the water. It had been so long since I swam like that. My whole body rejoiced, from my fingertips to my flanks, my crotch to my toes. Now I was flying through the water, my hair streaming behind.

It was late at night when I arrived at my husband's home. I was lying there, my wet hair spread out on the floor, when he came back.

"Welcome home," I said.

"Is it you?" he said. "Can it really be you?" He dropped his big backpack on the floor and began fondling my body, exploring every part with his hands. I had just emerged from the water, so I was stark naked.

"You were trying to go back to the ocean, weren't you," he said. His fondling grew rougher. I knew his behavior was outrageous, but I let him do what he wanted. After all, I had been handed over to him.

He kept at me throughout the night, abusing my body as he pleased. I didn't feel anything. None of the elation I had experienced with my first husband remained, not a speck. When light returned to the sky and the red, overripe sun began to ooze over the horizon, he finally released me.

From then until he departed on his next trip, my husband rarely used me, and then only as if he had suddenly recalled my presence. Instead, I was left to lie unwanted like all the other objects he had collected on his travels.

I slept quietly among his sculptures. Those of women usually portrayed the upper half, those of men the lower.

When I opened my eyes, he was often seated at a desk in the middle of the room, either eating or smoking a cigarette, or jotting something down on manuscript paper. All I could see from where I lay was his back. It was thick and somehow desolate.

The night before he left on his next trip, he handed me over to my next husband. First, he stripped me naked and jammed me into a crate. Then, heedless of its weight, he hoisted the crate on his shoulder and carried me all the way to my new home. My body was twisted every which way, my limbs at all angles— I could barely breathe as I bounced along.

When we arrived at my new husband's home, my old husband threw the crate down on the floor of the entranceway. My hair popped out one end, my feet out the other. My new husband cried out in surprise. I had smelled the sea while in the crate. The odor came from my own body.

I crawled from the crate. I looked up at my former husband's face. It showed no emotion whatsoever. My new husband thanked him, and he left. I watched his thick back disappear down the road. It looked desolate somehow.

"A STORM IS COMING," my fourth child says.

"Even though it's winter?" I ask.

"It's a really big one," she says, shaking her head. "We've got to escape."

"Escape to where?"

"To the ocean."

Startled, I look at her face. Flames seem to be shooting from its center. There should be no flames, yet there they are. Her face is shining. At that moment I realize she is about to leave for good. The other three had left, but they still came back from time to time. This one wouldn't. I would never see her again.

"What will you do when you reach the ocean?" I ask.

"I don't know. But I'm half from the ocean anyway. Originally."

"There's nothing there," I say.

"There's nothing here on land either."

"There are men, aren't there?"

"Yeah, such as they are."

Such as they are. For many long years men have looked after me, passed me around, made me do their bidding. I want to tell all that to my daughter, but I doubt she will understand. Then why didn't you leave earlier? she'll ask. The fact you didn't leave means that you really didn't want to. What could I possibly say in my defense?

I tried to remember my first man. But I couldn't. Why have I spent so long so far from the sea? I thought of the husband with the desolate back who had jammed me into a crate and carried me off. Was he still scouring the ends of the earth in his search? Or had he died long ago?

That husband had lavished my body with endless caresses before he packed me in the crate. Each of my husbands seemed to have grown sad as time passed, regarding me with eyes of unquenchable longing. Once he had climaxed inside me, though, this one briskly crammed me in a box, deaf to my groans. I'll show you what real suffering is, he muttered as he jammed me further in.

Were any of them from the sea? Did any have true names?

A storm is on the way. Every night my fourth child says this.

WHEN THE STORM FINALLY HITS, it blacks out our whole neighborhood. Both video shops in front of the station close their shutters. The supermarket closes before its usual 10 pm too. I grab my umbrella and walk to pick up my fourth child at her workplace to take her home. The wind is strong—it is all I can do to hang on to the umbrella. The awning of the video shop is flapping madly. Eyes sparkling, my child is standing beneath the wet and darkened awning. She is drenched too.

I stop and look at her from a slight distance. Water is streaming from her large white body. She is laughing happily. As the rain pelts her, I can hear her peals of laughter.

"Are you leaving?" I ask her.

"You bet," she answers with a laugh.

"Don't go."

"I'm going."

"But there's nothing good about the ocean."

"You needn't worry about me."

Still laughing, she runs out into the rain. I stand and watch her, still from a distance. My child is leaving me. My eyes see nothing but her. Her back is growing smaller. The way she runs is strange—she seems to be dancing, yet there is something uncertain in her stride. When she reaches the river beyond the tracks she leaps in headfirst, not bothering to remove her clothes. The river is a torrent in the storm.

I see her head sink beneath the surface, then rise again. I am rooted to the spot as she drifts away with the current. I try calling her back, but my voice is lost in the wind. I can't even hear it myself.

Soon she is out of sight. I call her by her true name. I can feel a trace of her return. It timidly joins me under my umbrella. For a second, her warmth envelops me. Then she is gone. I weep.

The blackout lasts all night. My husband doesn't come home. I lie on our bed thinking of the fish that live in the sand at the bottom of the ocean, imagining their almost imperceptible movements.

"The sea?" my husband says.

"Take me there," I ask him.

"What will you do there?"

"Return. I want to return."

"So, the time has come, then."

My husband puts me in the car, and we set off for the sea. A gale is blowing. It has been blowing nonstop since the night my fourth child left. We drive from Setagaya to Tamagawa Avenue, then get on the Metropolitan Expressway. The wind pounds the side of the car, making it shake. When we reach the Tomei Highway the traffic suddenly gets heavier.

At Atsugi, we exit the expressway and take a road through the mountains to Ōiso.

"You seem to know the way," I say to my husband. He nods.

"I come here sometimes," he says.

"Why?"

"To look at the ocean," he says. Sadness is written on his face. He too is yearning for something.

The wind is getting stronger and stronger. Not a soul can be seen on the beach at Ōiso. The fishing boats are moored out on the water. The sky is leaden. A dull light stretches out from the horizon.

"Are you alright with me going back?" I ask my husband.

"That which comes from the ocean must return to the ocean," he answers. "Keeping you here has been exhausting for all of us," he continues. "Go ahead—I won't try to stop you."

Hearing those words makes me weak in the knees. I have forgotten the sea for so long. Indeed, I am hard put to recall my true name.

The trees on the other side of the road are whipping back and forth in the wind. The sign for a fishermen's lodge comes crashing to the ground. I put my foot in the water, my body shaking. The image of my fourth child's form melting under the video shop's fluorescent lights comes back to me with perfect clarity. I can feel the water soaking my shoes. Where in the ocean would my child be by now?

Quietly, I step out further. A few steps away from shore. Now the water reaches my thighs.

I can hear the shoreline murmuring loudly. All sorts of things are being blown about in the wind. Hundreds of winged insects are plastered to my body.

Now the water is up to my neck. Is my husband still watching me from the beach?

I look back, but the waves block my view. My clothes have melted away at some point, and a pelt of jet-black hair is beginning to cover my body. The smell of the sea envelops me. I can feel my forelegs and my hindlegs sprouting muscles and my torso thickening. My neck is growing longer; a thick mane of hair sprouts from my head.

I am a sea horse once again, swimming the seas. I pass the moored fishing boats and race toward the horizon, gaining momentum as I go. Days and nights pass as I speed along. When I reach the northern reaches of the ocean, I can picture my fourth child swimming ahead. Her laughter rings in my ears. On and on I run. To that point in the ocean where day and night come to an end. 🐵

© Scott Waters

Tomoka Shibasaki

———————

A woman hears
an announcement
on the radio that war
has broken out,
relatives arrive at her
house seeking refuge,
when the war ends
they leave, then a civil
war breaks out

translated by Polly Barton

THE WOMAN HEARD the announcement on the radio that war had broken out. Since the beginning of the year, there had been talk that things might come to this, yet the declaration still seemed to arrive out of the blue.

The woman's house was not far from the border, but it lay midway along a mountain road that ran between one town and the next. When she heard the announcement she was alone, and her surroundings perfectly tranquil. The sun continued to shine on the trees that were just coming into bud and the birds continued their chirping, just as they had before the announcement. The day was warm and balmy.

Six months later some of the woman's relatives, who had been living in the city, showed up at her door, seeking refuge. The city was subject to the occasional air raid. The area where they lived was still untouched, the wife of the family explained feverishly, but they'd decided to leave when there was bombing in the area around the factory where she worked. The children, perturbed by the sudden change in surroundings, sat quietly in a corner of the room. The wife explained that her husband had been sent to a military base near the front line, where he would work not as a soldier but as some kind of communications technician. He was the woman's uncle, but she hadn't seen him since somebody's funeral over ten years ago.

It was the first time the woman had met her uncle's wife, who turned out to be a friendly, talkative type. The woman preferred spending time alone, and at first found the distance between herself and the wife hard to navigate. But the two women were similar in age, and after a couple of weeks they began conversing casually about the things going on around them, just like school friends.

At the beginning of the war, their country had an overwhelming advantage over the other country, and both the government and the news channels expressed their certainty that it would be over in a matter of months. The people in town, too, echoed this sentiment. Everybody, the woman and the wife included, thought the same, although deep down they likely knew that this was no more than wishful thinking.

After a year had passed, the price of groceries and other everyday items began to increase, and their availability dropped off. The woman grew vegetables on the land around her house, so the situation wasn't desperate, but an acquaintance who had been providing her with milk began showing reluctance to continue. The woman's relative was earning a little money from helping out on a nearby farm. By that point communication from her husband had grown patchy. The children were still too young for school, but perhaps understanding the significance of the adults' grave and tired demeanor, they occupied themselves quietly in the corners of the house and the garden.

When the woman's relatives had been in her house for exactly two years, the city was devastated by bombs. The extent of the damage was even worse than was reported on the radio and in the newspapers, and they heard from people in the city that there were virtually no buildings left standing. The base where her husband was working had also been hit, the wife said without altering her expression. The wife had had no contact from her husband since a letter informing her that he'd been moved to a different base on a remote island, but neither had she received an announcement that he'd been injured or died.

At one point, the enemy troops came as far as the neighboring town. The woman was at home at the time, and the children were also safe at the school they'd just begun attending, but the wife had gone to the town to deliver produce from the farm and didn't come home. They heard the sound of shells echoing, and as night came, a number of planes skimmed low through the sky overhead. A faint haze of smoke drifted through the air, and there was a horrible smell. In the direction of the town, the sky was a blazing red.

It was two days later that the wife returned. She'd lost the duffel bag she'd been carrying, and there were bruises and cuts on her face and legs, but she didn't mention what had happened in the town. Nor did she say anything about where she'd been and what she'd seen.

Yet in the end, that was as far as the enemy invasion progressed. They had extended the front line so far that it had impeded the chains of supply and command, said the owner of the farm where the woman's relative had been working. After a while, it was announced that the situation had turned against the enemy.

When the war came to an end a year later, nothing at all remained of the city where the family had been living. The houses, the city hall, the schools, the libraries, the churches—the air raids had left them all in ruins.

It's just the roads that are left, the wife said, after waiting until spring to go and see the state of the city. Only the shapes and the names of the roads are the same as before. Only them.

In the summer, just as the wife had decided to carry on living with her children in the woman's house, her husband came to find her. He had lost a lot of weight, and his face had aged so much that he looked like a different person. He'd sustained a serious injury and been sent to hospital, where he'd caught an infectious disease. For a long time it had been unclear if he'd pull through. Someone had recommended him for a job as a technician in a factory in a port town, he said, where they could now live as a family. For a week after his arrival, the man also lived in the woman's house, eating fruit and vegetables grown locally, and after he'd been restored to life somewhat, the family moved to the port town.

From then on, come the summer, the wife would bring her children and visit the woman's house. Both the wife and the children were delighted that they now had somewhere to spend the summer, and every year the woman looked forward to the season when her relatives would come. The man's work was going well, the woman said. It seemed as though things had finally settled down.

Ten years later, a coup d'état led to a change in the political system, and the country was plunged into civil war. Anti-government forces began appearing close by the woman's house, and she secured the help of people that she knew to move to a country on another continent. In the news she read and saw on TV, it seemed the situation in her home country was only getting worse. She heard from her relatives now living in the port town that they were also thinking of leaving. By that point, the region where the woman had been living was occupied by anti-government forces.

The woman's relatives moved to a different country. They couldn't speak the language there, but it was a small developing nation, and the man had found a good job, said the last letter that the woman received from the wife.

It took almost ten years before the situation in their native country stabilized. Neither the woman nor the wife had any idea what was happening in each other's lives. It was another few years before the woman managed to return to her country. She now had no relatives left there, and stayed only a few days, just to see her native country one last time.

The ship arrived in the port town where her relatives had lived right after the war. The country was now reliant on the financial support of a larger nation, and the port town, which had once been old and shabby, now boasted an amusement park and various tourist facilities. The woman searched for the name of the street on which her relatives had lived, and eventually found what she thought was the place. It had become an entertainment district for tourists, with most of the old buildings now converted into hotels. The woman remembered the wife's words at the time of the first war: *Only the shapes and the names of the roads are the same.* She decided then and there not to go to the valley where she'd lived.

Looking out at the sea from the boat on the way home, the woman thought about the summers when the wife and her children had come to visit—those peaceful, bright summers.

In a country far off across that sea lived the wife and her children. Shortly after arriving there, her husband had died from the aftereffects of the disease he'd contracted during the war. Her children were both married, and had three children between them. The wife was soon to give up her job at the garment factory, where she had worked for many years, and move in with her elder son's family. During her lunch break, she liked to sit on the bench in the factory garden, which was perched on top of a hill, and look out at the sea. She thought about the country that lay far across that sea, to which she would never return. There were many things she didn't want to remember. But thinking about the days she spent in the woman's house in the valley gave her a feeling of calm. When she thought about those times, she always felt that somewhere far off, the woman was thinking the same thing.

A young married couple now lived in the woman's house in the valley. The road in front of the house had been converted into a highway, and the couple ran a cafeteria for long-distance truck drivers. They were deciding what to name their baby who would soon be born. 🐵

by Satoshi Kitamura

The Overcoat

That evening Akagi and I went to a bar.

He joined his friends at the table while I took a rest in the hallway.
The place was crowded and warm.

I must have fallen asleep. When I woke up, it was chilly and quiet.

I went to the bar, but there was no one there.
Where have they all gone?

How on earth could Akagi go out without me on this freezing night?
Wherever he was, I had to find him.

I walked around the parts of town we frequented—

the back streets, the cafes, and the park—but there was no sign of him anywhere.

I was getting worried.

Akagi might be in trouble . . .

Then I came across a stray dog. And it gave me an idea.

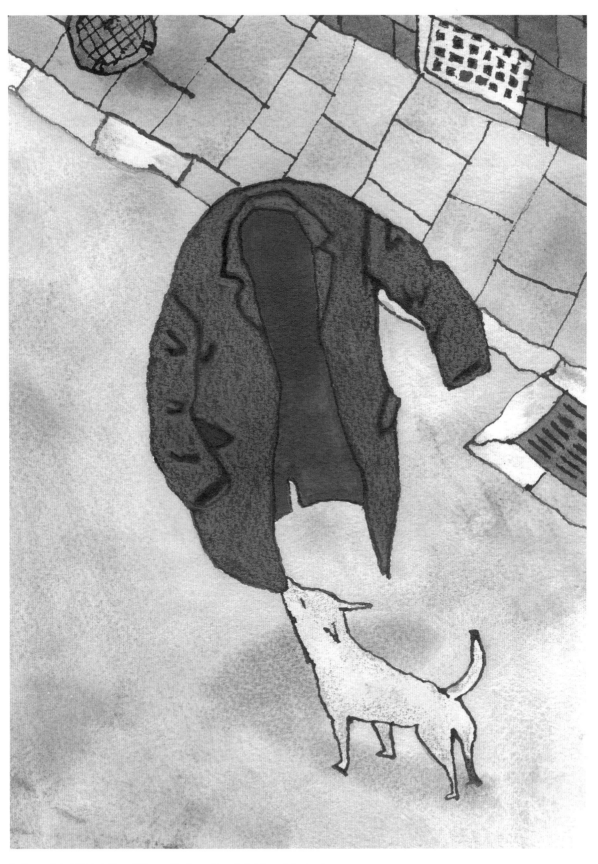

I thought, if I let it sniff my lining, it might be able to trace
the path Akagi took so that I could find him.

The dog started to walk with its nose to the ground.

It seemed to have caught Akagi's scent. Every now and then the dog stopped, sniffed around, and then continued on.

This might work, I thought, and followed the dog.

The farther we went, the surer the dog's steps became.

It increased its pace.
I was breathless trying to keep up.

Suddenly the dog turned into an alley.

I was puzzled. Is this where Akagi is?
What made him come here?

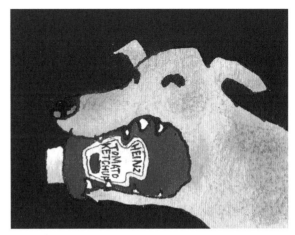

The dog started to root around in a pile of trash.
He found something, and showed it to me proudly . . .

Yes, Akagi had once smeared me with ketchup from a hot dog,
but that wasn't what I was looking for. The dog was useless!

Now I had to go home, but where was I?

I realized that I had no clue which way to go.

I made a guess and walked for a while, only to find myself back in the same place.

It started to rain, and soon my wool got completely soaked, making me colder and heavier. I felt desperate.

Then I saw a light in the distance.

When I walked toward it, I saw three worn-out overcoats standing around a fire.
One of them waved its empty sleeve at me, inviting me to join them.

That was what I did. And in that moment,
I felt certain that I would never go home or see
Akagi ever again.

Kikuko Tsumura

———

Hell

translated by Polly Barton

I'VE KNOWN MY FRIEND Kayo since middle school, and we ended up dying on the same day, in a tour bus accident on our way back from a hot spring. Everyone else survived—the driver, the other people on the tour, the tour conductor, and the guide. Kayo and I were the only fatalities, dying on impact. I don't know exactly what happened to Kayo, but in my case, a rectangular tin of rice crackers came flying at me with considerable force, and its corner struck my head, delivering the fatal injury. The tin contained fifty-four crackers, so it was seriously heavy. I should really have asked the gift shop to send it on for me. Kayo and I had copious quantities of luggage between the two of us, and I'd gratefully commandeered the empty seat across the aisle from us for the presents we'd bought. What I'd thought was a piece of good luck ultimately backfired on me.

Of course, dying at the end of the trip was not what I'd envisaged, but overall it had been great fun. Kayo and I had been firm friends ever since finding ourselves in the same class in the second year of middle school. Traveling with chatty, good-natured Kayo turned out to be just as enjoyable as I imagined. We bought a ton of souvenirs, and said to one another that we wanted to do it again—several times more, in fact, while we were still mobile. Quite honestly, talking to Kayo was hugely entertaining, even without any traveling involved. As we entered the twilight years of our lives, we found ourselves with a lot of free time on our hands, and whenever we met, we'd end up talking for ten hours at a time. We got through about fifteen cups of tea per session.

As for how old Kayo and I were when we died, I find that now that I'm in hell, I don't really know any more. In hell, your appearance reverts to the point in time when you were at your most sinful. It seems that my sinning reached its peak at the age of thirty-four, and so I assumed my thirty-four-year-old form permanently. I haven't seen Kayo at all since we lined up together to be assigned to one of the various hells, and I can only guess she's been placed in a different one. When we were standing in line, Kayo and I started talking about how the nose hair of the demon monitoring the lines was sticking out like crazy, and we got overexcited. I think there must have been complaints from the people around us, because at some point said demon asked Kayo to move to a different line. After dragging her heels for fifty days or so, Kayo eventually said, "I guess the demon's got a job to do, just like everyone else. I should probably cooperate." And with that, she walked off. At the time I wasn't particularly concerned, figuring I was bound to bump into her again soon, but my calculations in that regard were clearly off, and to this day I still haven't seen her. I do miss her from time to time, but my hands are so full just getting through the assignments I've been set here in hell, particularly when the cycle of ordeals I have to complete enters one of its tougher phases, that it's not exactly a wracking ache or anything. I don't know what the other hells are like, but I get the sense that the one I'm in is quite a strenuous one. Or maybe it's less strenuous and more whirlwind. I suppose I only have my sins in the previous world to blame for that.

The demon I've been assigned to is called Mr. Gonda. By some quirk of fate, he's also the guy with the nose hair who moved Kayo to another line, although his nose hair isn't sticking out anymore—quite possibly because Kayo and I talked about it so much. What I will say is that he seems like someone so outpaced by life that it would come as no surprise if his nose hair did start sticking out again at any minute. He originally worked in a different hell together with his wife, but the environment there had exacerbated her eczema, and so he'd transitioned over to this hell we were in currently, where the air is comparatively cleaner. It seemed as though for Mr. Gonda, this move marked some kind of fall from grace or demotion or something—in any case, a deviation from the career path he'd imagined for himself, which occasionally made me feel bad for him. Incidentally, it turns out that the role of overseeing the entrance lines that he was carrying out when Kayo and I died is a rotating position that comes around once every fifty years— a bit like washroom-cleaning duty, which we each had to do every three weeks back when I was working in an office.

Mr. Gonda's behavior towards me is quite intimidating. I guess that makes sense, given he's a demon. When he was introduced to me as my supervisor,

I stuck out my hand and said, "Oh, you're the person who was overseeing my entrance line!" but Mr. Gonda ignored me entirely. I was amazed to discover that there was a demon assigned to every resident in the hell where I've been placed—even in care facilities on earth there was almost nowhere with such a high staff-to-resident ratio, and it seemed to me surprising that people in hell would be shown such hospitality. When I articulated my admiration in this way, though, Mr. Gonda made no response whatsoever. Yet having no other suitable topics of conversation up my sleeve, I kept repeating the same thing, day in and day out for three hundred days, and eventually he replied that this hell and the adjacent one were brand new, so they had more employees than the others. Oh, there's another new hell next to this one, is there? I asked, surprised. After enquiring for another three hundred days what kind of hell it was, I finally managed to elicit the information that the place next door was a hell for "chatty bastards who never shut up." Chatty bastards, not gabby bastards, then? I asked, but as usual, Mr. Gonda just ignored me.

The various departments in hell weren't given titles in the way that, say, Accounting and Admin and so on are within the structure of a company, so it was hard for me to know for sure, but it appeared that the hell into which I'd fallen was a hell of excessive narrative consumption. Gluttony is of course a well-known sin, and usually understood with reference to food, but it seemed as though my hell was one reserved for the specific sin of gluttony in terms of stories. Certainly, my consumption of both factual and fictional narratives during my lifetime had been pretty momentous. At peak times, I'd watched a minimum of three episodes of a TV drama and one documentary per day, seen three films a week, and read ten novels a month. I would be sure to watch whatever matches Manchester City, Schalke 04, Athletic Bilbao, and Cerezo Osaka were playing. When the Grand Tours were on—the Tour de France, obviously, but also the Giro d'Italia and Vuelta a España—I would mostly do without sleep, while in winter, I watched mogul skiing, Alpine skiing, and ice hockey. I trawled through advice forums on the internet, eavesdropped on the conversations of people sitting next to me in cafes, and had something of a pastime of reading world history timelines. To make things worse, I'd been a novelist by trade. Mine had been a life marked by a voracious consumption of stories from across the board. Since Gutenberg's invention of the printing press, there had been a steady rise in the number of people demonstrating a great rapaciousness for narrative, while presenting little evidence of other vices—and so, following a long period of consideration, the decision was taken to add a new division of hell to address the issue.

It appeared that the administration's policy was to provide a hell that fit each individual—a purgatory with a personal touch. The reasoning was that simply thrashing people and making them walk great distances and yelling at them indiscriminately wasn't necessarily effective in prompting them to reform their sinful ways, and so the residents were given assignments to carry out that were appropriate to their particular situations.

I was no exception in this, and my days were chockablock with ordeals. Last week, on any given day, I would die at least three times between getting up and going to bed. In the morning, I was shot over an inheritance dispute; at lunchtime I had my neck wrung for having said something careless along the lines of "If they have no bread, let them eat cake" to some embittered types; in the evening I was killed in what was made to look like a motoring accident for refusing to break off an affair. I was also murdered for a panoply of other reasons: to ensure my silence over an embezzlement, for being a tyrannical business owner, out of revenge. I was assassinated for being a VIP, and killed in a case of simple mistaken identity.

What I discovered from being murdered in so many different ways was that, although the experience was largely an unpleasant one, being mistaken for someone else was the most infuriating way to die, and the most tawdry, lacking as it did any sense of

catharsis. Of course I was dead already, but when I was killed anew I would feel pain and suffering for a while, until the fearful knowledge that I was about to die would overlay itself on the knowledge that I was already dead, and at the very instant that this feeling reached its zenith, Mr. Gonda would come to collect me. Before I knew it, the fear and suffering would abate, and I'd be able to move again. That said, I would only be moving over to the next murder scene, so it was hardly cause for celebration.

Mr. Gonda explained that the reason all this was happening to me was that I'd watched crime dramas on TV, day in and day out. Feasting several times daily on the sight of people being killed and their crimes being solved was a vice sufficient to send a person straight to hell.

In my case, being murdered repeatedly wasn't the only form of content in my purgatorial experience—there was a whole selection of other trials in store. In fact, the trials would usually change around once a week. The week before I was murdered multiple times a day, my task was to sit and quietly read novels. Yet not only was I assigned a daily quota of four hundred pages, but also the last few pages of each book were torn out. In other words, I was forced to read the books in the full knowledge that the ending was missing. As a former novelist, I understood that a story wasn't all about its finale, and yet not knowing how the stories ended was really tough. Whenever I realized there might be something crucial written in the final pages, I'd start to fret. As I fretted, I had to make a start on the next book. Thanks to the fretting, my progress was slow. Yet I still had a vast number of pages to get through to meet my quota. My eyes became tired, I grew bored by the very act of reading, and, knowing that I'd never discover the ending, my impulse was often to just put the volume down—but that wasn't permitted in hell. When the books were thrillers or the like, then the pages would be ripped out from a point calculated to ensure that I couldn't possibly figure out who'd done it. Eventually I started asking Mr. Gonda who the culprit was. Needless to say, he didn't reply, but I'd explain to him my reasoning, about which I'd scribbled notes as I was reading, and watch the shift in his facial expressions. Using this technique, I gradually acquired the pointless skill of being able to judge whether or not my inferences were correct. Most of the time, though, they weren't. A fat lot of good all that crime-drama watching had done me.

As a special assignment on the final day of reading week, I was forced to read the handwritten manuscript of a novel that my mother had written during her teenage days. The title was *The Adventures of Miss Margarita, The Phantom Thief.* Margarita is a Texas girl, initiated into thievery by her notorious father. After her father's death, Margarita sets out on a quest to steal famous paintings from around the world, approaching her professional and romantic conquests alike with tremendous verve. Not only did the plot sound vaguely familiar to me, but it contained numerous elements that had me shaking my head, such as how the French prime minister who pursued Margarita and fell in love with her was twenty-three years of age, and the way that Monet, Manet, and Degas were thoroughly confused through-out (the book featured Degas's *Haystacks* and Monet's *Olympia*), and how Margarita's mother, currently incarcerated, was a Ukrainian politician and billion-aire who owned a gas company, and the prevalence of monsoons in the American South, and so on. According to Mr. Gonda, it was a veritable tome of a work spanning twenty B5 notebooks, of which I'd read just a single one. Which meant I had another nineteen to go. I wanted to die. Although I was, of course, already dead. Incidentally, my mother had had no professional connection to books whatsoever: she'd worked in the admin department of a bank. While I was alive, I'd never heard her express any interest in writing a novel.

And now this week, I have found myself switching roles every twelve hours or so, vicariously experiencing all kinds of extreme situations. Yesterday morning I assassinated JFK, and in the afternoon I myself was assassinated by Jack Ruby. Tomorrow I am supposed to be repairing the outer wall of a space station. I endured a humiliating experience at Canossa, too. I was aware to a certain extent of the fate that would subsequently befall my rival, Pope Gregory VII, and yet being there, fasting and barefoot during the blizzard, supplicating the entire time, proved to be really hard. All I could think was, *I'm gonna get him back for this one day.*

Then, first thing this morning, I was Zinedine Zidane in the finale of the 2006 World Cup. It was the very last match I'd play before retiring, which just so happened to be the World Cup final—and there, on that most gloried of stages known to humanity, I head-butted Materazzi. Oh my god, I'm gonna head-butt him, aren't I? I thought. And then I did it. Recalling it now makes me feel like I could develop a stomach ulcer in a second flat. Since coming to hell, there's been an almost constant flow of things that feel horrible, or are hard, or a pain in the ass, but with the head-butting episode, I experienced for the first time a sense of true remorse for my actions. Even if my own life had been so incredibly peaceful and I'd barely hurt a fly, when it came to other people's terrible experiences I had overconsumed.

I told Mr. Gonda about this remorse of mine, but he showed no sign of being moved in the slightest as he led me without a word to the next installation. Now I was somewhere in the Alps. I was on a bike, and I was absolutely exhausted. Luckily, I was going down-hill—but it appeared that descents were not my forte as a cyclist. An unpleasant tension overwhelmed my body, and all my muscles stiffened. In the overall standings, my rival in the yellow jersey had a twenty-three-second lead, and behind me were close to two hundred riders. Summoning up the dregs of my strength, I attempted to break away from my nemesis, who was having an off day. It was the twentieth day of the Tour, and if I didn't make up the time between us now, there was no hope for me. If only I could be prepared to fight to the death—but wait a minute, I thought. I'm already dead, so what does it matter if I die again? If I could just channel that spirit into pedaling, then maybe, just maybe, I'd be able to over-take the leader.

Yet the fact remained that riding downhill was not my strong suit, and so I was pedaling with some trepidation. If I could somehow overcome this challenge, then the greatest of all honors awaited me. An announcement came through on my wireless radio that my rival seemed to have regained form a little and had broken away from the pack behind me, and I began to panic. I'd been scared pretty consistently up to this point, but knowing I had to go even faster made me more scared still. But this was a race. I stood up out of the saddle and pedaled hard. That was when the chain slipped off. The excess momentum made me lurch to one side, and my bike followed, tipping in that direction too. Now the front wheel slid at an angle across the smooth road surface, and I felt every cell in my body curling up into itself. There were no railings on the side of the road. Still mounted on my bike, I went careening over the cliff. As I plummeted, thwacking into trees on the way down, I let go of the handlebars, and the front wheel reared up to strike me between the eyes. Being a Tour de France racing bike, it was light enough, but still, having your own bike strike you in the face as you're tumbling down a cliff is a truly cruel fate to endure.

I'm sorry, I thought. I don't know if this was repentance, as such—I just felt, simply, that I'd been in the wrong. I'd gotten too much enjoyment from other people staking their lives on doing things. I'd felt as much respect for those people as it was possible to feel, but really, that had just been an excuse as I derived excessive pleasure from their plight. For that, I was truly sorry.

Down I rolled to the bottom of the valley, down, down, like a little rice ball. When my bike reared up to strike me, the thought *I'm gonna die* had formed in my mind, so I guessed that in terms of purgatorial content, I was dead. Maybe I'd fallen into a spot that was hard to access or something, because there was no sign of Mr. Gonda. And so I kept on lying there, face down on the forest floor. My body throbbed all over, and the shock of having slid off the road had rendered me immobile, but lying there endlessly was very boring. Being bored and in pain at the same time was the absolute worst. An amount of time that I could only describe as interminable went trickling by, interminably. My body wouldn't move. But I was fully conscious, so I tried counting to a hundred in all the languages I knew. When I'd exhausted that, I started playing the word chain game in my head.

"Hey! You okay down there?" By the time I heard a familiar voice calling out to me, I'd already given up on the word chain game and returned to the world of my present reality, wondering if something bad had happened to Mr. Gonda, and that was why he hadn't come to find me. The familiar voice wasn't Mr. Gonda's. Are you okay? Can you breathe? The person who hurried over, whose feet I could hear tramping through grass, was none other than Kayo.

Well, well! I thought, and raised my head, only to find that the pain in my body had gone.

"Nom-Noms! I can't believe it's really you! How long has it been?"

My surname is Nomura, and back at middle school everyone called me Nom-Noms. I was aware that nicknames functioned on the principle of making a long name shorter, and I'd secretly found it slightly questionable how mine was lengthier than my real name, but while I was alive I'd not once complained about it. The truth was, I'd always had too much other stuff that I wanted to say.

Kayo reached out a hand, asking me repeatedly if I was alright, and I said repeatedly that I was, waving my hands and nodding my head as I picked myself up off the ground. Kayo looked really very young. My guess was that she'd reverted to her last year of high school. That was the year she'd had to have surgery during the summer holidays to remove a polyp from her vocal chords, which had developed as a result of talking too much. Even then, she'd carried on talking all day, every day—even when her voice grew hoarse, even when it made her cough. I guess that means we had a lot to say, but as to what Kayo and I and our other friends actually talked about, I have no memory whatsoever.

"I'm on this program at the moment where I'm made to live alone in a mountain cabin, and can't say a word to anyone, and my god it feels good to talk. Such a relief, I can't tell you!" And with that, Kayo went on to fill me in about all the things that had been happening to her since she'd been sent to a different line by Mr. Gonda.

It transpired that Kayo had been assigned to the next hell along—the one that Mr. Gonda had told me was for "chatty bastards who never shut up." Of late, she'd been living with no conversational partner in a mountain cabin not far from here. Kayo referred to this as "conversational fasting"—I didn't know if this was the official name for it, or something she'd come up with herself. She said that after a while, she'd gotten used to having no one around, and it wasn't so bad, but the previous assignment, where she'd been made to witness all kinds of spectacles on the proviso that she couldn't talk to anybody about them, had been really hard.

"I was taken along to a public screening of a World Cup match, and I got really into it, and then Zidane head-butted Materazzi, and then they showed a TV interview where he was explaining his actions, and he was wearing a jacket with another jacket on top of it, and I had no idea what was going on, but I wasn't allowed to speak to anybody about it! Even leaving aside the head-butting, what was with that jacket? It was just so strange, like, did nobody think to say anything to him? Or was that his idea

of a cutting-edge fashion choice? Goodness, that was stressful!"

After that, Kayo said, she had become a citizen of Dallas in 1963 and witnessed Kennedy's assassination. As she watched Jacqueline Kennedy get up on the back of the car, she was absolutely desperate to turn to the person next to her and say, "Well, things are going to be tough for the country now, aren't they? What are we going to do about Vietnam? And what will Khrushchev think when he hears about this? Honestly, if I was Jackie, I think I'd get down under the seat—what would you do?" Yet the rules of this punishment meant that she couldn't say any of that.

"If I do break the rules, the inside of my mouth grows so dry that I think I'm going to die. I mean, I'm dead already, but, you know."

"Ah, dry mouth! The bane of any talker's existence."

I figured the reason that Kayo seemed unconcerned about talking to me when she was supposedly on a conversational fast was that I was a resident of a different hell. I could only guess that this valley into which I'd fallen was an intermediary zone between our two hells. Kayo went on to relate various other shocking moments that she'd witnessed, but when I told her that I might have had something to do with the Zidane thing and the Kennedy thing, she nodded and said, Hmm, I guess they must share some stuff among the hells, to save on expenses.

When the conversational fasting in the mountain cabin was over, Kayo was apparently going to move on to a kind of purgatorial content where throughout her waking hours she had to make nonstop conversation with her demon about topics like the cracks in the walls, the grain of the floor, and the shapes of the clouds in the sky. The demons weren't really supposed to tell the residents about what ordeals were coming next, but apparently Kayo's demon, whose name was Mr. Saionji, was extremely talkative and had let the cat out of the bag.

"Mine's called Mr. Gonda, and he barely opens his mouth!"

"Oh, trust me, that's way better. My guy really gets to me sometimes. I want to say, look, you told me that yesterday, can't you write about it in your diary or something instead?"

Kayo might have been a real talker, but she was also a good listener, and to have aggravated her this much, the demon's talking habits must have been quite something. By the by, that Kayo and I could talk for ten hours a day stemmed from the fact that as well as being talkers, we were both also pretty good listeners. When two such people get together, they are bound to keep on talking until they are physically spent. Some might wonder if they wouldn't run out of things to talk about, but there were always more things to discuss, thrown up by the incidental details of the main story. Where we were concerned, talk sprung eternal.

Kayo confessed that Mr. Saionji's degree of verbosity had her occasionally regretting that she had talked so much in life. Holding this up alongside my own recent experience of feeling remorse about my past actions, it was clear that hell was, in fact, having an effect.

"Honestly, all he does is moan. You'd think someone would give up being a demon if they hated it so much, but apparently he went through considerable effort to get the job in the first place, and he has to make a living somehow, and it's kind of enjoyable. Well, that's great then, if it's enjoyable, I say, but then he's all, Oh, but it's not *all* enjoyable. It's the fact that it's not always enjoyable that's the problem, and we're off again."

Aside from his professional issues, Mr. Saionji also had concerns about his family and his health. For the most part Kayo just listened to him patiently, but when his moaning transcended the limit of her tolerance, she ended up giving him advice, which then invited a backlash of *no, but*'s from him. Even when Kayo had finished her trials for the day and went to bed, Mr. Saionji would send her text messages about his problems, and sometimes, when things got really bad, would even follow her to the bathroom and stand outside the door, talking all the while.

"And to top it all, he's having an affair."

"Do demons do that?"

Mr. Saionji's most pressing worry at the moment, it transpired, was whether the person he was having said affair with—a colleague at his same hell—was really into him or not. Depending on the answer to that question, he was considering whether or not to steal her away from her husband.

"Steal her away?! What kind of language is that?"

"Honestly, that's the kind of thing he says. 'I'm afraid I might end up stealing Kimiko away from her husband.'"

"Surely that's not stuff he should be sharing in such detail with other people?"

Although Mr. Saionji's purported reason for talking to Kayo was wanting a woman's perspective on the matter, he then met whatever she said with a chorus of *no, but*'s. It sounded as if there was genuinely no point at all in responding to him.

"I feel as though talking about him in this way might make him sound kind of intriguing, but he really, *really* isn't. He's unbelievably dull."

I'd been half-suspecting that that might be the case, and my intuition proved correct. I hung my head on Kayo's behalf. Having a profoundly uninteresting demon who talked a lot but had no capacity for listening to anything that anybody else said consulting with you endlessly about his love life—that really was hell.

"He's a good person at heart, though."

"Yeah…"

The majority of people are "good people at heart," and so as a decisive reason for not turning one's back on someone, this is therefore a bad one. And yet, people love to use it as a reason for not taking action.

"And that's why I can't give up on him totally, and as long as I haven't given up on him, I'm forced to listen to what he says and take it seriously, and so it's just endless."

It seemed that Kayo now found herself in a hell of incessant talking—of a totally different kind to the one where she'd talked with me and her other friends until she developed a polyp. Although it had to be said that, even before her death, Kayo had been a magnet for those kinds of people.

It wasn't clear what Mr. Saionji was saying to others about Kayo, but of late, other demons had started turning up to confide in her. Kayo would listen and make all the appropriate noises, but she was getting really tired of it. Demons had all kinds of problems too, it turned out. There were those like Mr. Saionji's, where the answers to their issues—*she's just using you to appease her loneliness*—were evident in a split second, and there were more serious concerns like, *however hard I work I don't get a raise,* or, *I feel like I'm not cut out for this job,* and all other sorts of complaints besides: *vegetables are expensive, I'm not sleeping well, I wanted to work in the lake-of-blood hell and not here, my back is all knotted, I'm always tired, I don't mind my job but I can't be bothered to do the housework,* and so on, and so on. Still, it all sounds like fairly peaceable stuff, I said, at which Kayo screwed up her face and shook her head.

"I've only told you about the ones that are easy to explain. Honestly, I hear a lot of really tough stuff, thing that have no solution. 'I just can't stand so-and-so,' that kind of thing."

Kayo found it distressing when those seeking her advice brought up unexpected details from other people's pasts as reasons for being unable to get on with them: *so-and-so used to be a member of the local gang,* or, *so-and-so was her boss's lover,* or, *so-and-so used to be a member of the Railfan Club.* Yet when she thought to confide in someone else about those things she'd been told in confidence, her mouth would get unbelievably dry. As long as she continued contemplating telling others, her mouth would remain dry, regardless of how much water she drank. It sure was hell.

"Stop telling me this stuff, I keep thinking, but they don't stop."

"Maybe it's part of your whole hell experience?"

I went on to tell Kayo how things were in my hell. Kayo said she didn't much like the sound of dying repeatedly, but reading my mother's novel sounded genuinely fun. The demon guy looking after me is the one who was managing the lines, I told her. Isn't that a weird coincidence? Oh, the guy with the nose hair, Kayo said, nodding in recognition.

After a while we heard the sound of a music box playing "Massa's in de Cold Ground" coming from the direction Kayo had appeared. Oh, is it five already? Kayo asked. I better get back, I'll see you soon, okay? We swapped contact details and she disappeared back into the forest. Almost as soon as she'd gone, Mr. Gonda came to collect me, and I thanked my lucky stars he hadn't shown up while she was still there. We got on the bus, which only came once every two hours, and went home.

This was, after all, narrative hell, so of course there had to be some kind of fracas in boarding the bus as well. Just as it pulled up to the stop and we started to get on, Mr. Gonda's phone rang. Mr. Gonda wasn't a particularly moronic type, by and large, but now he stood stock-still and steely faced halfway up the steps, saying things into his phone like, "Oh, you can't come home? What, it's run late again? You're doing a lot of overtime at the moment, aren't you?" and generally abandoning the process of boarding the bus, so that the demon driver grew irritated and shouted at us, "Are you guys getting on or what?"

"We're getting on, we're getting on," I said, forcing a smile and applying pressure to Mr. Gonda's back, but he didn't budge an inch.

"No phones allowed on the bus, you know!" the driver harped on.

"He'll hang up right away! Please just drive off," I said, at my wits' end. With all my might, I pushed Mr. Gonda inside, and eventually the driver shut the doors.

"You've got your health to think about," Mr. Gonda was saying now, his tone such that it was hard to tell if he was angry, or sad, or both. "You should be taking it easier." When he finally removed the phone from his ear to hang up, I caught a glimpse of the caller's name—or at least the last part of it: miko. In a flash it occurred to me: what if this was the same Kimiko that Kayo's Mr. Saionji was having an affair with? At the appearance of this thought, I immediately felt the sweat pricking my scalp. Of course, Mr. Gonda's wife's name could have been Mamiko or Emiko, I told myself—in fact, there were any number of names ending in "miko." And yet I couldn't get the idea out of my head. It was a long bus ride, and I was unable to relax one iota.

The following day, I spent the morning in outer space, and later on I became Julius Caesar. Cleopatra was delivered to me rolled in a carpet, and I was assassinated by Brutus. While going through the motions of being Caesar, I remembered how the English tended to pronounce his name "seizer" instead of the Latin way, "kai-sar," that we use in Japanese, which was something I'd thought about around two hundred times while still alive.

When I was through with my assignments for the day, I saw I had a text from Kayo. "I'm supposed to be discussing the cracks in the wall with Mr. Saionji," she wrote tragically, "but he won't stop talking about what he should do about Kimiko, so we're making no headway, and I'm not allowed to go home." I deliberated about whether to confide in Kayo my suspicions that Kimiko might be Mr. Gonda's wife, but not wanting to cause any more chaos, I instead wrote her back: "Why don't you try saying something along the lines of, 'Ooh, this crack looks exactly like the Chao Phraya River! You know, I hear that

when you're making fried rice, nothing beats Thai long grain.' And then you could go through all the rivers that you know like that, so as to stop him getting a chance to talk?"

"Got it," Kayo texted back. Five hours later another text arrived, "Managed to somehow finish for the day," which came to me as a great relief.

This exchange marked the start of a long-running state of affairs whereby Kayo was prevented from carrying out her assignment by the verbosity of Mr. Saionji the demon. Whether this situation was a paradoxical one, or was in fact perfectly in line with the logic of hell, was hard to determine. The ordeals one faced in hell were of course the outcome of one's sins while living, but how Mr. Saionji conducted his personal life had nothing to do with Kayo. "If the program of ordeals is like the job I do in regular

working hours," Kayo said in outrage, "then listening to Mr. Saionji is like unpaid overtime I've no choice but to accept." Besides, unlike unpaid overtime, Mr. Saionji's advice-seeking truly had no end. And it couldn't even be properly termed advice-seeking, since he barely listened to anything that Kayo said.

The truth was, Mr. Saionji simply enjoyed speaking about himself and Kimiko. Listening to Kayo, I found myself itching to explain in no uncertain terms to Mr. Saionji that he wasn't as enamored with Kimiko as much as he was with talking about her—but I also understood that Kayo had her relationship with him to consider. Every time Kayo texted, I'd send her ideas for conversational gambits that might be good openers for longer conversations. On the grain of the wood, she could say: "It looks just like the contours of a map, doesn't it! I wonder what this mountain range is called. I'll bet it's pretty perilous," while of the clouds in the sky she might comment: "They rather remind me of the stuffing of soft toys or something. Did you have many stuffed animals when you were a boy?" Yet even with all my suggestions, it appeared as though Kayo was having a hard time of it.

She wished she could return to her days of conversational fasting in the mountain cabin, she said. Not speaking was tough, but being around people who spoke far too much was no picnic either. When Kayo had worked in an office, she and the younger colleague who sat next to her had moaned constantly about their high-stress workplace as they went about their tasks, both going home three hours after the official end of every day; now Kayo had begun to reflect that maybe her colleague had found the situation less than desirable, but had been unable to say anything. While alive, Kayo said, that thought had never once occurred to her. Was the current Mr. Saionji–Kayo dynamic reproducing the one that had existed between Kayo and her colleague, she wondered. Although I was pretty certain that Kayo's complaints were more interesting to listen to than Mr. Saionji's.

Nowadays, as I made my way through the purgatorial content I'd been assigned, I would be scheming up ways for Kayo to outtalk Mr. Saionji, and sending them to her. Kayo didn't put all of my conversational gambits into practice, but she implemented about half of them, and it seemed that her performance was improving somewhat as a result. It came to me that this was pretty similar to the work I'd been engaged in while alive. Even in hell, I was carrying out writing-related tasks. By creating these alternative realities in my head, I found that I had somehow grown able to take a more objective stance on all the dramatic events I was forced to experience vicariously. When I subsequently moved on to a program that consisted of sitting on a cloudy beach and doing absolutely nothing, I began thinking more than ever about Kayo, Mr. Saionji, Kimiko, and Mr. Gonda.

Because of Mr. Saionji, Kayo had been unable to meet her talking quota and had failed her program. At the end of each day she would be given stats about her talking performance and had been issued a warning on this basis: How was it possible, she was asked, that Mr. Saionji the demon had greater possession of the conversation than she did? Kayo said that she was willing enough to make conversation about meaningless minutiae, but putting up with Mr. Saionji was a serious trial.

She was having such a miserable time of things that I confided in her that I suspected the wife of my demon might be the person Mr. Saionji was having an affair with. "Why on earth didn't you say something before?!" Kayo said, before answering herself: "I guess it's not the sort of thing you would say, as an adult, if you weren't sure about it, is it." She asked me to tell her in more detail about Mr. Gonda, but knowing very little about him, I could only fill her in on how, for reasons related to his wife's health, he'd given up on working at the hell where he was previously stationed and which he'd seen as the cornerstone of his future success, and moved instead to this newly developed one. "Is that all you've got?" Kayo asked,

somewhat grimly. "Okay, well, I'll give it a go." What exactly it was that she intended to "give a go" I had no idea.

It later transpired that, audaciously enough, Kayo had attempted to give Mr. Saionji a lecture. When, as the two of them sat staring at the cracks in the wall, Mr. Saionji had started up with his usual brand of nonsense, saying how much he longed to sail down the Danube River with Kimiko, Kayo had pressed him as follows: she'd heard that Kimiko's husband had given up on his hopes of a bright career for the sake of Kimiko's health, coming out all this way to a new hell. Kimiko's resolve might appear to be wavering at the moment as a result of her being so busy, but did Mr. Saionji really think she was likely to give up a marriage like that? Or to put it another way—was that kind of sacrifice something that he himself thought he was capable of?

This news seriously impressed me. Whatever else might be said of them, demons were demons at the end of the day, which meant they carried iron clubs at all times and wore tiger-pelt loincloths that lasted for a hundred years—there was no way I could have done something like that. But Kayo had gone and done it. Trust a talker to manage such a thing. This, surely, made her the talker to beat all talkers.

As it happened, Mr. Saionji's reaction had not been to strike Kayo with his iron club (it turned out that demons could be penalized with things like suspensions for striking residents with their iron clubs without good reason). Instead, his face had taken on a meek look. "I think I'll sleep on it," he'd said, and slunk off home. It turned out that Mr. Saionji was actually younger than Kayo—we had been of quite a venerable age when we died—so maybe that went some way toward explaining his deference.

From that point on, Mr. Saionji stopped talking about Kimiko almost completely, and instead took to sighing all the time, and saying things like, "Ahh, I should take some holiday and go away somewhere. I'd love to visit Tohoku." In response to this, Kayo managed to bring the talk back to the crack on the wall by commenting: "No, no, you should get yourself somewhere completely different . . . like the Amazon!" She then went on to talk about how the CEO of Amazon was apparently really strict when it came to giving presentations in meetings. With this, she took the upper hand in the conversation for the first time in ages, and managed to boost her possession rating.

Now that the problem with Kayo and Mr. Saionji was cleared up, I suddenly found myself on my diversion-less beach with a lot of time on my hands. The sky was forever clouded over. I spent the days alternating between walking and lying splayed out on the sand. Sand was really all that there was on that beach—there weren't even any marine creatures. If the level of sensory information I'd been receiving while I was Heinrich IV suffering outside the castle at Canossa was five thousand, then I was currently down to about two. Enduring a surfeit of stories was hard, but enduring their total absence was also hard. While I was alive, I'd dealt with a dearth of stories in my life by inventing them myself, but on the beach I had no means of recording anything I made up. When I tried to write in the sand, my letters were dispersed by the wind or washed away by the waves almost immediately. When I made to speak out loud, I found that the sound of my own voice would gradually break up against the pleasant sound of the waves, and eventually disappear.

On the beach I didn't get hungry and I didn't get tired. I suppose it was good for me physically, but inside my head there was a tangled mass of black yarn, squirming around and seemingly growing in size. In the attempt to effect some kind of change, I'd grind my teeth, or scratch at my arms, or jump around like crazy. Mr. Gonda, presumably knowing that his mere presence would constitute an influx of information, had absented himself entirely.

Day after day I lay sprawled out in a star shape on the beach, shaking my arms and legs, rolling from side to side, making up new lyrics to old songs. At some point, it occurred to me suddenly that it might be good to go running into the sea, which was the only thing that constituted a change around here, and sink down to its deepest depths. Getting up to do just that, I found Mr. Gonda beside me. I hadn't seen him in such a long time. Here on the beach I was unable to count the days, so I was unable to express the length of time in any way other than saying how very, very long it was.

"Ms. Nomura. It's been a while."

"It has."

Mr. Gonda stationed a small table in front of me, on which he placed an eighty-page A5 notebook and the kind of rollerball pen that I'd often used while still alive.

"I made up with my wife."

"That's good to hear."

"She told me what happened."

I could only guess that this statement meant that Mr. Saionji had broken off with Kimiko after hearing the information Kayo had obtained from me, and that Kimiko had then related the whole affair to Mr. Gonda. Did nobody hide anything from anybody any more? I thought. Trust the affiliates of chatter-box hell.

"It seems like you really helped me out, so I've decided to repay the favor."

With his iron club, Mr. Gonda gestured to the table and nodded. "I want to think about why it was that things turned sour between me and my wife, and try and make our relationship better in the future, so I'd like you to write me two thousand possible causes, and two thousand ways of fixing things."

"Okay."

I sat down and straight away wrote, "Because your nose hair was sticking out," and then I got stuck. The black woolen ball inside my head showed signs of easing up with its indignant knotting and tangling, but this was still hell and no mistake. It turned out that, whether too few, or too many, or whether you were forced to produce them yourself, stories meant suffering regardless. 🐵

Mieko Kawakami

———

Seeing

translated by Hitomi Yoshio

Except for waking moments, I want to be fully asleep
Except for sleeping moments, I want to be fully awake
April my beloved April was April
April that saw me   that saw April   in April

No reason for sorrow
No longer any reason for sorrow, yet
Addressing an envelope—sad
So many straight lines—sad
Baby hairs golden, lashes fluttering—sad
Books heavy—sad, so many flowers blooming—sad
Stories hypnotically dark, strange endings bloom
All learning is sudden, always
The children's ages immersed in water
With each memory, eyes grow big, dark iris expanding
Lashes become heavy
How long can you keep your eyes open, you wonder
You can't keep them open for long, so don't worry, okay?

Round things can't be stacked, but triangular ones can,
square things are even easier to stack, soft things can
be piled up. Hey, did you know? The world has so many
colors. And all the things I will never see are what make
up most of me.

Hideo Furukawa

Decline of the Aliens

+

Sheep After Sheep

translated by Jordan A.Y. Smith

DECLINE OF THE ALIENS

THE HISTORY OF HUMANKIND came to an end. To gloss this sentence with a bit more specificity, we might add: "came to an end *rather easily.*"

Humans were no match for the Ship.

And they were dominated.

From the moment another species came to dominate them, humans simply recognized this simple truth: *Our history is over.* And recognizing it, they prospered.

Yet, being dominated is not prosperity, we should note.

This being the case, perhaps it's better to say that humanity was fruitful and was multiplying as it had been up to that point.

On Earth. On this planet, this land.

Humans were under observation from the Ship. This observation merits emphasis. Thus we say, they were under SURVEILLANCE.

This SURVEILLANCE did not involve any actual interference. So could it really be called an invasion?

ONE DAY, the bottom of the Ship blocked out the entire sky. Of course, since this refers to *the sky around all of planet Earth,* it was night in some regions and daytime in others, and it was really a multitude of Ships. They appeared over every single continent (including the Antarctic Peninsula below the sixty-ninth parallel, so one even appeared over Palmer Land), and their behavior was a kind of declaration: *From now on, to our Ships, Earth's sky is an ocean.*

Humanity was robbed of its sky.

Put another way, humanity was forced to begin referring to *the sky* as *the ocean.*

Of course, a Sky Guardians resistance organization arose, but they were never victorious in battle.

In the beginning, some conjectured that the inhabitants of the Ships must be fish.

But they were not fish.

They neither lived in water nor breathed through gills.

They were land-dwelling beings who breathed through lungs, with developed sweat glands, sebaceous glands, and four long limbs. Moreover, they possessed a language.

The humans (on the side that had suffered the Ships' attack) thought those on the Ships must also be human. At first, that's what the Earth humans thought.

But one thing clearly distinguished the ape superfamily Hominoidea from the crew of these Ships. These non-fish creatures lacked the sense of sight.

They had no eyes, no organ for seeing.

The humans knew they were not fish.

Thus, they came to call them "Aliens," while regarding them as akin to Devas or Angels.

HUMANITY RECOGNIZED THAT being dominated by the Aliens signified *the end of human history.*

In allowing the sky to be rechristened as the "Ocean," with Ships that sailed it freely, humanity had meekly surrendered. Until that moment, humanity had taken over every patch of land on the planet and, at least psychologically, had dominated, had even monopolized the oceans—and then the arrival of the Ships robbed them of the sky. The *sky* is the *ocean.* If we're to consider the entire atmosphere as Ocean (which is actually what it became), then the zone beyond that region is what we would properly understand as the Heavens. The zone from which the invaders arrived— Aliens from Heaven.

Visitors from beyond our world.

The crew of the Ships.

And these sightless Aliens immediately began to construct their empire.

AT THIS POINT, my description of the Aliens rather abruptly mentions that they have *no eyes,* but neglects to address gender, which they most certainly do have. In fact, their language makes clear distinctions between masculine and feminine speech. And whoever is chosen as head of the empire must rigidly adhere to feminine speech. Even if the Alien holding imperial power has been raised as a male, by using feminine speech *he* would become *female.* As in, he would transform physically. This may be redundant, but the use of masculine language could also transform female Aliens into males.

It was not an emperor but an *empress* who ruled this empire, so feminine pronouns were the default when referring to the Alien in the ultimate seat of power. If we're to speak generally about an Alien, rather than saying, "He has no eyes," it would be more appropriate to assume feminine, and say, "She has no eyes."

Other than that, the most distinguishing feature of their language is that it lacks a written form.

AS THE ALIENS BUILT THEIR EMPIRE, all the existing nations (of Earth) were refashioned as vassal states. These vassal states were issued an edict to "Carry on with all activity as you were."

Naturally, the majority of humans obeyed these orders—there were already upwards of two billion dead after the war of resistance—but the Aliens noted something odd about their obedience. The vassal states maintained their existing governments while acknowledging (sometimes grudgingly) the Superior Government of the empire above them, but there were some who believed in an Even Higher Power. These humans considered the Aliens as another species alongside humans and placed the existence of God above them all.

And it turned out that there were different Gods.
Religion had survived.
Multiple religions, with multiple Gods.
There were many Gods in existence.
Sometimes, one God would denounce the others, declaring them not the genuine God.

THE ALIENS thought about it.

Is there no religion that from the beginning has accepted multiple Gods?

A bit of research turned up one rather easily.

Buddhism had made the leap beyond vassal state borders to become a world religion.

However, Buddhists didn't refer to their God as a God. He was known as the Buddha. There were many manifestations of the Buddha: Nyorai, Bodhisattva, and others.

The Aliens decided to convert all the cities of the planet so that they submitted to the will of the Buddha—or Buddhas. The Aliens decided the "Higher Power" above them could be used as a psychological crutch, as long as the Buddhas were the guardian deities of the cities.

At this stage, the Aliens began to show interest in the intersection between the Ocean (which had traditionally been called "the sky"), the land, and the ocean (as it had always been called).

To that point of intersection, they summoned the musicians.

AT THIS STAGE, there's one issue that requires more than a sentence to explain: what stratum of humanity could best process and respond to a language, such as that of the Aliens, that gives no thought to visuality? The task was put to those who most excelled in audio sensibility. Of course, smell, touch, and taste were all important senses, but in the Aliens' language it was hearing that was most crucial. Initially, the nations of the world (nations currently under imperial control as vassal states) found that the people most effective in dealing with the Ships, in negotiating or bargaining with the Aliens, were the linguists and musicians. Particularly the musicians, who merely had to play some music to smooth out situations and appease the Aliens. Just by singing, or plucking a few strings, they took in the other's language as a performance (in the musical sense), and they blended in to form responses.

Thus, on a global level, this signaled the rise of musicians capable of interacting with the Aliens.

These musicians could easily board the Ships. They were invited, even. As humanity—as representatives of humanity.

Moreover, they served as the Aliens' emissaries, moving freely among the vassal states. That is, they traveled. In order to bring all kinds of reports back to the Ships. To bring back news to the Alien members of this empire.

THE YEARS PASSED. The Aliens gradually grew weaker.

It was only natural, as the Aliens were simply a foreign species, not immortals. So they began to die of old age. Their decline came in stages.

Even for the empress, there was no escape from the stages of aging and death.

The day came when the empress could no longer enjoy a peaceful night's sleep.

How the empress longed for such sleep.

And she wanted to know, *How vast is this empire I am governing?*

The Alien empress commanded, summoning all the most feminine diction, personal pronouns, and sentence endings to embellish it, "I do want to know. Someone please do fetch me a report on it."

They summoned the finest musicians and sent them off.

Where was the empress's Ship anchored?

It was floating in the zone above the Kanmon Straits just off Shimonoseki, between Kyushu and Honshu, the main island of Japan.

That area was the ocean (in the original sense of the word), and the site of an ancient battle, a battle fought also on the ocean, and on the shore was a Buddhist temple that had held funeral ceremonies after the battle and continued to perform rituals for the appeasement of the dead souls. Legend had it that some who had wanted to be mourned and celebrated were denied such ceremonies, and so they left behind their curses.

The empress proclaimed: *Summon the musicians, who travel the lands of Earth, and put this thing called writing, which is incomprehensible to us, onto their bodies—tattoo the words on their skin. Since writing itself is meaningless, we treat these letters as passports issued by the empire, passports of the flesh. And you must emphasize the ears. Because hearing is crucial. So no need to write on the ears. And their names, all of them, must start with Hou, like Hou-ichi from the beautiful legend. Call the first among them Houichi.*

In this way, the reporter musicians Hou-ichi, Hou-ni, Hou-san, and so on, came to be selected and sent out by the dozens. One after another.

SHEEP AFTER SHEEP

SOME SISTER CITIES ARE publicly recognized, whereas others are concealed. Cities in different nations that establish a special relationship and, on the surface, sing of "cultural exchange" and "goodwill" missions may have ulterior motives, such as becoming preferred trading partners or military allies. Or the bonds may be spiritual, or religious. And with secret sister city relationships, absolutely no mention is made of their sisterhood.

Soon after the invasion of the Alien Ships had put an end (for the time being) to human history— actually, two years, two months, and two days after—Kyoto and Ulaanbaatar became completely secret sister cities.

Ulaanbaatar is the capital of Mongolia. And Mongolia, now an imperial vassal state, had two things about it that pertain to this tale. The first was sheepherding. The second was Buddhism. Mongolia was the biggest home to Tibetan Buddhism outside Tibet.

Every religion has heretical beliefs, or heretical sects.

After all, it is humans who act on this religious faith, and thus far we've been speaking on the Human Level.

LET US SHIFT TO THE OBJECT of religious conversion. Namely, the Buddha level.

The Buddhas held a clandestine meeting. And every type of Buddha was in attendance, from Bodhisattva to Nyorai, though exactly which Buddhas attended was kept strictly confidential. But the majority were distressed Buddhas, I can say. Distressed in what sense though? Because they were suffering from three of the "Four Sufferings" (of living, aging, illness, and death, they were now free from only the first). That is, all the participants were Buddhas who had begun to age.

"I never would have imagined this," remarked one we'll call Buddha 1.

"The Four Sufferings minus one . . . so we're afflicted by the Three Sufferings," commented Buddha 2.

"In other words, we Buddhas will die one day, and our numbers will dwindle," stated Buddha 3.

"I wonder about that," said Buddha 4. "As long as we can give birth to new Buddhas, there's no problem, right?"

Incidentally, this conversation was being held in real time, though the participants were not all in the same space. Like a video conference.

"That's not necessary," declared Buddha 5.

"Not necessary?" parroted Buddha 4.

"I've heard a rumor. Something about the generation of our origins, one after another."

"I've heard as much too. That Shakyamuni is being reborn, is that it?"

"And Buddha Shakyamuni manifestations are multiplying. There are even some imperfect Buddha manifestations, is that it?"

"The Buddha is never imperfect."

"Indeed, indeed," they signaled agreement, with Buddhas 6 through 8 and Buddha 2 having done the talking up to this point in the discussion.

"It does make me think . . . ," mused Buddha 3.

"About what?" asked Buddha 9.

"Our teachings, the Dharma. After all, Buddhism itself is a doctrine of equality," replied Buddha 3.

Buddhas 9, 8, 7, 6, 5, 4, 2, 1, and the other attendees grew quiet.

They remained silent. And then—

Just as Buddha 10 opened his mouth to say, "Egalitarianism is—"

"Opposed to any thought of dominance," Buddha 11 completed the sentence.

"As in, defy it," said Buddha 12.

"You mean . . . the empire?"

So it was secretly decided that the immaculate will of Buddhism was to raise the flag of rebellion against the empire.

THE BUDDHAS MADE UP THEIR MINDS. They decided to enter the Human Level. A conclusion like this is so deeply within the Buddha Level that its meaning lay beyond comprehension, but in sum, it meant that an incident was about to occur in the human world. Going back to the Buddha Level again, one of the Buddhas declared that they had heard another rumor. Hou-gojūichi (the fifty-first in the group of Hou musicians) had appeared, and was himself a clone of the Buddha Shakyamuni. Another Buddha affirmed this information to be true. However, when they checked with the Aliens, they discovered that there seemed to be no number 51 in the Hou group—it was simply missing. One Buddha said that there were others in the Hou group using those digits, such as 5 and 1, and another Buddha pointed out that there was a 511 and a 501, and another said that if we think in terms of mathematical elegance, there should be five hundred and one and then another five hundred. With that, it was set.

What was set?

On Earth, there was already a temple with five hundred and one, and another five hundred. In the human world. At the Human Level, in Japan. In Kyoto. And to zoom in even closer, we're talking about Higashiyama in Kyoto. The temple's name was Rengeōin. But it was known by the name of its main hall, the Sanjūsangendō (Hall of Thirty-Three Bays). And Sanjūsangendō has another name as well: Sentai Kannondō (Hall of a Thousand Kannons). Inside it, just as the name implies, stand a thousand statues of the Bodhisattva Kannon. And between the two groups of five hundred statues of the Thousand-Armed Kannon in the standing position, there was one enormous statue of the Thousand-Armed Kannon in the seated position.

Five hundred and one, and five hundred.

So, what is equality?

ON THAT DAY, in the night, an incident occurred on the Human Level. In Sanjūsangendō, where as I've explained were 1,001 Kannons, there were also statues of the God of Wind and the God of Lightning, and of the Twenty-Eight Heavenly Deities. These twenty-eight were the guardians of the Thousand-Armed Kannons. The first guardian had a snake draped around its neck. It had five eyes. And was holding a biwa lute. This was the God of Music, and that night, this heavenly statue *moved*.

It began to strum the biwa.

As if on cue, the 1,001 statues of Kannon—that is, the Bodhisattvas enshrined on the Human Level—each began to move their thousand arms.

At the same time, from the higher Buddha Level,

a message was transmitted (to each of the thousand earthly Kannon statues), saying, "Equality requires freedom."

A FREE LANGUAGE LEADS to independence. And independent language leads to crossing borders. Being able to cross the border of one nation to enter another is one way of defining national sovereignty. At this point, our story returns to Ulaanbaatar. To the nation of Mongolia. Which is known for the widespread practice of sheepherding. And the widespread practice of Tibetan Buddhism. Ulaanbaatar, the Mongolian capital city. A capital where a heretical sect would one day take root.

A sect whose practitioners rendered Buddhist statues into wild, exotic forms.

IF THOUSAND-ARMED KANNONS and five-eyed Heavenly Deities were to be permitted, why not a thousand-legged sheep statue? This line of thought seems to have produced the statue of the Thousand-Legged Sheep, which they worshipped. At first, it was thought of as akin to one of the mythical birds and beasts that were used as pedestals for Buddhist statues, with a Bodhisattva or Wisdom King sitting astride it. But it inspired such a miraculous sense of awe that it came to be worshipped in and of itself, and that moment was the birth of a new sect. The sect had its sights set on Kyoto. Particularly on the Sanjūsangendō, with its 1,001 statues of the Thousand-Armed Kannon. It was this sect that united Ulaanbaatar and Kyoto in a complete sister city relationship.

And it was in that role that the miracle-producing Thousand-Legged Sheep statue linked to a certain *something* in Kyoto.

NOW, RETURNING TO the Buddha Level. The Buddhas agreed that to speak of this in terms of the *Lotus Sutra* would require a metaphor. That is, this must all transpire like metaphors. And the Buddhas determined that at the Human Level, in Higashiyama in the city of Kyoto, in the hall of Sanjūsangendō where the 1,001 Thousand-Armed Kannon statues would have to begin to stir, to stand, and to *cross over the border*.

They would have to depart from Japan and enter another country.

They would have to seek protection from their sister city.

So they flew to Ulaanbaatar. In a blink.

By using the Thousand-Legged Sheep statue as a channel.

In a single instant, the Thousand-Armed Kannons teleported out to Ulaanbaatar, the capital of the Imperial Vassal State of Mongolia. One of them stayed inside the Thousand-Legged Sheep statue, while the remaining thousand of them—or rather, the remaining five hundred and five hundred of them—went on in search of other bodies that could house them. Or rather, they sought out bodies they could *possess*. And they selected living bodies found in pastures at the outskirts of Ulaanbaatar—the sheep, one thousand of them.

Thus it came to be that *five hundred and five hundred Kannons all found homes inside the sheep, where they found themselves free.*

To this day, on land, on Earth, there are many Shakyamuni "clones," and one thousand sheep that are also Buddhas. 🐵

_____

Note from the translator: "Decline of the Aliens" and "Sheep After Sheep" are excerpts from Hideo Furukawa's novel *City of Ears*.

© Taiyō Matsumoto

TRAVEL
A Monkey's Dozen

Unlike a baker's dozen (one extra!), a monkey's dozen is one short.
In this section you will find eleven delicious treats:
stories, essays, a Noh play, and a selection of poems about travel—
the special focus of this issue.

Tatsuhiko Shibusawa

———

The Dugong

translated by David Boyd

ON THE TWENTY-SEVENTH DAY of the first month in the sixth year of the Xiantong era, Prince Takaoka left Guangzhou on a ship bound for Hindustan. By the Japanese calendar, the year was Jōgan 7, and the Prince was sixty-seven. At his side were two Japanese monks, Anten and Engaku, both of whom had accompanied the Prince during his stay in Tang.

Guangzhou was one of the liveliest ports in the South Sea, rivaling even Jiaozhou (present-day Hanoi), or "Lūqīn," as the Arabs knew it. As far back as the Han dynasty, when it was known as Panyu, the port of Guangzhou boasted a great many treasures: rhinoceros horn, elephant ivory, tortoiseshell, pearls, jade, amber, aloeswood, silver, bronze, and cardamom. In Xiantong 6, the port was no less vibrant. Moored cheek by jowl were ships from Hindustan, Arabia, Sihalam (Ceylon), Persia—even the Kunlun boats of the Southern Lands. The men of the port were no less exotic, with eyes and skin of every color. Suntanned sailors stripped to the waist bounded across the decks in a veritable showcase of the world's races. Although it would still be four centuries before Marco Polo or Odoric would travel to this part of the globe, there were already "white savages" (Europeans) on some of the ships. Even if only to witness the strange people passing through, the port of Guangzhou was a sight to behold.

In broad strokes, the Prince planned to leave this port aboard a small ship, then head southwest via the route known as the Guangzhou–Yi Sea Pass. He and his companions would then disembark in Jiaozhou, the heart of the Tang protectorate of Annan, at which point they would follow the Annan–Hindustan Road to their destination. But this road was forked; one of its paths led over the Annan Mountains toward Funan (Siam) while the other wound through Kunming and cut across the Dali Plain, ending in Pyu (Burma). The Prince and the others had not yet decided which path they would take. Moreover, it was not out of the question to continue the voyage by sea rather than by land. Sailing past the coasts of Champa (Vietnam), Chenla (Cambodia), and Pan-Pan (the Central Malay Peninsula), one could bypass the Cape of Luo-Yue (near Singapore) and enter the Indian Ocean through the Strait of Malacca. But whether land or sea, all courses harbored unforeseeable dangers. That being so, there was little to be gained by planning ahead. For now, they would consign their fates to the wind, moving as far south as possible. At this juncture, there was no need to think about anything else.

It was never very cold near the equator, even at the height of winter, and the wind here remained warm. The Prince was on the deck, standing straight as an arrow. He was well into his sixties by this point, but appeared at least ten years younger. He looked out over the bustling port of Guangzhou, from which they were to depart at any moment. Just then, a child slipped between the legs of the stevedores carrying cargo. Spotting the boy as he snuck onto the ship, Prince Takaoka and Anten exchanged puzzled looks. Like the Prince, Anten had the bearing of a contemplative monk, though he was in fact a sharp-eyed, brawny man of about forty years.

"Mere moments until our departure and some strange child suddenly appears!"

"I'll go and have a look, Highness."

The boy who was dragged before the Prince had bright cheeks and delicate limbs like a girl. Right away, Anten began to question him in the local language. Although Anten hardly looked it, he was in fact a highly skilled linguist who regularly served the Prince as an interpreter. The boy gasped for breath as he started to explain: "I'm a slave and I've run away from my master. Should my pursuers find me, they will almost certainly kill me. I seek shelter for but a moment. If this ship were to set sail for some remote place, however, so be it. I would not regret leaving this land, not in the least. On the contrary, if you would so much as allow me to bail out bilgewater, I would be grateful beyond words." Such was the boy's earnest plea.

The Prince looked to Anten and said: "It would seem as though a little bird in need has flown into our arms. How could we turn him away? Let's bring him with us."

At this, Anten voiced his concern: "As long as he doesn't slow us down. . . . If you wish it, Highness, I suppose I have no objection."

Then Engaku came along and added: "We could never be so cruel as to abandon him. This is a voyage to Holy Hindustan, after all. It must be the Buddha's Will."

Just as the three monks had reached an agreement, the shipmaster screeched from the yardarm: "Unmoor! Hard to starboard!"

The ship slid into the heart of the bay. Meanwhile, on the wharf, two or three men who seemed to be searching for the slave boy yelled at the departing ship. Overjoyed at narrowly escaping with his life, the boy threw himself at the Prince's feet, choking on tears. The Prince took the boy by the hand and said: "I will call you Akimaru. Until a few years ago, I had a page by that name, but he fell to the plague back in Chang'an. Be my second Akimaru."

In this way, the Prince's entourage came to three: Anten, Engaku, and young Akimaru. Engaku, by the way, was five years Anten's junior. He was a polymath well-versed in Taoist medicine and herbology; his encyclopedic knowledge set him apart from his countrymen, and had won the Prince's respect on numerous occasions.

The ship set sail in the direction of the Leizhou Peninsula and Hainan Island. It drifted across the open sea like a solitary leaf, rushing forward and slowing as the wind willed. At times, the water seemed like oil. Was the ship moving or simply floating in place? It was hard to say. In other moments, the ship ran across the water with such speed it seemed as though the vessel would surely fly apart. It was as if the wind and waves in these parts had some sort of mysterious power, a force that no ship could possibly resist. Every day, like clockwork, a terrible squall hit the ship, enclosing the travelers in curtains of slate gray. It was impossible to tell the sky from the sea, and at times it even seemed as though the ship were sailing across the frothy sky.

Struck by the mystique of the ocean, the Prince said, to no one but himself: "As we head south, things will occur that we could never have imagined back in Japan. Perhaps the world itself will turn upside-down! But I must not be startled. As we approach Hindustan, things will only become stranger and stranger. And isn't that exactly what I wanted? Hindustan approaches! Rejoice! Soon it will be within my grasp."

At the bow of the small ship, the Prince bathed in spindrift as he spoke. Spat into the darkness, his words were immediately taken by the wind, shattering like little objects as they rolled away across the sea.

THE PRINCE WAS NO OLDER THAN SEVEN OR EIGHT when he first heard of "Hindustan." The word made him quiver with sweet intoxication. Hindustan—it was a magic philter to the boy. It had been none other than his father's consort, Fujiwara no Kusuko, who whispered those three syllables in his ear at night.

Before the Prince's father became Emperor Heizei, Kusuko and her daughter had entered the Eastern Palace as scribes. In no time, Kusuko had stolen the Crown Prince's heart and, when he later ascended to the throne, their attachment became increasingly evident, despite the fact that Kusuko was already a married woman. Those years saw the height of Kusuko's favor. Night after night, she shared a pillow with the Emperor. There were rumors that Kusuko had beguiled him, but she remained unshaken by the scandal. At the time, the Emperor was thirty-two and at the peak of manhood. No one knows Kusuko's age. What we do know is that Kusuko had a daughter whom she intended to present to the court for marriage to the Crown Prince, meaning her daughter had to have been of marriageable age. It is fairly clear that Kusuko was somewhat older than her lover. And yet Kusuko didn't seem to age at all. It was rather curious how perfectly she retained the radiant beauty of youth. As suggested by the name Kusuko, which contains the character for medicine, she had a profound knowledge of Chinese herbs; she was no less expert in the art of lovemaking. And, if the persistent rumors were true, she also drank cinnabar and made use of secret arts to retain her youthful appearance.

The common noun "kusuko" traditionally referred to the attendant of a poison-taster. That this word would become Kusuko's name tells us much about her character.

As it happens, it was also during the reign of Emperor Heizei that the hundred-volume *Classified Formulae of the Daidō Era* was compiled. Medicines and poisons, we must not forget, played a crucial role in the power struggles of the day.

Emperor Heizei was very fond of his eight-year-old son, Prince Takaoka. He often took him with Kusuko on trips to the nearby mountains. In court and at home, the Emperor often allowed Kusuko and the young Prince to remain in his company. Unbeknownst to the Prince's mother, the boy often stayed at Kusuko's home with his father. Kusuko made no special effort to endear herself to the boy. She easily won his heart with the sort of closeness often enjoyed by partners in crime. It was almost as if the two were friends, sharing some secret. On occasion, when the Emperor had to tend to some official matter, Kusuko chose to sleep next to the little Prince. Lying beside him, Kusuko told the Prince all kinds of stories, animating his young dreams.

"Can you tell me the name of the realm beyond the sea, Highness?"

"Koryŏ."

"Right, Koryŏ. And what about the one beyond that?"

"Tang."

"Tang. Right again. They also call it Xidan. And then comes?"

"I don't know…"

"Really? Far beyond that, there's a land called Hindustan."

"Hindustan…"

"Right. That's where the Buddha was born. You know, in Hindustan, there are fantastic animals in the fields, curious plants in the gardens, and celestial beings in the sky. And that's not all. Everything in Hindustan is the opposite of what it is in our world. Our day is their night, our summer is their winter, our up is their down, our man is their woman. In Hindustan, rivers run backwards and mountains sink into the earth like gigantic holes. What do you think, Highness? Can you imagine so strange a place?"

Kusuko loosened her silk kimono as she spoke, revealing one of her breasts. She took the Prince's hand and placed it on her breast. This had been a custom of theirs for some time. Kusuko would smile and slip her hand between the Prince's legs, clasping his boyish testicles, rolling them around like a pair of Baoding bells. The Prince was in ecstasy but remained quiet, allowing everything to happen as Kusuko willed. Were it not Kusuko—had it been one of the many other women serving at the palace—no doubt the Prince would have shuddered in disgust and pushed her away.

That this never happened only shows that, as risqué as it may sound, there was not a hint of coquetry or debauchery in Kusuko's act.

"Highness, I believe you'll grow up and take a ship to Hindustan. No, I'm almost sure of it. I can see the future. But I'll be long dead by then—no longer a part of this world."

"What? Why?"

"I can't say, but I know I'll die soon. I can see it in the mirror of my heart."

"But you're so young, Kusuko!"

"Oh, Highness, you say the kindest things. But I'm not afraid of dying. My soul will move on. I'm tired of being human anyway. The next time I'm born, I think I'd like to be hatched—"

"From an egg?" the Prince interrupted.

"Yes, like a bird or a snake. Doesn't that sound nice?"

Then Kusuko stood up. She took something from her bedside cabinet and threw it across the dark garden, then said, as if singing:

"Away, away you go! Off to distant Hindustan!"

The Prince's eyes lit up as he watched Kusuko.

"What was that? What did you throw? Please tell me!"

Kusuko laughed. "Something that will make its way to Hindustan. After fifty years in the moonlight of the jungle, I'll be reborn from it, as a bird."

But the Prince wasn't satisfied. He persisted: "But what was the thing? That glowing ball!"

"Hm, I wonder. Why don't we call it the egg of my rebirth? Or, it being mine, we might call it a medicine ball. . . . Really, I have no idea what to call it. Some things are like that, you know."

That image of Kusuko was burned into the Prince's memory, like a figure in a shadow play. A woman on a moonlit veranda, tossing a small ball of light into the darkness. Polished like a jewel over the years, that memory shone even more brilliantly with the passage of time. Had that episode really taken place? Was it only a phantasm? As he got older, even the Prince wanted to doubt the authenticity of his memory, but something wouldn't let him. Whenever he thought about it, he told himself that there was no way his memory of that night could be so clear were there not some degree of truth to it.

What she said to him that night was like a riddle. But only four years later, in the fall of the year Daidō 5, a struggle broke out between allies of the recently retired emperor, the Prince's father, and those who sided with the newly enthroned Emperor Saga. Kusuko took her own life amid the chaos, and that shook the Prince to his core. Kusuko was with Heizei when his camp moved on the emperor. She shared a palanquin with him as they advanced east from Sentō Imperial Palace in Nara to Kawaguchi Road, but Saga's mighty army blocked their path, leaving them with little choice but to turn back. It was then that Kusuko and Heizei parted ways. Alone in a roadside hut in Soekami village in Koseta, Kusuko poisoned herself and died. Untimely, to be sure, her death was nonetheless a fitting one for a specialist such as herself. Centuries later, scholars would speculate that it was monkshood—aconitum— that Kusuko used to commit suicide, but no one knows for certain.

Before that tragic struggle, Prince Takaoka was heir presumptive to the throne. It was immediately clear to all, however, that as a result of the uprising, he would never become emperor. It made no difference that Heizei took the tonsure—the Prince was still the son of the instigator. The whole capital sympathized with the Prince, but for a twelve-year-old boy like him such political matters meant little. Undoubtedly, what opened a bottomless hole in the Prince's heart was Kusuko vanishing like a star and taking that sweet image of Hindustan with her.

When the Prince reached his twenties, without warning, he shaved his head and renounced the world. It was a decision that might well be traced back to the image of Hindustan that Kusuko had instilled in him when he was a boy.

Of course, some prefer the more sober view that, beginning with the Kusuko Incident, the Prince became increasingly frustrated by the political world, and that it was this frustration which drove him to pursue Buddhism, as similarly desperate conditions had driven the Prince's nephew, Ariwara no Narihira, down the path of eroticism. Yet this banal interpretation cannot adequately account for the rather unique Buddhist views that the Prince held throughout his life. For him, the entirety of Buddhism converged on a single point: namely, Hindustan. There can be no doubt that the Prince was a true practitioner of exoticism in the original sense of the word. That is, he reacted strongly to the foreign. Certainly, from the Asuka period onward, Buddhism might as well have been called an "imported culture" in Japan. A great many Buddhists were drawn to the exotic afterglow of Buddhist practice. Yet for the Prince, Buddhism was this and nothing but. It was like an onion, layer after layer of the exotic in its purest form, with Hindustan at its core.

The great saint Kūkai was a dandy and a Hinduphile in his own right, so a strong connection between these two preeminent Buddhists should hardly surprise us. Kūkai opened his Abhiṣeka Hall on the grounds of the Tōdai-ji temple in the year Kōnin 13, fifteen years after returning home from Tang. The Prince, who was twenty-four at the time, wasted no time in getting close to the Shingon Buddhist trailblazer. In fact, it was in that very hall that the Prince performed the Abhiṣhekam of the Two Realms and received the title of Ācārya. In the years to follow, the Prince became known as one of Kūkai's most esteemed pupils; when his master passed away, Takaoka was one of the six elite disciples chosen to attend the forty-ninth-day rites and accompany his remains to the Oku-no-in shrine on Mount Kōya. He was then thirty-seven.

I have no intention of writing an exhaustive biography here, so I will skip over some of the details. Nonetheless, there are a couple of moments in the Prince's earlier years that merit additional attention. For one, there was the reconstruction of the Great Buddha at Tōdai Temple. The Buddha's head fell to the ground in the fifth month of the year Saikō 2. The Prince and Fujiwara no Yoshimi were put in charge of its reconstruction. The task took seven years to complete. The Buddha's eyes were finally opened during the third month of the year Jōgan 3. The ceremony held to celebrate its completion was lavish beyond all description. The Prince was then sixty-three.

Takaoka traveled widely. In addition to his stay at Tō-ji in the capital, there were legends of his travels to other locales: Yamashina and Daigo Ogurusu to the east; Saihō-ji to the west; Kongō-in monastery to the north. Although Saihō-ji later became a Rinzai temple, it had in fact belonged to the Shingon sect until the Kamakura period. For a time, the Prince was also in charge of the gigantic Chōshō-ji temple in the village of Saki in Nara, near his father's final resting place. From there, the Prince frequently climbed Mount Kōya, the most sacred peak in Shingon Buddhism. There are also traces of the Prince's pilgrimages at Shingon temples throughout South Kawachi and South Yamato.

The Prince's apparent distaste for the madding world—or perhaps his fondness for seclusion—earned him the sobriquet Prince Dhūta. The Prince, whose real name was Takaoka, was known by a dizzying array of nicknames. While later generations would know him by his religious name, Shinnyo Shinnō, he was also known as Prince Zen, the Zen Prince, and the Fallen Prince of the Buddhist Path. The Prince had still stranger names, as well, including the Pill-Bug Prince. This curious title seems to refer to the Prince's tendency to turn inward and reflect. Yet this was the very tendency that made the Prince the greatest exote of old Japan.

As we go about retracing the Prince's footsteps, there is one more point we cannot afford to overlook. The very same month as the ceremony celebrating the reconstruction of Tōdai Buddha, the third month of Jōgan 3, the Prince sought permission to embark on a pilgrimage around Japan. The Prince's request appears in the records as follows: "After more than forty years as a priest, I have little life left to me. Before dying, I wish to see the mountains and the woods. I wish to finally witness the profundity of the Dhūta sites." These words hit home even today. According to the same petition, the Prince's entourage would have included five monks, three apprentices, and ten youths. They would have traveled to the western extremes of Japan's main island—the San'in and San'yō regions—and neighboring islands, as well. But this pilgrimage never came to pass. Why is that? Although it would seem that the Prince wanted to travel within Japan, he knew deep down that such a journey would never satisfy him. So, the same month, he submitted a second petition. This time he sought Imperial Consent to leave Japan and enter the Tang empire.

On the ninth day of the eighth month of the year Jōgan 3, only five months after the Great Buddha's eyes had been reopened, the Prince had already presented himself to the Kōrokan authorities in Dazaifu. It would appear that things had changed course rather quickly. Now the Prince appeared to have forgotten all about his earlier plans to make a pilgrimage around Japan—his heart was set on Tang. In the seventh month of Jōgan 4, the ship that the Prince had ordered from the Tang merchant Zhang You Xin was completed. Almost immediately, the Prince led a group of sixty—monks and laypeople alike—aboard the new vessel and set out for Tang. One of the sixty souls on that ship was Anten, the monk who would later accompany the Prince on his journey to Hindustan.

The ship waited for favorable winds near Tōchika Island, then sped across the East China Sea, arriving at the port of Mingzhou on the seventh day of the ninth month. From there, the group made their way to Yuezhou, where they waited a year and eight months for permission to enter the Tang capital. At last, on the twenty-first day of the fifth month of Jōgan 6, they were granted access, at which point the Prince entered Chang'an from Luoyang. By then, most of the Prince's companions had been allowed to return home to Japan. According to the "Brief Record of Prince Dhūta's Entry into the Tang Empire," it was the Japanese monk Ensai who told Emperor Yizong of the Prince's journey, which greatly impressed the Tang sovereign.

Without even stopping to rest, the Prince, who had only entered Chang'an in the fifth month, had already begun making the necessary arrangements to journey to Hindustan by summer or fall of the same year. It appeared that the Prince had been intending to travel to Hindustan all along. The initial pilgrimage in Japan and even his entry into Chang'an were no more than opening moves made to that end. It is extremely unlikely that the Prince met with the high priests in Luoyang and Chang'an, and only then came to the conclusion that he would have to travel to Hindustan to further pursue the Buddhist Law. The Prince was not one to wait. Once he entered Chang'an, he immediately set about making the connections that would allow him to begin the final leg of his true journey.

It was in the middle of the tenth month of the same year that, with the permission of the Tang Emperor, the Prince embarked from Chang'an in the highest spirits, following the quickest possible route to the port of Guangzhou. According to Sugimoto Naojirō, who documented the trip in considerable detail, "The Prince headed south from the capital, crossed Mount Zhongnan, then exited into the Han River Basin. Next he advanced to Xiangyang, from which point he would have taken either the Qianzhou Mountain Pass or the road to Chenzhou." Whichever the case, four or five thousand leagues separate Chang'an and Guangzhou, so the Prince and his companions must have spent approximately two months on horseback. No doubt Anten and Engaku were with the Prince by this time.

The group's arrival in Guangzhou coincided perfectly with the end of the northeast monsoon season. As already mentioned, it was the twenty-seventh day of the first month of Jōgan 7. Things being what they were, the travelers wasted no time boarding a southbound ship.

NOW, ONCE THE SHIP HAD PASSED between the Leizhou Peninsula and Hainan Island, the Prince and the others noticed that the water below was blue-black and sticky as birdlime. Alas, there was no sign of the fabled monsoon. In fact, the ship was barely moving at all. A thick vapor shrouded the vessel, significantly limiting visibility. Making matters worse, it was stiflingly hot. At night, however, small dots of light that looked like fireflies would appear on the water: Noctiluca scintillans—also known as sea sparkles. Although quite common in the area, the sea sparkles provided all on board with a rare moment of relief; if not for them, the boredom would have simply been too much to bear.

As it was, to deal with the boredom, the Prince sat down on the deck and started playing the flute he had acquired in Chang'an. He didn't expect much from the instrument, but it had a surprisingly fine tone. Notes poured out of it; like smoke, they floated out over the sea. Just then, the water began to bubble up— it was a glabrous creature, rearing its head above the waves. It seemed the animal had been summoned by the sound of the flute. The Prince didn't notice the animal at first, but Anten did. He asked the shipmaster about the strange creature, and the shipmaster explained: "It's a dugong. They're very common in these parts."

Hoping the visitor might put an end to their stupendous boredom, the shipmates hoisted the peach-colored animal onto the ship, whereupon the shipmaster fed it cinnamon rice cakes and wine. Apparently sated, the dugong began to doze off. Not much later, drops of dung that looked just like rainbow-colored bubbles began to slip out of the sleeping animal's anus. The bubbles floated in mid-air, then vanished with a pop.

Akimaru seemed particularly smitten with the dugong. Timidly, he asked the Prince whether they might keep the animal on the ship if he promised to look after it. The Prince laughed and gave his consent. From that day on, the dugong ate and slept with the rest of the crew.

One day, Anten watched from the shadows as Akimaru played with the dugong. The boy looked serious. He was facing the dugong, speaking to it. Of course the animal could only flap its fins in response, but it seemed as though Akimaru was trying to get his pet to talk. Akimaru broke up his words as he spoke, enunciating very carefully: "Sov...ajemto...nhi."

Anten was on the verge of laughing, so he turned away. There he saw Engaku, who asked: "That's not Tang he's speaking. Is it some tribal tongue?"

In a low voice, Anten answered: "Yes, I picked up on that, too. I believe it's Uban, a language of the Bird folk."

"Uban..."

"Spoken by the Luo-Luo of Inner Yunnan. You know, Akimaru's face is flat and round, not unlike the Luo-Luo..."

Before even ten days had passed, the dugong was speaking something that sounded vaguely like a human tongue, if fragmentary and imitative, all thanks to Akimaru's passionate instruction. Of course, the animal's words were unintelligible to all except Akimaru. That said, an animal learning a human language is surely something special. Reckoning this augured well, the Prince was pleased.

It was right around then that the wind began to blow furiously. The ship was suddenly sailing over the water with incredible speed. Once the wind picked up, it roared continuously, all day and all night. The small ship was beyond control now; there was nothing the crew could do except watch helplessly as the wind pushed the ship further and further south. No doubt they had gone well beyond Jiaozhou. That the ship did not capsize was a blessing, to be sure. Under the deck, the shipmates came together as if in prayer. The Prince and everyone else on board became seasick; only Akimaru and the dugong remained curiously unfazed.

At last, the wind died down again. After a good ten days moving south, they finally caught sight of blue sky through a break in the clouds. Then the lookout yelled at the top of his lungs: "Land ho!"

These two words filled the crew with new life and they ran to the gunwales to see the reflection of the mountain island floating in the water before them. No, this was no mountain island. It was a jungle coast that ran along the horizon as far as the eye could see.

"Where are we? I imagine we've come a good deal south of Jiaozhou."

"I doubt we're anywhere near Jiaozhou now. This is probably Nhât Nam, the place they call Champa, home of the Viets. Well, well...It would appear that powerful wind carried us to some far-flung land!"

"I suppose the name Champa refers to the champak tree that appears in *The Vimalakirti Sutra,* among other texts. Apparently its flowers are extremely fragrant, drawing Garuda to them from miles away. In Sanskrit, the tree is known as campakā."

"Ah, Engaku. You truly are well-versed in the sutras. There must be many gold-flowered campakas here. Look here, see these trees? I have no idea what they're called, but their roots run right up to the water's edge. Ah, we've landed!"

The ship ran right up to the coiling mangroves on the shore, practically running aground. Everyone on board took in the heady, luxuriant smell of plant life for the first time in weeks—it was as if they had been given new life. Land at last! Even the dugong waddled off the edge of the ship, demonstrating its desire to accompany the others ashore.

Into the thick wall of wilderness ran a faint trail. The Prince and his companions cut through the giant ferns and tangled roots of the dark jungle. Eventually, a vista opened up before them: they had found a field of dead grass, and there were men there.

They had to be Viet. Four or five men sitting in a circle, talking and eating. Upon closer inspection, they could see that the men were using their hands to eat fish and meat; every now and then, they would place a straw in a ceramic bowl and snort some kind of liquid from it. Each of them did this in turn. Seeing this from a distance, the Prince was unable to contain his curiosity. In a low voice, he asked Engaku: "Those men are doing something strange. What do you make of it?"

"I've never seen it with my own eyes before, but I imagine this is the famed Viet custom of nose-drinking. For the Viets, drinking alcohol or water through the nose holds an indescribable charm."

Just then, the Prince broke wind. The Viets heard it where they sat. They stopped their nose-drinking, looked over, and began shouting. Even Anten, who fancied himself quite the polyglot, was not familiar enough with the language to engage them. There was nothing that he or Engaku could do but stand there.

The Viets, however, didn't cast even a glance at Anten, Engaku, or even the Prince. Their eyes were fixed on young Akimaru. All of a sudden, one of the men reached for the boy, grabbed him, and ran off. Akimaru struggled to break free, but his captor was a giant, easily twice his size. No matter how Akimaru flailed about, the man didn't even flinch. Needless to say, the others could hardly stand by and watch as the man made off with one of their own. Anten was the first to give chase.

When he was younger, Anten was always getting into fights. He had even been expelled once from a temple. This past gave Anten confidence in his physical strength. Quickly, he swept the legs of the giant man out from under him; the Viet fell to his knees and dropped Akimaru with a thud. Anten then head-butted his opponent square in the chest, sending him flat onto his back. Anten moved with such speed that the other men had no time to intervene.

Stunned, they staggered away in retreat. There was no way to know if they would be coming back, but they were gone—at least for the moment.

Akimaru was lying unconscious on the grass. The Prince was the first to arrive at the child's side, where he saw something he wasn't meant to see: Akimaru's clothing had been ripped open from shoulder to chest, exposing a pair of breasts. They were in no sense full, but they were unmistakably the breasts of a young woman.

That night, the travelers set up camp in a clearing in the jungle. Sitting by the fire, the Prince, Anten, and Engaku put their heads together to discuss this development: "What do you make of three Buddhist monks taking a woman on a voyage to Hindustan? I know how it sounds, but now that we know Akimaru is a woman, we have no choice but to ask her to find her own way."

"I had a feeling Akimaru's presence might be a hindrance. As we make our way from Yunnan to Hindustan, dangers abound. I seriously doubt a woman's fragile feet could withstand the trek anyway…"

The Prince listened in silence as the others spoke. When they had finished, he said with a smile: "No, there's nothing to worry about. Man or woman, what's the difference? We all know Akimaru was a young man at first. He only became a woman once we set foot in this land. Who's to say she won't return to being a man as we come closer to our destination? If we can't cope with such minor miracles, I truly doubt we'll ever be able to make it all the way to Hindustan. Whatever the case, it's no bother for us to take Akimaru as far as she can go."

The Prince's logic didn't sit well with either of his companions, but he had spoken with a force that put the matter to rest. Anten and Engaku felt ashamed for having given so much thought to such a trivial matter.

At first, the travelers could handle the heat, but after spending a night in the jungle, it began to take its toll. It was unlike anything in Japan—as the rays of the sun beat down on the Prince and the others, walking on without shade was simply unbearable. As such, the travelers made straw hats to lessen the effects of the sun.

Akimaru made a second hat for the dugong to wear, as if being out of water wasn't painful enough for the marine animal. While the dugong managed to keep pace with the others for some time, the heat ultimately proved to be too much. Completely drained by the merciless sun, the dugong died that afternoon. Moments before dying, the dugong looked to Akimaru and said in clearly human language:

"What a joy it's been. I couldn't say so until it was time to die. But I will die with words on my lips. Even when I go, my soul will not vanish. We'll meet again soon—somewhere in the Southern Seas."

With those strange words, the dugong shut its eyes. The others dug a hole in a corner of the jungle and carefully lowered the dugong's body into it. The three monks dutifully chanted the sutras. Then the Prince remembered the flute he had been playing when the animal first appeared. He had an idea—he would play the instrument now, in the dugong's memory. The crisp notes flowed out like a fountain, cutting coolly through the jungle.

Just then, a strange creature appeared, shouting: "What a racket! Is that a flute? I was having such a pleasant nap until I was disturbed by some damned flute. Unbelievable!"

The creature was darting all over the place, and what a creature it was! Its mouth was like a long pipe; its tail was bushy and spread out like a fan; its legs looked like they were clad in straw chaps or fur boots. Repeatedly, the creature flicked its tongue out of its mouth. As it moved around nervously, its tail swept across the ground like a skirt, sending a cloud of dust into the air.

The Prince placed his flute back in its brocade bag. Flabbergasted, he asked Engaku: "Engaku, you must know. What is the name of this strange-looking creature?"

"I have no idea. There's nothing like it in *The Classic of Mountain and Sea*. It simply defies imagination. But, from what we've seen, it seems to have a decent command of language, so I'll ask it a few questions to shed some light on things."

Engaku stepped toward the creature and glared at it: "Lo, ignorant beast, you dare to call the Prince's flute-playing a racket? Such insolence! Perhaps you are unaware, so I shall inform you: This is Prince Shinnyo, third son of Emperor Heizei. Years ago, he left the courtly world and has since attained the title of Master Sage-Priest of the Dharma Lamp. If they have a name for you, tell us now, in good grace!"

The creature seemed unruffled: "I am a great anteater."

At this, Engaku began to redden with anger: "Come now, be serious! There are no great anteaters in these climes. It simply isn't possible."

Engaku looked so bellicose that the Prince had to interject: "Now, now, Engaku. There's no need to lose our tempers. Why should an anteater's presence here bother us at all?"

"Highness, you know nothing! That's why you can say such foolish things. At risk of anachronism, let me explain: the great anteater will be discovered roughly six hundred years from now, when Columbus arrives in what will then be called the New World. So how can we be staring at one here and now? Can't you see that its existence defies the laws of time and space? Think, Highness!"

The anteater thrust its snout between the two men: "Wrong, wrong! It's stupid to think that the existence of my kind hinges upon being 'discovered,' as you put it, by Columbus or by anyone else. Don't underestimate us! Our kind has lived on this planet longer than yours. We can make a home wherever there are ants. To restrict us to the New World—doesn't that smack of anthropocentrism?"

Unflinching, Engaku responded: "Alright, then. Tell me: when and how did you arrive here from the New World? Answer me this, or I shall have to consider your existence a flat-out falsehood."

"The Amazon River Basin, the birthplace of my kind, is on the exact opposite side of the planet from where we stand now—"

"Meaning?"

"Meaning that we are the Antipodes of the great anteaters of the New World."

"Pardon? *Antipodes*?"

"Yes. You see, on the opposite side of the planet are animals that look like us, living upside-down, opposite our feet, almost like a reflection in water. These are our Antipodes, and we are theirs. One need not ask if it was us or them that came first. We break down anthills to search for ants to eat, just like they do in the New World. Take a look around and you'll find no shortage of anthills here. The abundance of ants vouchsafes our right to live here."

Now the Prince cut into the conversation: "Enough. I'll settle this matter. There is surely some logic to what the great anteater says. Engaku, don't get your back up. Antipodes, eh? You might say we're on our way to Hindustan to see these Antipodes of which you speak. Thus, in my eyes, encountering an anteater such as yourself here is no less than a sign. You mentioned anthills a moment ago, but I have yet to see any. O noble anteater, if it's no trouble, would you mind showing us one of these hills? And while we're at it, I would love to watch you feast."

At this, the anteater became quite amiable. He agreed to lead the travelers into the jungle. Akimaru, ever the animal lover, followed right behind the anteater as they marched toward the largest anthill in the area.

After about a league, the jungle opened up and there it was. Once they arrived, all eyes were riveted on the towering mass. None had ever seen so strange a thing. It looked just like a giant pine cone shooting out of the earth. How could this massive structure have been built by mere insects? It seemed more like the ruins of an ancient civilization.

The Prince happened to notice a round object of some sort embedded in the anthill. What was it? A glowing green stone about the size of a peach, lodged just high enough that a person could reach up and grab it. Once he saw the stone, the Prince couldn't put it out of his mind. He had to ask the anteater about it. Their host had just clawed a hole into the hill and was in the act of extracting a meal of ants with his long tongue, but being questioned by the Prince, he turned to answer as follows:

"According to the lore of our kind, this stone came from across the sea a very long time ago. They say it flew through the air and smashed right into the hill— where it has remained ever since. There seems to be no way to wrest it free. On nights when the moon shines brightest, the stone, apparently jade, glows green. Moreover, when the stone in the hill is lit up like that,

you can see the outline of a bird inside, waiting to be hatched. It would seem as though the bird in the stone has grown larger with time, nourished by the moonlight. Legend has it that someday the bird will break free from its stone shell. But, when that bird spreads its wings and flies off, our kind will perish. I know it sounds absurd, but that's legends for you."

Though stoic in mien, the Prince was deeply moved by this. He turned to Engaku and asked nonchalantly: "When is the next full moon?"

"The gibbous moon is waxing. Should only be a couple of days, I suppose."

On the night of the full moon, the Prince made sure the others were all asleep in their cots, then made his way through the jungle. The moon was still rising when he arrived at the black anthill, which looked even stranger now than in the light of day.

The Prince waited with bated breath. About half an hour later, when the moon sat in the very middle of the sky above him, he saw the stone in the hill begin to glow. No, not just glow—the stone grew so blindingly bright that it was impossible for him to look away. There really was a bird inside, bathing in the brilliant light. It looked as though the bird might break out of the stone at any moment.

Just then, the Prince had a strange thought. He didn't really believe it himself, but part of him wondered if throwing that stone back toward Japan before the bird broke loose might make time run backward, causing the past to appear again before his eyes. Yes, it was a ridiculous idea. The Prince was thinking about Kusuko, no doubt.

Away, away you go! Off to distant Hindustan!— Kusuko's words hummed in the Prince's ear.

He had to fight temptation. While part of him wanted to see the bird escape its stone egg, there was that other part of him that wanted nothing more than to experience the sweet past once more. There was a chance he could be reunited with his beloved Kusuko and, ultimately, that temptation proved too great. He reached up to grab the bright stone buried in the wall of the anthill. The Prince pulled at it with all his might and wrenched it free. But it tumbled to the ground, whereupon the light inside vanished. It had instantly been reduced to an ordinary rock.

That night, the Prince returned to camp in the lowest of spirits. He kept to himself what had happened at the anthill. Later on, however, when he casually mentioned the anteater in conversation, everyone—Anten, Engaku, and Akimaru—gave him blank looks, as if they had no idea what he was talking about. But how could that be? It seemed as though the others had never encountered such a creature. 🐵

Note from the translator: "The Dugong" is the first chapter from Tatsuhiko Shibusawa's 1987 novel *Takaoka's Travels* (*Takaoka shinnō kōkaiki*). The novel follows a Japanese prince as he travels through Southeast Asia on a pilgrimage to the birthplace of the Buddha.

The Takaoka character is based on a ninth-century prince who lost his status within the courtly world of Kyoto after his father conspired against the emperor. Forced from the capital in his youth, Takaoka became a Buddhist monk, as disgraced princes typically did in those days. Decades later, in his sixties, he set sail for China. History lost sight of Takaoka once he arrived in China, but it is with that moment that Shibusawa's historical fantasy begins.

At the start of the novel, Takaoka leaves the Tang Empire. He then visits several Buddhist kingdoms, each more bizarre than the last. As the narrative "progresses," miracles and anachronisms abound—or perhaps, the story suggests, the Prince is only dreaming. The Japanese monks accompanying the Prince on this long and difficult journey are constantly frustrated by these supernatural developments; the Prince, on the other hand, appears to revel in them. As the retinue comes closer to the holy land, the rules of the physical world are further upended, and the Prince finds exactly what he has been looking for, even though he is—in a very real sense—lost at sea.

Shibusawa (1928–1987) completed *Takaoka's Travels,* his only full-length novel, not long before dying at the age of fifty-nine.

Haruki Murakami

Jogging in Southern Europe

translated by Ted Goossen

THE MOST INCONVENIENT THING about this extended stay in southern Europe is making my daily run. Jogging is not a custom here, so you seldom see people running. The exceptions are purse-snatchers on the lam (they really do exist here!) and backpackers late to catch the local bus, which comes only twice a day. So I get all kinds of really weird looks when I trot leisurely down the road. "What the hell is he doing?" they ask, gawking as I pass by. Some stop dead in their tracks, mouths hanging open. The farther out you go into the countryside, the more extreme the reaction. The concept of jogging, indeed of physical exercise itself, is a product of urban culture, so many here simply can't wrap their heads around it.

When we were living on the island of Mykonos, I used to run from the port of Hora to the beach on the other side of the island, which meant crossing a (very steep) mountain. It was winter, the off-season, so it was pretty deserted. If I passed anyone on that mountain road, it was usually a farmer or an old woman astride a donkey taking their vegetables to market. The winter winds of Mykonos are sometimes so fierce that you can feel yourself being pushed backwards down the slope. Time and again, someone would call out to stop me. They couldn't fathom what it was that compelled me to jog over the mountain. "What are you running for?" they wanted to know. Greeks have an abundance of spare time, and they are a curious people.

A group of three called out to me one day, two old women dressed in black and a man of about fifty. He was wearing a hat and had a donkey on a rope. They appeared to be farmers, stocky and deeply tanned by the sun. They were chatting at the entrance of a small farmhouse, but, true to form, their jaws dropped and their eyes zeroed in on me as I went running past. "Here we go again!" I thought. Sure enough, I was already 150 feet down the road when they called out to me. "Young man, come back!" they addressed my retreating back. It was rudimentary English, but English nonetheless. Grumbling to myself—What the hell do you mean, "young man"?—I trotted back to where they were.

"Hello," I said.

"Hello," the man answered.

"Hello." "Hello." The women greeted me. One wore thick glasses; the other was as big as an elephant. They were staring at me warily, my jogging shoes, my T-shirt. I could tell they weren't going to let their guard down easily.

"Um, why are you running on this road?" the man asked. He seemed to be their spokesman.

"Because I love running," I replied in Greek. I had been asked this over and over again, so I had the phrase down pat.

"By which you mean," he went on, stroking his beard, "you're on no particular errand?"

"No, none at all."

The three looked at each other for a few moments, debating how to take my words. Meanwhile, I killed time mopping the sweat from my face, looking around at the scenery, and so forth. The wind was strong, and if my sweat dried, I was likely to catch a cold, but I had to wait until they had finished their conference.

"How far will you run?" the man finally asked.

"To Super Paradise Beach," I replied.

"That's quite far," he said.

"Well, yes, um, you could say that."

"Running all the way?"

"I like running."

"But why do you have to run to the beach?" the heavy-set old woman broke in. My god, I wasn't getting through to them at all. Maybe my crummy Greek was to blame.

"I like running, you see," I repeated my words more firmly.

"Running is bad for your health," the old woman with the Coke-bottle glasses put in.

"Mm-hmm," the other woman agreed.

That was news to me, but judging by their deep frowns they were certainly convinced on that point.

"Look, I'm strong as a bull," I said, flexing my biceps. I was getting desperate. Good grief, I thought, what the hell am I doing?

I tried, they tried, but regretfully we just couldn't make ourselves understood. It was futile, like trying to shout across a valley in a gale. There was no common ground. The man shrugged and spread his arms in defeat. The old women slowly shook their heads from side to side like stunted giraffes. We all fell silent. The donkey's flanks were quivering.

"Say, why don't you come inside for a glass of ouzo," the heavy-set woman asked. Now there was a fine idea! All I needed on my morning run was a shot of strong liquor. I hadn't gotten through to them at all.

"Thank you so much," I said with a bright smile, "but I had better be on my way."

"Ouzo is good for you," said the old lady with the glasses.

There was no way to end this conversation, so I chose a random moment and jogged off. When I glanced back over my shoulder, they were still standing there, their eyes fixed on my departing form.

THE SECOND PROBLEM about running in southern Europe is the dogs. There are scads of them running free. And they're not used to joggers, so when they see a suspicious character—i.e., yours truly—running by, they set off in hot pursuit. At least with people, there is always the possibility of talking things out, however frustrating that may prove to be, but dogs usually exist beyond language. They just don't listen to reason. If worst comes to worst, your life may be at risk.

I was running on the outskirts of a Greek town one day when a big black dog came after me, putting me in real danger. No one was around, and I thought that this might be the end for me, but just then a taxi appeared out of nowhere and inserted itself between me and the dog, saving me.

I had numerous run-ins with dogs when I was living in Palermo, in Sicily. There was an excellent running track not far from the Palermo racetrack, a real blessing for a jogger like me. The problem was the dogs I encountered in the fifteen or so minutes it took me to get there. How were others dealing with the problem, I wondered? Then it hit me that everyone else drove their cars to the track, did their run, and then hopped back in their cars to go home. I didn't own a car, so I was the only one arriving on foot. My particular nemesis was a large and vicious white dog who lived next to the gas station that I passed en route. No sooner did he see me than he would take off in my direction, barking all the way. He was always waiting in the same spot, and he always chased me. Though his owner was usually nearby, all he did was sit back and watch. I shouted and gestured at him, but he ignored me. Sicilians can be quite heartless and stubborn in situations like this. Their attitude seems to be, go ahead, dog, bite the damned outsider. Serves him right!

For the first few weeks, I carried a stick for protection when I went out running, but that led to yet another problem. You see, the authorities had recently snared a high-ranking mafia boss, and he was standing trial at that very moment. In retaliation, the mafia had gunned down several government officials in the streets, and so the whole city of Palermo was heavily patrolled, with policemen on every corner. Each carried an automatic handgun and wore a bullet-proof vest and a tense expression. To go running past those guys with a club in my hand was asking for trouble, no matter how I looked at it. The dog was scary, but the cops were scary too.

This left me with just two options: I could either give up running or rise to the challenge and confront the dog head on. Of course, I chose the latter. I don't scare easily—if the critics couldn't stop me writing my novels, I figured, no damn dog could prevent me from making my daily run. Well, that may be a bit over the top, but I did feel capable of besting a mere dog.

It was thus that, one morning, I trotted straight up to where the dog was sitting. I glared at him, and he glared back at me. I bent to his level and gave him my "watch out, you son of a bitch!" look. He answered with his "try and make me!" face and a low, rumbling growl. I had never tried to stare down a dog before, so I was a bit worried at first how it would turn out, but before long it became clear that I had the upper hand. A look of puzzlement came into his eyes. Never had a human adversary made the first move like this, and his doggy brain was confused. Now I had him. Sure enough, after five or six minutes of staring at each other like this, he averted his gaze. Seizing the opportunity, I drew to within a few inches of his muzzle and shouted at the top of my lungs (in Japanese, of course).

"I'm warning you! Don't ever mess with me again!"

The white dog never chased me after that. In fact, I would sometimes chase him just for fun. Now he was the scared one, since he always ran away. I learned that chasing dogs is actually quite a lot of fun.

THERE AREN'T MANY JOGGERS IN ITALY, but there are a few. They are a breed apart, though, from their brothers and sisters in places like the United States and Germany. Japan too, for that matter. I've jogged in towns and cities around the world, and among the so-called advanced countries Italian joggers stand out as a tribe unto themselves.

First of all, they are terribly clothes-conscious. I run in whatever I find comfortable, but Italians start off by putting together a stylish outfit. From old folks down to children, they take great care in crafting their "look" and then spend the money to make it happen. I stand in awe. It would be great if their running rose to the same level, but I remain to be convinced on that score. Nevertheless, it is something to see a runner decked out in a jogging suit by Valentino, with a Missoni towel wrapped around his neck.

The second striking feature of jogging in Italy is that solitary runners are rare. Instead, most run in groups. I'm not sure why—a dislike of doing things alone? a national fear of solitude? a need to be constantly talking?—but it blew my mind at first. I have no problem with people running in groups, nor do I wish to dictate "correct behavior," but the fact remains that there are just too few Italians running alone. Single runners constitute a clear majority in other countries —probably 80 percent of the total—while the rest usually run in organized groups; but the numbers in Italy are completely reversed. Smiling and chattering, they all seem to be having a fine time. If someone needs to stop to pee in the bushes, the rest jog in place as they wait for him. I know it's none of my business, and I shouldn't carp about people who are clearly enjoying themselves, but stopping so someone can pee? I can't buy into that. I mean, that's what children do! Americans wouldn't wait. Germans wouldn't stop to pee in the first place. Running is the same every-where, but the culture of running differs depending on where you are. Watching how the Italians do it, I can see why they lost the war.

I heard the same opinion when I was traveling in Malta, the scene of many hard-fought battles in World

War II. Although Italian planes had bombed Malta, the Maltese seemed to bear Italians no animosity. That's because the bombing caused no real damage. "Italians go all out for just three things—eating, talking, and flirting with women," one man told me. "But that's it. When they attacked us, they were so afraid of our antiaircraft guns that they dropped their bombs from a great height. Then they turned around and went home. They flew so high, though, there was no way they could hit anything. Instead, their bombs fell in the fields or in the ocean. But they didn't care. They had been ordered to drop their payload, so that's what they did. As far as we Maltese were concerned, Mussolini could rant and rave all he wanted, but Malta would never surrender. Then came the German bombardment. That was sheer hell. Their dive-bombers flew so low they could hit whatever they wanted. Our whole city was destroyed. So you see, in that way the Italians weren't bad at all."

I agree entirely. Italy is, in that sense, a wonderful country. The sort of country where few can be bothered with something as pointless as running.

In Germany, by contrast, you find even sex workers out for a jog. I know that it sounds like something from Ryu Murakami's collection of stories *New York City Marathon,* but I actually encountered one such woman in Hamburg who said she jogged around Lake Alster every morning. It was the same route I was running, so just to check, I asked her what her time was, and it was damn fast. When I told her how impressed I was, she shrugged. "You see, my body is my capital," she said. She had it right. For a novelist as for a sex worker, our bodies are our capital.

"Do you run alone?" I asked

"Of course," she said.

Hey, Italians. Did you hear that? In Germany, even prostitutes run. By themselves no less!

It was rare, but there were occasions when I saw an Italian jogging alone. Some were silent. Others, though, were only too eager to strike up a conversation. They would fall into stride beside me and pester me with questions like, "How far are you running?" and "Shall we run together?" Those guys were a real pain! They couldn't stop talking, even after I made it clear that I spoke almost no Italian. At first, I thought they might be gay, but I was wrong. It appeared they were just lonely with no one to talk to.

ROME IS THE WORST CITY in southern Europe for joggers, hands down. It's not that there are no good places to run. There are. For example, there is a wonderful path through the Villa Borghese gardens, spacious and with a great view. The path that runs along the River Tiber is also a winner. The problem is getting to those places. Indeed, finding one's way there is a bit like passing through hell. Far from being places to walk, the sidewalks are crammed with parked cars, there is dog shit wherever you look, cars zoom past, the air is bad, people jam the streets—by the time you reach your destination you're already exhausted. I thought getting to Central Park in New York City was bad, but it's the epitome of refinement compared to the chaos of Rome.

Then there are the groups of obnoxious teenagers, who seem to be everywhere. Theirs isn't the deep-rooted malevolence of the young knife-wielding heroin addicts of the South Bronx. In Rome they simply suffer from an excess of energy, which comes bursting out in all sorts of unpleasant ways. And they are spoiled rotten. For one thing, they are sexually precocious—a newspaper survey reports that most become sexually active at about age fifteen. In that area, at least, they seem focused. I don't know anything about Italy's school system, but it is common to see groups of high school and junior high school students out in the middle of the day, knapsacks hanging over their shoulders, smoking cigarettes and making out as if they hadn't a care in the world. They don't have money to spend, but they do have lots of time and energy, so when I come jogging by, they see a turkey ripe for plucking, the perfect way to pass the time. The screeching and hooting never let up:

"Hey, Japanese, pick up the pace!"

"Hey, Japanese, enough running—we want kung fu!"

"Ichi, ni, san, shi!"

Everybody yells things like that—it's a real show. Some mimic my running, others pretend to be doing kung fu, others just leap wildly about. In other words, they behave like the rowdy monkeys in an old Tarzan movie. I don't get all that angry since I know they're not bad kids at heart, but they can still bug me, like when a group starts in on the theme song from *Rocky*. Japanese high school kids don't act out that way. Sure, I sympathize with all they have to put up with—the exam hell, the rules and restrictions, the obligatory club activities, the hysterical teachers—and wish they could escape the crushing weight of the circumstances they are placed in. Nevertheless, when I see those Italian kids I want to grab them by the scruff of the neck and shout, Why don't you stop horsing around and go to school? Think about others once in a while!

It would be ridiculous and pathetic to scold them like that, though, so I pretend I can't hear and go jogging past.

Rome is really just an enormous village. People there are far less informed than those living in New York, or Tokyo (or even Milan for that matter). Although Rome may be backward, its youth are full of life. Their boorishness may tick me off sometimes (I was ready to throttle two or three of them!), but compared to the average young Japanese I see milling around Harajuku, their darting eyes sparkle—the Italian kids seem tuned in to what is going on around them. In cinematic terms, they fast-cut from one thing to the next in perfect rhythm. When they look at something, they really see it. Those typical Japanese kids I'm talking about are different. Some dismiss what's taking place in front of their eyes as of little interest, or assume it's something they know already. Others get jumpy, in the same way that they use their remote controls to restlessly skip from one TV channel to the next. They are constantly under stress, and frantically trying to keep up with the huge quantity of information the metropolis offers. There seems to be no middle ground. At least that's how it strikes me. In that sense, the spoiled brats of Rome have it lucky. There's not that much information to keep up with and a whole lot of fun stuff taking place around them. So they can just sprawl about the square, singing out to passersby: "Hey, old man! How's it hanging?"

When I'm traveling, I love running in the towns I'm visiting. I think a pace of about 6 miles an hour is perfect for looking at the scenery. Cars are too fast—I miss seeing small things, not to mention the odors and sounds of the road. Walking, on the other hand, takes a bit too much time. Every town has its own air, its own feel. Its citizens also react to me in various ways. The street's twists and turns, the sound your feet make, the width of the sidewalk, how the garbage is set out—all are different. In a really interesting way. I just love relaxing as I observe the look of each town on my run. Running marathons is fun, but this is fun too. I have the distinct sensation of being alive, surrounded by other living beings. It is a sensation one is prone to lose otherwise.

There are those who search out a popular drinking place when they arrive in a new place, and others who look for a woman to sleep with. I run. It is through running that I attempt to feel something that is mine alone. Sometimes it works, and sometimes it doesn't. Nevertheless, I keep running. I enjoy it, and there's the pleasure of discovering new vistas too. Like cracking open a new writing pad to that pristine first page. 🐵

Note from the author: I know things have changed in the thirty-five years since I wrote this!

Laird Hunt

Whale Leg

TRAVELING NORTH FROM TOKYO to Kumagaya one early morning, I'm sure I've fallen asleep, because I think I'm hearing whales, big ones, calling out to each other across the deep. I open my eyes and the whales are still there, singing from the connection between the train cars. It's just elaborate squeaking, I think, but still I stand a moment, eliciting barely a glance from my fellow passengers, and go over to listen. I hear it again—lower, then higher, a strange aquatic keening—long enough to determine that it's not coming from the connection between the cars, but then it stops abruptly and I return to my seat. I don't shut my eyes this time; instead I reopen my copy of the *Japan Times,* one of two I've brought with me, and return to my reading.

In today's paper there are articles on the Chinese love of high-end Spanish ham and on the "ghost" ships "full of" bones and corpses washing up on Japan's coast. In the paper I bought last week, there are quick hits on a five-year-old girl who has passed a written test to become a ghost expert; two escaped emus that have now been caught; and an exorcist paid millions of yen who has been arrested for telling parents to take their diabetic son—who died as a result of the advice—off insulin because he had the "God of Death" in his stomach.

"Jesus Christ, that's too much!" the man sitting next to me says.

"I know, it's outrageous!" I say and turn toward him, preparing to smile and ask him, if it seems appropriate, how he speaks English so well, only he hasn't been looking at my paper and isn't addressing me. He is instead looking at the stain he has just made on his suit pants, near the knee, by opening his jet-black can of coffee too quickly. The stain he has made is more than a little whale-shaped. It looks like the whale is swimming in a perfectly pressed dark-green sea. But what kind of whale is it? Beluga? Gray? Sperm? Humpback? I can't quite decide, and before I can open my mouth to ask him what he thinks, he has taken a packet of tissues and a bottle of sparkling water out of a handsome cognac-colored briefcase sitting on the seat next to him and begun dabbing at the little whale, which quickly becomes a dark, amorphous blob. I am preparing, a little sadly, to return to my paper to continue reading when the singing starts up again. It sounds deeper, longer, and sadder this time. In the meantime, the amorphous blob on the man's pants has reformed as a whale, but is much bigger now. The whale looks like it is far below the surface and might not breach for a long time.

"Aha!" I say rather loudly and clap my hands.

The man, startled by my outburst, turns his head and looks over the top of his glasses at me.

"It was your leg," I whisper to him. "It was your leg singing to us all along." 🐒

From the modern Japanese
translation by Seikō Itō

—

KUROZUKA
A Noh Play

translated and with an introduction
by Jay Rubin

BLACK MOUND OF DEATH:
AN INTRODUCTION

A NOH PERFORMANCE IS ESSENTIALLY A DANCE structured around a public recitation of a narrative text, with actors and chorus speaking or chanting their lines at musically predetermined moments, fluidly switching between first person and third person. Only in the Kyōgen "comic" interlude of *Kurozuka,* in which the chorus is silent, do actors speak as characters, as in Western drama. No attempt is made to distinguish between lines delivered by the chorus and those delivered by the actors. See the introductory remarks to *Fujito* in *Monkey* 2020 for more on this subject.

Most schools of Noh call this play *Kurozuka* (Black Mound), but old records and the present-day Kanze school call it *Adachigahara,* the name of the locale in which the action is set. The playwright Komparu Zenchiku (1405–c.1470) may have had some hand in adapting it from legendary material, but nothing definite is known of its authorship. It is traditionally classified as a play of the fifth category, in which the central character is a demonic being to be quelled, bringing the day's program of plays to a spectacular conclusion.

This translation first appeared in the December 2020 issue of the magazine *Shinchō,* where it benefitted greatly from the attention of Maho Adachi and other members of the editorial staff.

ON THE PLAIN OF ADACHI—Adachigahara—in the deep north of Japan, stands a huge black mound that has been there as long as anyone can remember. Legend has it that a demon, an *oni,* lives inside the mound. No one has ever seen her, but when night falls, strange things begin to happen, and people disappear.

KUROZUKA

THESE TRAVEL ROBES OF OURS are *suzukake,* the ecclesiastical garments worn by intrepid *yamabushi* mountain priests such as us. We make our way on pathways so overgrown, our *suzukake* sleeves are always damp with dew—and damp with tears as well.

Here I stand before you, a high-ranking preceptor of Buddhist doctrine, an Ajari, by the name of Yūkei. I am the leader of this *yamabushi* band from the Eastern Light Monastery in Nachi, Kumano.

The Way of the *yamabushi* is to renounce the secular world and to practice our ascetic discipline deep in the mountains.

We *yamabushi* from Kumano travel as pilgrims to province after province, as befits the work of any priest.

Yūkei, having recently sworn a vow, departs now for the provinces with his men.

Leaving our home temple behind in Kumano, we travel down the Kishū Road, walk past the shore of Shiozaki, and by the time we pass the beach at Nishiki no Hama, our robes drooping all the more though we retie the cords that bind them day after day until, before we know it, we have arrived in Adachigahara in far-off Michinoku, known to us only as a name. Yes, here we are on the plain of Adachigahara.

"Having traveled swiftly, we have already arrived in Adachigahara in Michinoku. The sun has set, so let us find lodgings here."

"Yes, let us do so."

Having agreed to look for lodgings, Yūkei and his men hear a woman's voice emerging from a humble cottage:

Surely nothing can be sadder than the days of one who lives in wretched loneliness. Tired of living through the days that fall upon me comes the fall when daybreak winds cut through my flesh and no rest comforts this breast of mine, another day gone by in emptiness, my only moments of life those few I doze through in the dead of night. Oh, this life of constant turmoil!

Yūkei calls toward the cottage: "Hello, I wish to speak with you."

"And who might you be?"

"We are Buddhist pilgrims traveling through the provinces. Overtaken by nightfall in the midst of our travels, we have lost our way. We beg for a single night's lodging."

His *yamabushi* companions join him in saying, "Oh, mistress of this dwelling, hear our plea! Having come to Adachigahara for the first time, and the sun having set, we have no way to find lodgings. Please take pity on us and take us in for the night."

The woman then replies, "How can I put you up here in the fields so far from human habitation where fierce winds blow into my bedroom and moonlight shines through the roof?"

Yūkei says, "We need rest from our travels tonight, even if it means pillowing our heads on grass. All we ask is one night's lodging."

The woman thinks, *In this cottage that even I find appalling?*

The *yamabushi* are determined to stay here, and though she has closed her brushwood door, she takes pity on them and says, "If you insist, you may stay here." She opens the door and steps out to welcome them.

She gives them crude mats of sedge and grasses. "We sleep on these tonight?" Yūkei and his men wonder, and though they all but forced their way in for the night, each lies alone on his travel robe, sleeves soaked with dew, restless in this wretched hovel, sad and lonely travelers.

Yūkei then speaks: "Please tell me, mistress, what is this unusual object you have in your home?"

"Oh, that? That is called a spinning wheel. We poor women use it in our work."

"How interesting. Please be so good as to show us how you use it."

"I am ashamed to have you travelers look upon the humble work I must constantly suffer through."

Yūkei admires the deep kindness of their lodgings' mistress as the night deepens.

"The moon is shining in," says the woman, looking up.

"Into the room," Yūkei says, moved.

Spinning thread, the woman thinks to herself, *Spinning beautiful linen thread like this again and again, pure white linen thread again and again, I want to bring back the good old days again and again.*

Spinning linen thread, I perform my lowly labor into the night.

Oh, the backbreaking toil of keeping oneself alive!

The woman laments, "How shameful of me! Though born a human being with full potential to earn the Buddha's salvation, I have wasted my days pursuing this sad and painful life."

Yūkei hears her lament and mutters, "What heartbreaking words! Please recognize that saving one's own life is the very first means by which one may eventually seek to attain Buddhahood."

Though you spend night and day without letup prolonging your life like that in this dismal world, as long as your heart lives up to the True Way, your harsh life can become the connection through which you are eventually saved by the Buddha, even if you do not pray for it.

Whereupon the woman says, "A human being is but a fleeting combination of the four states: earth, water, fire, and wind. Once so combined, the person enters the cycle in which life is endlessly reborn, rotating through the Five Realms: Hell, Hungry Ghosts, Animals, Humans, and Heaven, plus the sixth, the Realm of the Warring Demons, all of which are products of the heart's delusions. When we consider the fleeting nature of humanity, we see that no one is young forever, that all of us inevitably age. Yet why do we not all come to despise this transient, dreamlike life of ours and renounce it for the life of a priest? My own heart is so uncertain, but resenting this truth would do no good."

As she spins thread on her wheel, the woman sings to herself of many threads.

They say the one who visited the house of the Twilight Beauty on Gojō in Kyoto was the famous Prince Genji, whose hat was festooned with blue and white threads worn in deference to the gods.

And lining the route of the Kamo Shrine's festival were . . .

. . . fringed ox carts decorated with colorful threads, I am told.

And the time of year when swaying thread-cherries bend their brilliant blossom-laden branches toward the ground . . .

. . . is the season when so many people come to see them: spring evenings, when I am careful not to stretch the threads I spin so much they lose their spring.

In autumn the thread-like plume grasses wear their silken crowns . . .

. . . and, spinning thread, they wait for night—in hopes of seeing the moon?

And now, as this humble woman spins her thread . . .

So long a life that does not go as planned.

Yes, long a bitter life I see, I raise my voice like a plover on the Akashi coast, crying all night alone, crying alone all night.

Before long, the woman says, "Listen, everyone!"

"Yes, what could it be?"

"The night has grown so cold, I will go up the mountain to gather wood and build a fire to keep you warm. Please wait here. I will not be long."

"We are grateful for your thoughtfulness. Please come back soon."

"Yes, I will be sure to come back soon."

She starts to leave but suddenly halts. "I do have one thing to say, however. Until I come back, do not look in my bedroom."

"No, of course not! We are not the sort of people who would look into another person's bedroom."

"Ah, I am glad to hear that. Be sure you do not look. And that goes for the others as well."

"Yes, we understand."

She takes a few steps, pauses a moment, but then disappears.

SOON AFTER SHE GOES, the priests' servant begins to speak.

"My oh my, though she lives in this deserted place in the depths of Michinoku, the mistress of this house is such a kind person! That she has allowed us to stay here at all is remarkable, but in addition she has taken it upon herself to go out alone into the mountains at night, although she is a woman, to gather wood and start a fire for us because the night has turned so cold. Surely there is no one else like her. On the other hand, she took on such a menacing aspect as if she had become a different woman, and so I watched her very closely. As I had expected, she started to leave for the mountain, but then she turned back and said, 'Be sure not to look into my bedroom.' Granted, there are many different kinds of people, but no one should be saying things like that to a high-ranking preceptor, an Ajari no less. I will say this to the Ajari himself, and then I believe I will take a peek into the mistress's room."

The servant presents himself to Yūkei.

"Good Master, I wish to speak if I may. Though she lives in this deserted place in the depths of Michnoku, the mistress of this house is so kind that she has generously allowed us to stay here. In addition, although she is a woman, she has taken it upon herself to go out alone into the mountains at night, to gather wood to start a fire for us because the night is cold. Surely there is no one else like her, but what does the Ajari think?"

"What you say is true. Surely there is no one as kind as tonight's host. Though a mere woman, she goes up the mountain in the middle of the night to gather wood to build a fire for us. It is remarkable."

"And yet, as if she had become a different woman, she took on a menacing aspect as she left. I watched her very closely. She started to leave for the mountain as I had expected, but then turned back and said, 'Be sure not to look in my bedroom.' Granted, there are many different kinds of people, but no one should speak like that to a high-ranking preceptor, an Ajari no less. This is so very strange, I will go take a peek into the mistress's room."

"No no, I gave her my solemn promise. I forbid you to do that."

"I thought you would have no objection."

"No, I forbid it. Now the night is deepening, and I must have some sleep. You, too, go to sleep over there."

"Yes, Your Holiness."

The servant tries to sleep, but he says to himself, "What is the meaning of this? I thought there would be no objection, but His Holiness tells me not to do it. He insists so strongly, though, I'd better not look. I'll just go to sleep."

He lies down but sits up again right away.

"What is happening? I'm trying to sleep but I can't. I'm too worried about what the mistress said before."

He looks at Yūkei.

"The Ajari appears to be sound asleep. I'll just go and take a peek at the mistress's room."

"What are you doing?"

"I'm rolling over in bed."

"Calm yourself and go to sleep."

"Yes, Master."

He stretches out in bed but he cannot sleep.

"What is happening? I thought he was asleep, but he was wide awake. Oh, well, it's hopeless. This time I'll be sure to sleep."

He tries again to sleep.

"What's this, what's this? I want to sleep but I can't. I'm too worried. Oh, now I see at last the master is sleeping. This time I will slip past the Ajari and look into the mistress's room."

"Where are you going?"

"Oh, I had a scary dream that someone was taking me away. I'm sorry I woke you up. Now I will go to sleep."

"You're so annoying!"

"Yes," he says, bowing his head to the master with both hands on the floor, and lying down again.

"Oh, what a sharp-eyed master he is! This time I was sure he was asleep, but he woke up again. What can I do? Ah, yes, they say of a man's heart and the pillars of the Great Buddha Hall, the stouter the better. All right, I'll do my best to sleep."

But soon he wakes, approaches Yūkei, knocks on the floor, and clears his throat, "Ahem!" He does this several times until finally he stands and moves past the master's bed.

"Yes, I did it, I did it! I managed to slip past him! My old habits are at work again. If someone tells me to look at something, I don't want to look at it, but if someone tells me *not* to look at something, I can't stand not to look at it. All right, then, let me hurry and look into the mistress's bedroom."

He opens the bedroom door but immediately closes it and staggers back, hardly able to walk.

"Oh, how frightening, how frightening! No wonder she was keeping it hidden! Skeletons beyond counting! Corpses piled to the rafters! Souls of the dead flying around the room like luminous spheres! If he stays here, the master will lose his life. I must warn him now!"

He immediately presents himself to Yūkei.

"Master, I looked!"

"What are you talking about? You looked at what?"

"I looked into the mistress's bedroom, and there were skeletons beyond counting, corpses piled to the ceiling, and luminous spheres flying around the room. If the Ajari stays here, she will take his life, too. Hurry and leave this house!"

"I expressly told you not to look. This is outrageous."

"Yes, Master."

"As wrong as you were to do it, I feel I must look inside."

"Please do so immediately. Meanwhile, I and the others will go out first and try to find other lodgings."

"Yes, please do so."

"Oh, how frightening! Let us hurry out of here and find lodgings. We're saved, we're saved, we're saved, we're saved!"

KUROZUKA continued

THE SERVANT LEAVES and Yūkei approaches the bedroom.

"How strange. I take a good look at the mistress's bedroom through the cracks to find countless corpses piled up to the rafters, pools of pus and blood everywhere, the stench of swollen corpses, scraps of putrefying skin and fat. This must be the dwelling of the demon said to hide out in the black mound of Adachigahara!"

His fellow *yamabushi* also speak: "How frightening! This horrible scene must be what the old poem described: 'A demon hides in the black mound of Adachigahara in Michinoku.'"

Frightened out of their wits, Yūkei and his men let their legs carry them in all directions, scattering in confusion.

At that point, who should appear but the demon woman herself!

"You *yamabushi* there! Stop, I say! You have revealed the contents of my bedroom I tried so hard to conceal. I am here to vent my rage. Clouds of smoke arise from the flames of anger burning in my breast just as the Qin Dynasty's Xianyang Palace was burned by Xiang Yu."

The demon throws down the firewood she has been carrying on her back.

From fields and mountains, the wind bears down on the hut.

Thunder and lightning fill heaven and earth.

Clouds cover the sky and rain pours down.

The demon will devour them in one gulp.

Her footsteps draw near.

She swings her iron staff with such terrifying force it mows down everything around it.

Meanwhile, Yūkei and his men raise prayers with all their might to the Five Great Guardian Kings:

In the east, Gōzanze, Vanquisher of the Three
    Worlds of desire, form and formlessness with
    their poisonous greed, Hatred, and ignorance.
In the south, Gundari Yasha, Dispenser of
    Heavenly Nectar.
In the west, Daiitoku, Destroyer of Death.

In the north, Kongō Yasha, Devourer of Demons.

And in the center, Dainichi Daishō Fudō, the
    Immovable One.

They chant a powerful mantra: ON-KOROKORO-
SENDARI MATŌGI, ON-NABI-RA-UNKEN SOWAKA,
UNTARATA-KANMAN!

The *yamabushi* all stamp their feet and grind their
rosaries.

One who sees my body will aspire to Buddhahood.

One who hears my name will abstain from evil and
practice good.

One who hears my teaching will attain great wisdom.

One who knows my heart will become a Buddha in
the flesh.

"A Buddha in the flesh," the *yamabushi* say as
they attack and attack, investing all their prayers in
the punishing rope in Fudo's left hand until their
prayers have vanquished her: may she have learned
her lesson!

Beaten down by their rosaries, the demon casts
away her iron staff, crouches on the ground and says,
"Until now, I have been so . . ."

Yes, so ferocious until now, the demon has suddenly
weakened, shrinking down to human size. She
staggers, dazed, her footsteps wandering over the
plain of Adachigahara.

"I have always been so well hidden, living in the
black mound, but now in shame I stand revealed!"

Her horrible shrieks resound, but soon the wailing
storms drown them out. Her screams fade into
the fierce night winds that tear across the plain. 🐵

Note from the translator: In *Kurozuka,* the worst
human fears of death and putrefaction are played out
before our eyes with all the predictability—and thus
the archetypal sense of doom—of a Grimm's fairy
tale. Since this is all that awaits us, it implies, we had
better not waste the rare opportunity granted us
through birth into the human realm. Religious spells
may have chased the demon back out into the night,
but they have not dispatched her. She still lurks in
the black mound of death. Though it tells an entirely
different story, the 1964 film *Onibaba,* directed
by Kaneto Shindō, draws from some of this legendary
material.

Eric McCormack

The Trail

ON MY ARRIVAL FROM CANADA I rented a car at the airport and drove east for more than an hour along a winding road. The sky was overcast, as was usually the case in late October. At first, the landscape was quite pastoral, dotted with little farmhouses and weathered barns. Most of the fields had been ploughed for the approaching winter, while others lay fallow. Cows and farm horses grazed contentedly on the remaining grassy areas.

One very unusual sight caused me to stop the car and get my camera out. Overhead, thousands of black cormorants were flying towards the coast. Unlike geese, these big vampire-like birds uttered not a single cry. They flew a hundred feet or so above me, and the rhythmic swishing of their wings had an ominous sound. It took at least a full minute for them all to pass, so I got some good photos.

I drove on for another few miles into the more impressive Upland hill country. At a fork in the road, a signpost pointed south: RAVENSMUIR 10 MILES. This road was much narrower than the first and was lined with waist-high stone walls. No longer were there farmhouses or cultivated fields.

The road wound its way up a wide treeless valley between gentle hills. They rose at least a thousand feet on either side, their tops obscured by gray and blackening clouds. These hills had once been jagged mountains as tall as the Alps. Billions of years had worn them down, yet their former stature was still evident in these smooth mounds. Their colors mainly boiled down to just one: green, in its various shades. The occasional patches of white on the lower slopes were in fact grazing flocks of sheep. Alongside the road I was on, a narrow dirty brown river churned its way back towards the coast.

By around three in the afternoon, Ravensmuir was just ahead. I passed the town cemetery on the right side of the road. Its wrought-iron fence and entrance gate were rusty. Some of the gravestones were fairly ornate and dwarfed the others. Even in these remote towns the ranking of social classes survived death. Although, I couldn't help noticing how an overgrowth of nettles, thistles, and other weeds treated all the gravestones without discrimination.

The road now passed between the first of many low blocks of miners' row houses. They were built of a uniformly grayish stone, the color of the sky, and were uninhabited. Many of the windows were shattered, chimneys broken, and roofs caved in. Weeds protruded from cracks in the sidewalks in front of the houses, though the road I was slowly driving along was still in good condition. The only signs of animal life were the crows and sparrows that fluttered and swooped occasionally, going after insects, I supposed.

A HUNDRED YARDS OR SO FURTHER, I was in the heart of Ravensmuir—the town square. I slowed the car to a stop and looked around. This would have been the lively part of the town in its heyday. There were no signs of human life.

The dimensions of the square were just about right for a small town. It was the size of a soccer field, and completely overgrown. The trees had already dropped their leaves. Beneath them, some rusted frames of park benches remained. Wild grass had poked its way up through them.

Near where I'd stopped was a war memorial, a stone obelisk about six feet tall on a low pedestal. The names of the fallen were carved into the sides. At some point in the past the memorial had been defaced by graffiti. The spray paint colors were so faded that the names carved higher up were now quite legible. But not the names lower on the stone. Generations of thistles, dandelions, and all-conquering ivy had obliterated them.

Just like the miners' rows I'd passed on the way in, the buildings around the square had been ravaged by neglect. A boarded-up limestone kirk took pride of place on the north side. Its steeple tilted dangerously, as though in the midst of a slow-motion collapse. On the south side, a red-brick school, also boarded up, was surrounded by a chain-link fence. Through it, I could see the playground swings moving almost imperceptibly in whatever wind there was.

Around the rest of the square, boarded-up shops told the story of typical small-town life. Three of the names above them were still partly legible: MACFADDEN'S APOTHECARY, UPLAND GROCERIES AND SUPPLIES CO, THE HEATHER CAFÉ.

The biggest and ugliest of the cement-block buildings had a distinctive old-fashioned lamppost in front of it. The blue glass of the lamp was damaged, but still spelled out POL_CE STATI_N. On the walls, a number of obscene graffiti had faded but were still readable.

MY DESTINATION, The Ferret Inn, was at the southeast corner of the square. Its hanging sign, recently painted with the name and an image of a small brown ferret, jutted out above the doorway. I drove up and parked on the street in front. The building was of the same vintage as the others but had been given a makeover to look like a Tudor-era hostelry. The stone walls had been plastered and painted white, and the fake half-timbering had been given a fresh coat of black.

Walking the few steps from the car with my suitcase, I noticed how bracing the air was. The door of the inn was made of a heavy wood, so it took an effort to push it open and get inside before it shut.

The illusion of an old country inn immediately vanished. The lobby carpet and the walls were matching shades of a dull brown. The smell of stale cigarette smoke lingered in the air. The furniture consisted of vinyl-covered sofas and chairs, and flimsy round tables holding magazines.

I rang the bell at the reception desk. I could hear distant sounds from other parts of the inn. I waited a moment and was about to ring again, when a stern-looking young woman with very short red hair emerged from a door behind the desk.

I gave her my name and said I was with the Ministry Research Team. She checked a list taped to the counter.

"Ah," she said. "Welcome to The Ferret Inn." She had an efficient voice. "You're the first of your party to arrive."

I signed in and she chose a key from a slotted box on the wall behind her. She handed it to me. "The dining room doesn't open till six. I'll have coffee and biscuits sent up in a few minutes, if you wish."

I told her I wasn't at all hungry after sitting in a plane and a car for so long. What I really wanted to do was stretch my legs. Was there a decent walking trail nearby? That might give me an appetite for dinner.

"The best walking trail in Ravensmuir begins just at the back of the inn," she said. "You'll see it from the window of your room. It goes up through the hills and comes out near an abandoned mine. It's about an hour and a half away. From there, you can take the paved road back here. The trail's in a poor state in some parts. On your desk, you'll find a list of things to be careful of when you're walking. You should take a look at that before you go."

MY ROOM WAS ON THE THIRD FLOOR. It was small with an ensuite bathroom and a single bed. The carpeting was, unsurprisingly, brown. The small table, desk chair, and vinyl-covered armchair matched the furniture in the lobby. A flimsy wardrobe held some hangers on a rod, with two drawers in the bottom. A two-shelved narrow bookcase took up the remaining space in the room. On the top shelf sat a rotary telephone and an old directory. On the lower shelf lay several well-thumbed National Geographics and Reader's Digests.

From the window, I had a good view of that range of hills to the south. A wooden signpost marked the start of the walking trail. The trail itself, after a few yards, all but disappeared amongst the gorse and bracken. The wind was ruffling them and the sky seemed even more overcast than before. I'd brought a thick wool sweater and a pair of leather boots in my suitcase. All members of the party scheduled to descend into the mine the following day had been advised to bring them. Anyway, the prospect of bad weather on the walk didn't worry me.

I put on the sweater and boots, then looked over the warning list the receptionist had told me to read. It was basic stuff. Stay on official trails. Watch out for rabbit holes hidden in the heather—you could twist your ankle. Don't lie down for a nap—birds might attempt to peck at your eyes. Bogs that looked like harmless moss might just as easily be quicksands. Stay off them. They're often encircled by shriveled, blackened carcasses of sheep, sucked down and then expelled years later. Recently, a Paleolithic hunter with a bow and quiver of arrows still hanging over his shoulder had been disgorged by a bog near Ravensmuir. Finally, among the man-made dangers to be avoided were obsolete ventilator shafts that once provided air to miners in the tunnels far below ground. Their openings were just wide enough to fit the body of an incautious hiker. By the time the body hits the bottom, it's been flayed alive by the rough-hewn walls of the ventilator shaft.

The page ended with these words:

ENJOY A SAFE HIKE IN OUR BEAUTIFUL HILLS!

AS I PASSED THROUGH THE LOBBY on my way out, the receptionist called me over. On the counter lay a tiny LED pocket flashlight that resembled a cigarette lighter, as well as a hiking pole-cum-umbrella.

"The inn recommends these for walkers," she said. "Even if you don't leave the trail, a pole's always handy. If rain comes on, you can use the umbrella part. The flashlight's in case you get caught by darkness."

The pole looked heavy but was made of some light-weight metal. I made sure the flashlight was working and slipped it into my trouser pocket. I checked my watch. Right on three thirty. I thanked the receptionist and told her I'd be back before dark.

THE TRAIL LOOKED as though it wasn't used much. It began to wind up and around the hill, and soon the inn and the town were out of sight. It wasn't so much a trail as a crude muddy track, with protruding rocks and frequent puddles wide enough that I had to hop across them, leaning on the pole. The bottoms of my trousers were getting wet, so I tucked them into my socks.

Because I had to be careful where I put my feet, I became very aware of the insect life on the ground. Several times I stepped carefully over pitched battles between ants and different varieties of flies, mostly noisy bluebottles, fighting over the moldering remains of birds, or mice, or rabbits. The trail was now as narrow as a rabbit track.

After an hour or so, I'd no idea how far I'd climbed, but was enjoying the walk very much. A thousand feet or so below, I could see that road back to Ravensmuir the receptionist had mentioned. I pushed on knowing I'd soon be heading down that way. My stomach was beginning to grumble about not having been fed since the mid-Atlantic.

The wind had almost entirely disappeared now, but the cloud cover was even thicker and blacker— signs of impending rain. Fortunately, this final section of the trail now began descending in a series of gentle curves towards the road and the abandoned mine. I hoped I might find a place to shelter there if the rain started.

And indeed, within minutes, the first drops began to fall. I walked faster, but still had to be careful where I stepped. All at once, the sky opened and a heavy rain assisted by a howling wind battered me. I tried opening the walking pole's umbrella, but the wind blew it inside out.

Soon the rain had penetrated my sweater and was running down my face and into my eyes. I slithered down the remaining section of the trail as quickly as I could. I'd noticed a hut of some sort at the far side of what was left of the mine buildings. I splashed my way towards it through waist-high heaps of rubble with sodden weeds protruding from them. The only semi-intact remnant was one half of an intricate brick archway. The other half lay in pieces where it had fallen. I wondered if this might be part of the elevator building of the abandoned mine we were here to explore next day.

Soaked and shivering, I reached the hut at the rear of the site. It looked like a guardhouse and was made of rusted sheet metal, buckled with age. It sat on a cracked concrete slab. Perhaps this hut had been left intact for the occasional use of shepherds or hikers caught in the weather, drenched and desperate, just as I was. Its metal door was warped and rusted, as were the frame and hinges.

And it wasn't locked! A hasp for a padlock dangled, empty, beside a rusted, oval pull-handle. Which I immediately pulled on. But the door didn't budge. I yanked again, harder this time. No result. I dropped my hiking pole and pulled the handle with both hands. Then again, harder. It refused to give way, except for a little gap between the door and the frame. In desperation, I jammed the wet fingers of both my hands into that gap and pulled back with all my strength. The sheet metal of the door flexed just enough for me to squeeze my shoulder, then my whole body, inside, then snapped back into place behind me.

Oh, the relief to be out of that downpour! The hut was completely dark, but the sound of the rain drumming on the tin roof was now a comfort. The roof was leaking ever so slightly. I could feel the occasional drip on my head and shoulders, but that was nothing after being out in the storm. For a moment or two, I felt a great affinity with all those creatures that are at home in such dark places, secure from the elements.

A moment or two. Then, as I moved my feet on the gritty floor, an incredible stink assailed my nostrils. It was so vile, I instinctively started breathing through my mouth to lessen the smell. Was I in the den of a skunk? I remembered the little flashlight in my pocket, slid it out, and switched it on.

I saw right away that no skunk, or any other animal, had made its den in the hut. But the gritty floor I was standing on wasn't grit. It was a seething carpet of little black insects. Whenever I moved, hundreds of them crunched under my leather boots and gave off, stronger than before, the awful stink. Others had already clambered onto my boots. Some were climbing up the laces, then onto my socks towards my pants, which were tucked into them.

Those drips from the roof suddenly became heavier. I shone the flashlight upwards and lit up yet another nightmare. The entire ceiling was a swarming mass of thousands of these same creatures, their beady eyes now glaring red in the light. They had assembled into little stalactites, the points of them dripping onto my head and shoulders. I turned the light away. But they'd located me now and were landing in troops, crawling into my hair and around my ears and eyes. I swatted at them and blinked furiously to keep them out of my eyes. Some got to my lips and into my mouth. I spat them out, but the residual vile taste almost made me vomit.

I began hurling my body against the rusty door to force it open. But my feet, slithering on that mass of crackling bodies, couldn't get enough purchase and only produced a smell so palpable it might as well have been another foul, miasmic creature.

I shouted, I cursed. I threw myself again and again at the door till it opened enough to jam my boot into the crack. Tossing the flashlight into a corner, I used my hands and shoulder together to force the opening wider. Howling with the effort, I squirmed my way through the gap and tumbled out onto the concrete, as the jaws of the hut slammed shut behind me.

I IMMEDIATELY BEGAN THE EXTERMINATION. Many of the insects that were on my body when I burst out of the hut were now crawling back towards their home. I stamped on them over and over, crushing them to death.

Next I ran my fingers through my hair. I could feel dozens of them entangled there. I used my fingers as a comb and teased them out, one at a time, then nipped them, one by one, till they cracked and burst into a gritty residue.

I then went after those still clinging to the thick wool of my sweater. I pulled the sweater over my head and shook it as hard as I could, then stamped to smithereens the hundreds of insects that fell out. Those that refused to let go, I got rid of by the same procedure I'd used on my hair. I found others hidden in my trousers pockets, as well as several wily ones trying to elude me by hiding under my wristwatch. I slowly crushed them on the concrete with a handy stone. And so on, till I was satisfied none had survived.

Once I'd finished, I put my sweater on again and washed my hands in a nearby puddle. The foul smell lingered under my fingernails, reminding me of what I'd done. I took a deep breath of the clean Uplands air. The rain had diminished to a light drizzle, and there was still enough daylight for me to get to the inn by dinnertime. Dinner! I was now quite looking forward to it.

Walking back to Ravensmuir, I played over in my mind those brief moments in the hut and afterwards. I was thankful no one had seen me. I needed to work out to my satisfaction what caused me to react the way I did. After all, if my nerve had cracked so easily in that hut—on the surface of the Uplands, in daylight—how might I behave tomorrow as a member of a scientific expedition exploring the deepest bowels of the earth? We'd all been warned of "inexplicable phenomena" that had already scared off other rational, experienced scientists and engineers.

I'd always considered myself fairly rational. When I was at university long ago, a learned professor of entomology informed us that insects are made up of much of the same material as animals—including human beings. In fact, they might be considered our closest relatives. Tiny insects, visible only through microscopes, live on the bodies of our mothers, and hop onto us the moment we exit the womb. We become, in a sense, their new planet. They explore us and populate us. Desirable locales, such as our belly buttons, are for them the Promised Land, to be fought over in pitched battles. Even less attractive areas, such as our eyelashes, are like urban slums for these little relatives of ours. Sad to say, when we die, our entire population dies with us—unless they're lucky enough to escape to another planet.

During another of his lectures, the learned professor drew our attention to the practice of taking lecture notes with pen and paper. He compared that practice to ants secreting individual pheromone trails, recording the history of their travels for the benefit of their successors. Each ant, he said, has a distinctive odor in the same way as we have our distinctive styles of handwriting. Professional graphologists place such faith in the reliability of their science that human beings have been executed on the basis of it. Our professor smiled at the end of that lecture and assured us he was speaking metaphorically.

Now, on the road back to Ravensmuir, thinking of such matters, I wondered: what would have caused me, knowing what I know, to panic in that hut and lash out at these tiny creatures? They weren't evil, they were being themselves. It was my own five senses that had ganged up against my rational mind: the awful *smell*; the *sight* of the little red eyes; the horrific *touch* of them falling on my head and shoulders; the *sound* of them crunching under my boots; the disgusting *taste* they left in my mouth after I spat them out.

In that way, I'd been driven mad. We may congratulate ourselves on the superiority of our intellects, our reasoning powers. But in moments of crisis, those mental powers are no match for the five senses, which we share with all other animals.

Such an excuse for myself seemed plausible enough. But what about the sequel? Having escaped from the hut in a panic, I'd calmly, methodically, and deliberately destroyed every one of those insects that had come out with me. For a man who'd always liked to think of himself as someone who wouldn't hurt a fly, that should have been hard to justify. I'd just committed wholesale slaughter—murder of my nearest kin—

something we rightfully consider the act of a sociopath. I'd been fully aware of what I was doing as I performed my extermination of the insects, and it had given me great satisfaction. My state of mind in the hut I could excuse as being brought on by terror of the unknown. As for the way I'd acted after my escape—the painstaking elimination of each and every one of those innocent fellow creatures who'd clung to me? That was much harder to explain away.

As a matter of fact, I simply accepted the truth of it. But I was no longer sure exactly how I might react, tomorrow, on our descent into the bowels of the earth. What was the thing down there that had caused that first group of scientists to panic and flee in terror? Wouldn't it be wise for our group to pack guns along with our scientific tools? Or might the thing recognize —in me, at least—a kindred spirit, and welcome our intrusion?

I got back to Ravensmuir around five thirty. Daylight was departing, darkness was about to fall. And I was feeling very hungry. 🐵

—————

Note from the author: This is an excerpt from the novel I'm currently working on. In the story, frightening phenomena have been occurring at a long-abandoned coal mine, near the town of Ravensmuir in Scotland. In this episode, a science journalist arrives there the day before he and a group of scientists recruited by the government are scheduled to descend into the mine to evaluate the situation.

Five Modern Poets on Travel

selected and translated by Andrew Campana

Ken'ichi Kanan (1913–1945)

UNDER THE NIGHT CLOUDS

The car trembled
Lashed together with thin rope,
Our shoulders slammed against each other
The strike had been defeated
And we were being taken in
What could we do with the bitterness in our hearts?
"You can't smoke in there, you know."
One by one we were given our last cigarettes
I let the gray smoke fill my belly
Feeling something I couldn't put into words
As we rumbled down the bumpy road

I think the sun set soon after that
The green leaves that covered the road gradually
  darkened
As we sat, dejected—
But at that moment
We noticed an alarming commotion on the road
Bells rang out announcing a newspaper extra
Crowds starting to gather with unsettled expressions
Voices raised, talking about something
"Prime Minister Inukai has been assassinated!"
The man who told me this seemed devastated
We looked at one other,
Silent but eyebrows raised
It was May 15, 1932

The sun had set hours earlier at this point
The car sped up
And started to shake horribly
All we could hear was the groaning of the wheels
Where were we going now?
Through the film of the car window
There was only the muddy darkness
We were fiercely exhausted
And kept nodding off
But again and again, we startled awake
Our whole bodies drenched in terror
I braced myself for whatever they were going to do
  to us
But the bells announcing the news rang in my ears
And my shriveled heart continued to pound
The black clouds of night hung low in the sky
I knew this whirlwind would be raging
For a long time to come

The car curved through a sleepy street corner
And suddenly dropped its speed
Our shoulders slammed against each other again
We who were to be torn apart
Could do nothing but offer each other little smiles
Under the night clouds
Drinking in the pitch-black sky
The red lights of the prison
Flickered in the film of the car window.

夜雲の下

自動車が動揺すると
細引で縛られたまま
私たちの肩と肩とがごつんとあたる
争議は敗れた
送られる私たちは胸の苦汁をどうすることが出来たろう
「あちらでは吸えないんだぜ」
一本ずつもらった最後の煙草
言いようのない感慨とともに
蒼いけむりを腹の底までのみ
でこぼこだらけの道路を揺られて行った

やがて陽は墜ちたのか
道路にかぶさる青葉がだんだん翳ってくる
うなだれている私たちは
そのとき
道路のただならぬざわめきに気づいた
号外の鈴が慌ただしく鳴りひびき
気色ばんだ人たちがそこここに群れ
何か声高に話し合っていた
「犬養さんが殺されたんだって」
そう教えてくれた男は哀しげな表情をしたが
顔を見合わせた私たちは
思わずきっと眉があがった
一九三二年五月十五日であった

日はとっぷりと昏れて
スピイドを増した自動車は
ますますひどい動揺に喘いだ
車輪の軋りだけは微かにきこえるが
いまはどこを走っているのか
車窓のセルロイドには
泥のようにぬるぬるした闇だけだ
劇しい疲れにうつらうつらとなりながらも
ともすれば私たちは
おびえたように幾度も眼をしばたたいた
恐怖はびっしょりと全身を濡らしてくる
どうなとしやがれと観念きめても
さっきの号外の鈴が耳にこびりつき
しぼんだ心臓は急ぜわしくのたうちつづけている
黒い夜雲は低く垂れさがり
これからしばらくは
つむじ風が荒れるにちがいない

眠っている町角をカーヴすると
自動車は突然スピイドをぐっと緩めた
もう一度肩と肩がごつんとあたり
裂かれねばならぬ私たちは
しょうことなしにほんのすこし微笑み合った
くろぐろと空をのんでしまった
夜雲の下
刑務所の赤い燈が
車窓のセルロイドに点滅するのであった。

Kanoko Okamoto (1889–1939)

FOUR TANKA FROM
CHERRY BLOSSOMS

しんしんと桜花ふかき奥にいつぽんの道とほりたりわれひとり行く

Deep within
a dense rain of cherry blossoms
lies a single path
I will walk it alone

自動車の太輪の砂塵もうもうとたちけむりつつ道の辺の桜

Thick clouds of dust rise up
left by a car's heavy wheels—
cherry blossoms on the roadside

停電の電車のうちゆつくづくと都の桜花をながめたるかも

An electric train
stopped by a power outage—
all the better to enjoy
the cherry blossoms of the capital

春浅しここの丘辺の裸木の桜並木を歩みつつかなし

Early days of spring—
a gloomy walk
along the rows of bare cherry trees on the hillside

Kyūsaku Yumeno (1889–1936)

FOUR TRAIN TANKA FROM
CURIOSITY-HUNTING VERSES

ニセ物のパスで
　電車に乗つてみる
超人らしいステキな気持ち

Boarding a train
　with a fake pass—
an almost superhuman feeling

白い蝶が線路を遠く横切つて
　汽車がゴーと過ぎて
血まみれの恋が残る

A white butterfly crosses the distant tracks
　the train passes by with a roar
all that remains is bloodstained passion

自分が轢いた無数の人を
　ウツトリと行く手にゑがく
　　停電の運転手
動いてゐる
　さても得意気にたつた一人で

Picturing all the people
　he absentmindedly ran over
　　the conductor
thrilled with himself
　gets the stopped train to move again

青空の冷めたい心が
貨物車を
地平線下に吸ひ込んでしまつた

Below the horizon
the blue sky's cold heart
swallowed up a freight train

非常汽笛
汽車が止まると犯人が
ニツコリ笑つて麦畑を去る

Emergency whistle—
the train stops
and the grinning culprit
escapes through the wheat fields

Hisajo Sugita (1890–1946)

NINETEEN HAIKU

ゆく春の流れに沿うて歩みけり

I walked
alongside the flow
of spring's departure

梅林のそぞろ歩きや筧鳴る

Strolling through
the plum grove—
echoes of a water pipe

水上へうつす歩みや濃山吹

Taking steps
towards the water—
deep yellow roses

花の寺登つて海を見しばかり

I make my way up
to the flower-filled temple
just to see the ocean

蘆芽ぐむ古江の橋をわたりけり

In the old cove
I walked across a bridge
through the sprouting reeds

旅衣春ゆく雨にぬるゝまゝ

Travel clothes
holding on
to this last spring rain

歇むまじき藤の雨なり旅疲れ

The wisteria rain
just won't stop—
an exhausting journey

月の輪をゆり去る船や夜半の夏

A ship passes by
making the full moon shudder—
middle of a summer night

上陸やわが夏足袋のうすよごれ

Back on dry land
my summer socks
now a bit stained

夏羽織とり出すうれし旅鞄

Summer *haori* jacket
a pleasure to retrieve
from my travel bag

道をしへ一筋道の迷ひなく

A beetle shows me the way—
straight path,
no hesitation

湖畔歩むや秋雨にほのと刈藻の香

Walking by the lake
the faint scent of harvested algae
in the autumn rain

旅たのし葉つき橘籠にみてり

A wonderful trip
my basket filled with mandarin oranges
leaves still attached

城山の桑の道照る墓参かな

A path in Jōyama park
shining with mulberry trees—
visiting my father's grave

わが歩む落葉の音のあるばかり

As I walk
all that there is
is the sound of fallen leaves

枯野路に影かさなりて別れけり

On the road through dry winter meadows
our shadows overlapped
and then parted

雪道や降誕祭の窓明かり

A snowy path
lit by the glow
of a home at Christmas

柚子湯出て身伸ばし歩む夜道かな

Emerging from a yuzu bath
stretching, then heading home—
the nighttime streets!

北風吹くや月あきらかに港の灯

North wind blowing—
a clear moon
and harbor lights

Dakotsu Iida (1885–1962)

TEN HAIKU FROM
TRAVEL COMPOSITIONS

秋風や昼餉につきし山の蠅

Autumn breeze
sharing lunch
with a mountain fly

谷杉や雲をたのみに實をむすぶ

The cedar of the valley
depends upon the clouds
to bear fruit

奥山や雷雲いでて日のあたる

Deep in the mountains—
out come the thunderclouds
while the sun still shines

秋草や樹海出て逢ふ墓一つ

Autumn grass—
I walk through a sea of green
and encounter a single grave

地獄繪の身にしみじみと秋日かな

Like a painting of hell
deep within my flesh—
the autumn sun!

秋風やみだれてうすき雲の端

The edges of clouds
disheveled and frayed
in the autumn wind

岩けづる秋水翳り流れけり

Carving the rocks
the clear autumn water
darkens as it flows

観潮の帰航の雲に鴨引ける

After a day of tide-watching
the ducks make their homeward journey
through the clouds

夜にかけて卯の花曇る旅もどり

As the night falls
little white flowers darken
on my path home

駅前に穂家の麥干す薄暑かな

Sheaves of wheat
drying in front of the train station—
getting a bit hot, isn't it?

KEN'ICHI KANAN (1913–1944) was born in the town of Tamashima (now the city of Kurashiki), in Okayama prefecture on the Seto Inland Sea. After graduating from high school, he participated in leftist political movements, advocating for the rights of burakumin. He was imprisoned for these activities in 1932 and sentenced to ten months of hard labor. After his release, he moved to Tokyo to work as a journalist. He founded *Shiseishin* (*Spirit of Poetry*), a proletarian poetry journal. He later went to Japan-occupied northern China as a reporter, where he died of an illness shortly after being drafted into the Imperial Army.

 KANOKO OKAMOTO (1889–1939) is the pen name of Kano Okamoto, born in Tokyo. Her poetry was first published when she was still in her teens, and she was one of the early contributors to Japan's first prominent feminist journal, *Seitō* (*Bluestockings*), in the 1910s. She continued to write tanka throughout her life and eventually became a novelist as well as a scholar of Buddhism.

 KYŪSAKU YUMENO (1889–1936) is the pen name of Taidō Sugiyama, born in Fukuoka. He gained a reputation for wildly surreal and bizarre short stories and novels, often mixing detective fiction, horror, sci-fi, and Gothic tropes. He also wrote a long series of tanka in the same vein, some of which are included here.

 HISAJO SUGITA (1890–1946) is the pen name of Hisa Sugita, born in Kagoshima, on Kyushu. She founded *Hanagoromo*, a journal for women haiku poets, to foster a new generation of women in a largely male-dominated literary form. Her turbulent personal life made her the subject of many novels, plays, and television dramas in the decades after her death.

 DAKOTSU IIDA (1885–1962) is the pen name of Takeji Iida, born in the village of Gonari (now part of Fuefuki city), in Yamanashi prefecture. Yamanashi's landscapes provided the setting for his poetry throughout his life. He received enormous acclaim as a haiku poet for the grand, classically inspired style of his works—unusual in modern haiku—and was even called "the modern Bashō."

Hiromi Itō

———————

Itō Goes on a Journey, Making a Pilgrimage to Yuda Hot Springs

translated by Jeffrey Angles

I'VE BEEN THINKING CONSTANTLY about Oguri-san. Then yesterday I got an email from him. (Hold on, I won't tell you what it said just yet. Be patient!) I stood up and cried out in a voice that wasn't really a voice at all. I'm not exaggerating when I say he'd been on my mind every single day. I first met him through work. That's the reason I affix the polite suffix *-san* to his name and always use formal language with him, even though he's more than twenty years younger. I'd been brooding, really worried about him, so when his email arrived, I felt like I'd cast a spell that worked. I suppose I should call it "prayer," but I thought of him with such single-minded devotion that it felt more like a spell than a prayer. That's when I remembered. Perhaps it was the spell, but the other day I'd given him the charm I'd bought a while back when I was visiting the Thorn-Pulling Jizō in Sugamo.

I DON'T MAKE RIGHT TURNS. That's what I told him when we first met during the summer three years ago. I said I really wanted to go to the literary museum where he works, but the location was a problem. To get there, I had to follow the streetcar tracks away from Kumamoto Castle, go through the intersections at Suidōchō and Taikōbashi, then turn at Shin'yashiki, Miso Tenjin, or Suizenji, none of which had a special right-turn lane, and all the while I had to brave oncoming traffic and crossing streetcars.

I said, it's in my father's last will and testament—my Dad's dying words were that I should never make a right turn under any circumstances.

But Itō-san, you just told me that your father was alive and had a caregiver.

That's true, I said. I was just exaggerating, trying to show him how much I hate right turns. I also hate squeezing through narrow streets when there's oncoming traffic, but I still do it. Right turns across traffic, however, are where I draw the line. When I'm on one of those little streets where there's no right-turn lane and I'm waiting for a break in the oncoming traffic, which just keeps on coming and coming, ignoring me completely, I sense the cars behind me getting pissed, and I end up completely losing the courage to turn. If I do pluck up the courage to do it, I feel as if I'm taking my life in my hands, and by the time I get close to the museum, my fear has left me completely breathless. The parking lot is behind the gymnasium, and the museum is even farther, behind the library. To get there, I've got to make my way through bushes and thickets. My nails get broken, my feet get scratched and irritated, I get caught in spiderwebs and eaten by mosquitoes. As if that wasn't bad enough, the neighborhood is called "Izumi," which means "the spring." Every time it rains, the place quickly floods like water is bubbling up out of nowhere. I couldn't get to the museum even if I wanted to.

So Oguri-san taught me a way to get there by turning left in front of those intersections, veering right in front of Suizenji Park, then passing directly through all the stoplights. He also promised to clear a spot in the embarrassingly thick tangle of jasmine wrapped around the large camphor tree right in front of the museum, since that would give me a place to stop the car and enter.

After learning this special route, I started driving to the museum to see him whenever I returned to Kumamoto, even if I didn't really have any business there—I turned left, followed the road as it veered to the right, then proceeded straight ahead.

He really loved literature. He spoke passionately about all sorts of things, telling me how the museum built its collection and how the new displays were going to look. Until then, I never bothered to tell people I'm a poet, because as a poet I'd only just scraped by. The only reason people might have known I'm a poet was because I'd use my profession as an excuse to say things like, Hey, don't hate me, the reason I put the trash out on the wrong day was because, well, I'm a poet, you know. But with Oguri-san, things were different, his work involved putting together displays and exhibitions featuring the museum's literary collection, so I didn't hide my poems or books from him. We got lost in conversation, chatting on and on about famous poets like Kenji Miyazawa and Chūya Nakahara.

In the museum there were life-sized, papier-mâché statues of the novelist Sōseki Natsume and the haiku poet Teijo Nakamura sitting there quietly, and in the back stood a silent papier-mâché statue of the haiku poet Santōka Taneda. Once I started going to

the museum regularly, I got to know all the staff, and they would call out to me, Ah! Itō-san!

Twenty years ago, I moved to Kumamoto with a newborn in tow. My parents also left Tokyo for Kumamoto more than a decade ago, but in the meantime, I had relocated to California and returned to Kumamoto only a few times a year. My memories of Tokyo had faded. When I passed through Tokyo on my way to Kumamoto, I encountered new subway lines and lots of new places to visit, but they were all unfamiliar. When I talked about Tokyo, I talked about "going there," rather than "going home." On the other hand, if you asked me if I felt like I really belonged in Kumamoto, I probably would have said no. I lived like an orphan, depending on no one. I felt akin to the fleabane and goldenrod growing wild on the riverbank near my home in Kumamoto. But then, Oguri-san and his colleagues started calling out to me, Ah, Itō-san! And with that, everything changed.

Oguri-san and I'd been talking about going together to a festival dedicated to the poet Chūya Nakahara. It was held in Yuda Hot Springs in the city of Yamaguchi each year. I sent him an email suggesting we drive my car.

My car is bigger, he wrote back.

I responded, my car is a rental anyway, so we might as well use it.

The problem was that I wasn't comfortable making right turns or squeezing through narrow streets while there was oncoming traffic. It was impossible to drive the small backstreets of Kumamoto without having to give way to cars coming from the other direction. Renting a tiny, compact car was how I kept from killing myself.

I added, plus, even the smallest compact cars are pretty big these days.

Oguri-san accepted my offer. This whole exchange took place over email while I was in California.

Before long, another email came telling me something personal had come up on the afternoon we wanted to leave. I suggested we head out after he was done. Plus, I needed to make sure Dad had dinner. Would six o'clock work? He responded, I took off a half-day in the afternoon, I'll finish what I've got to do, then go back to work and wait for you. We can go whenever you're ready.

Aha, I thought. Every once in a while, the chance arose to ask him about his personal life. I tried to entice him into spilling the beans by asking, you got some dumb thing you've got to do that day?

He wrote back, I'll tell you on the road when we've got time to talk.

A little while later I arrived in Kumamoto. It was toward the end of April.

The camphor trees had grown. Wherever the camphor grew from the spaces between the rocks in the castle walls, it had bushed out, covering the stone. Not just there, though. Here and there all over town, the camphor had grown thick and looked out, dominating the city with its firm stare. No sooner did you notice the green clumps of camphor growing restless than the branches began to laugh with new leaves in shades of bright yellow and bronze, and before you knew it, the foliage was growing all over everything. The camphor trees didn't have any ill intent—they were just so hungry they couldn't stand it and resolved to grab and gobble up whatever they could. The gingkos were robust, thick, and completely covered with new leaves. The cherry trees weren't just green, they had a bluish hue to them, perhaps even the color of blue-green ocean water. The trunks and branches sucked in the color, and where the sunlight fell upon them, the trees sucked it in, turning a dark indigo. The rhododendrons had started to bloom, producing patches of color. It was as if red and white paint had been spilled on them—in places the colors mixed, in others they didn't, but in any case, the color seeped through the teal and viridian leaves. Sorrel, green with touches of red and yellow, had grown tall on the riverbank and shone in the light. The grass sweated and wound its way into whorls while the wild raspberries worked to produce sweet fruit. The trees and plants had pulled out all of the stops, giving birth and living life to their fullest.

APRIL 28. I TURNED LEFT, followed the road as it verged right, and reached the museum. Oguri-san was already waiting.

Hold on a sec, I'm going to move my car to the parking lot, then I'll be back, he told me, I've rented a parking spot for my car out back. The camellias are blooming back there, you want to come see?

I went with him. The space, which was behind the literature museum at the edge of someone's garden, was so tiny there was no way I could've gotten a bicycle in there, much less a car. The place was lined with huge camellias, which were blooming and dropping their open flowers. A long time ago, the goddess Izanami swore that she would strangle a thousand people to death every day, and her partner, the god Izanagi shouted back, well then, I'm going to make sure a thousand five hundred people are born every day. The blooming and falling flowers reminded me of that exchange. The camellias were at the end of their season, there's no way the number of newborn blooms could compare to the number of those that had already been strangled. Even while he was moving the car, the blooms were dying and falling off right before my eyes. *Sheets of metal eat senbei, and the spring twilight is calm. Low-thrown ash grows pale, and the spring twilight stills.*

Oguri-san was a big fellow, so he had to fold his limbs and stoop a little to fit in the passenger's seat. The tiny gray car got onto the highway and sped up. The forests of trees with their shiny leaves throbbed with life and new growth, while the wild wisterias wound around themselves reluctantly, eager to finish whatever they hadn't yet completed. Yellowish bamboo thickets stood here and there stupefied. Bright yellow rapeseed blossoms and white herons stood out against the background, but eventually, all of these things faded away in the encroaching darkness.

OGURI-SAN STARTED THE CONVERSATION, saying, let me level with you, I've developed a lump on my side, below my chest. I didn't know what it was, and it just got bigger and bigger. I went to the doctor, he did all sorts of tests, and he told me it was either cancer of the lymph nodes or some complicated illness named after the guy who discovered it. The illness they mentioned is rare and not well researched. It looks just like cancer but it's treatable if the lump is removed. The tests have taken forever, I was supposed to get the results today, but when I went to the clinic, they told me they couldn't really figure it out, so they'd send me to the university hospital. That just leaves me hanging for another two weeks. Calmly, quietly, he told me, I ought to know by the time the Golden Week holiday break is over. That'll be early next month. *In the slippery state of moonlight, is spring twilight that which submits?*

He told me, I've lost a bunch of weight. My appetite's just fine, I thought maybe the weight loss was because I was too preoccupied with work, so I didn't think much about it until the doctor brought it up.

The last service area in Kyushu was in Koga. I drove that far, and we changed positions there. As he drove, I stared into the distance. We saw a truck lying on its side on the edge of the road. The lights on the police cars were shining, shining, shining brilliantly.

It's hard, Oguri-san muttered, when things are so up in the air—all I do is think about it.

We chatted about all sorts of things—about champon noodles from Nagasaki, about the poet Chūya Nakahara, about my parents, about the displays he was preparing for the museum, but neither of us could avoid thinking about death, nothingness, and suffering. Nothingness, suffering, and death weighed heavily on our minds.

WE ARRIVED AT YUDA HOT SPRINGS. It was probably after ten in the evening. All the poets and other folks associated with the Chūya Festival were out eating, so we walked to the restaurant to join them. It was late at night, but *here and there, we could hear the sound of people scooping up water in the public baths.* On the street corners were steamy mini hot springs known as "foot baths" by the locals. Everyone was at the restaurant. I greeted them excitedly. My goodness, it's been so long! Looks like you've put on a bit of weight. So-and-so isn't here yet? He's supposed to arrive tomorrow.

Some people I knew, some people I didn't. I watched everyone bow obsequiously and exchange name cards, until a poet who I know really well said, there's an outdoor bath on the roof of the hotel, they usually turn the lights out at midnight, but apparently it's open all night.

It was almost one o'clock by the time I got to the hotel room. It was an ordinary hotel with Western-style rooms, and Oguri-san was in the room next to mine. I put on the cotton yukata the hotel provided and quietly tiptoed up to the hot bath on the roof. The light was shining on the women's side. There wasn't a soul there—no one had left their slippers at the entrance. I could tell there were a whole bunch of people on the men's side though—lots of slippers there. I guessed that's where all the poets were, probably Oguri-san too. It was a new moon and partly cloudy out. I slipped into the rectangular, jet-black bathtub and spread out my arms and legs. The water sloshing around my skin was just the right temperature— comfortably warm. I thought of Oguri-san's side, about suffering, death, and nothingness. I sank into the pool and watched the night slide by for what seemed like eons and eons.

CHŪYA WAS BORN ON APRIL 29, 1907, and every year on his birthday, the Chūya Nakahara Memorial Museum, built on the site of his birthplace and childhood home, holds a big festival in his honor. I won't say much about the festivities, but lots of people recited Chūya's poetry. We heard all his most famous lines. *Look, look, these are my bones,* and *On this bit of soiled sorrow,* and *Sheets of metal eat senbei,* and so on. I read too. *Will you flow, flow away?* And *One morning, I saw, a black flag, flutter, up there, in the sky.* That was why I was there—to read. I chatted with old acquaintances and the people I'd just met. *Here, tonight, a party like no other, Here, tonight, a party like no other.* Of course, Oguri-san was with me too. *It rains, it stops, the wind blows. The clouds flow, the moon hides. Ladies and gentlemen, a spring night. The wind blows, wet and warm.* I say he was "with me," but our circle of acquaintances didn't entirely overlap—*this time, and that time, are so far apart, and this place, and that place, are not the same*—so even though we were together in the same place, we spoke with different people. Nonetheless, I was thinking about him the whole time.

Yuaaaaan yuyoooooon—swinging back and forth. I imagined all sorts of things. Oguri-san's suffering. *Yuya yuyon—back and forth.* His death. *Yuyon.* And nothingness. *Yuya yuyon.* I imagined that even if I turned left, veered to the right, and proceeded straight to the literary museum, one day, there might not be anyone there anymore to greet me, Ah, Itō-san! *And so life puffs away like smoke, your life and mine puffed away like smoke. Yuya yuyon—back and forth, back and forth.*

In the middle of the night, I crept back to the rooftop bath. The lights were off, but I took a dip in the lukewarm water anyway.

And I rocked back and forth—*yuya yuyon.*

I thought of the cluster of banana trees behind the literary museum swaying back and forth—*yuya yuyon.*

Water flowed along, flowed along, feeding the banana trees, which drank up the water and spread. Over countless summers, they had spread in the heat and humidity. Over countless winters, they died back and grew quiet. The place was incredible, every time someone came to see me, I showed it to them as one of the sights of Kumamoto. I'd also take them to the eight-hundred-year-old camphor tree known as "Jakushin-san's camphor" because of the samurai-turned-priest buried beneath its branches.

THE NEXT MORNING while Oguri-san and I were eating breakfast, he suddenly stopped smiling and asked, do you want to touch my lump?

I extended my hand. *Yuya yuyon*—I hesitated, hand shaking back and forth. He lifted his arm, and just as he said, there it was—hard like a bean—but it wasn't just a single lump like I'd imagined. There were a few of them.

Oguri-san said, you see? Then he smiled again, but he looked like he might cry.

The previous night, when I went from the rooftop bath back to my room, I checked. Yes, I still had it—the substitute charm that I'd bought on my most recent pilgrimage to the Thorn-Pulling Jizō in Sugamo. That kind of charm was supposed to transfer your afflictions to Jizō, who acts as a substitute and takes them away for you.

Mom had told me you're supposed to keep it against the afflicted part of your body until it becomes soft, then you swallow it—it's also okay to burn it, put the ashes in miso soup, and swallow it that way. I'd bought the charm for Mom but giving it to her had completely slipped my mind.

I called out his name. *Oguri-san.* At that moment, every sound that issued from my mouth was a spell.

I have something good for you.

Something incredibly good.

I took the charm

Out of my wallet and put it

Trembling back and forth—*yuya yuyon*

In his hands.

As I spoke, I hid within my words a spell: *This is not just an ordinary talisman, no, it holds great spiritual merit, it is one of the Thorn-Pulling Jizō's talismans, and this one has the greatest power, Jizō will take away your suffering for you, so I bequeath it to you—place your faith in it.*

A FRIEND OF MINE CAME WITH US on the return drive. When she offered to drive, I stopped her, telling her that in America, it's not uncommon to drive five or six hours. I took the steering wheel, and we left Yuda Hot Springs behind.

It had rained the previous day, but that day the sky was completely blue. She suggested we stop along the way at Akama Shrine in Shimonoseki to enjoy the view of the sea, so I set my GPS and took off along the Chūgoku Expressway.

My friend kept talking about her boyfriend. *Although he is kind to me, I am firm in my ways,* and so nothing has happened between us yet, she said. I responded, he probably doesn't really want you, and honestly, it doesn't seem you do either. She said, no, I do. *I am fond of him, I've spent these nights and days submerged in the clear waters of affection and amicability.* Because I've been around the block a few times, I told her that wasn't enough—if she really wanted him, she had to go for it. We drove on the expressway for a while, then got off just before crossing over to Kyushu. As we followed the GPS's instructions, turning corners and driving straight, my friend continued talking about her boyfriend. She said to me, *I don't want him to think about anything when we're together, I don't like it even when he thinks out of consideration for me,* so I started teasing her. I teased her, and we had lots of fun laughing as we drove into the city. Oguri-san listened quietly in the back seat. The GPS told us we'd arrived.

My friend shouted, ah, there it is! There it is! Turn right! But since I had to turn right, I missed it. I kept going, made a careful U-turn, traveled back along the way we'd come and made a left turn. No one said a word.

My friend told us, some things here are amazing, but the rest aren't anything special. There's the statue of Hōichi the Earless and the mounds erected to the dead Taira samurai—they're totally creepy, like they're cursed, full of resentment somehow.

A famous naval battle had taken place just offshore in the late twelfth century. The result was the defeat of the Taira clan. The Genpei Wars, which dominated much of the late twelfth century, then came to a close. The shrine had been erected to appease the souls of the defeated warriors, and so on the grounds of the shrine were several memorial mounds dedicated to the Taira samurai whose bodies were never recovered.

Then a few centuries later, something incredible supposedly took place there. According to a famous folk tale, Hōichi was a blind musician who lived on the shrine grounds and recited stories of the Genpei Wars and the defeat of the Taira. The ghosts of the dead Taira warriors who were enshrined there began to visit Hōichi and asked him to perform the part of the story that described their own demise. Hōichi didn't realize at first that his patrons were ghosts, but when he did, the priest at the shrine took a brush and painted Hōichi's whole body with holy texts to protect him. The next time the ghosts came, they couldn't see anything but his two ears, which the priest had forgotten to cover with protective writing. As a result, one of the ghosts ripped off his ears and took them back with him to his grave. After that, the legend of "Hōichi the Earless" became famous throughout the country.

As luck would have it, the Festival of the Previous Emperors was going to be taking place there in the few days, and a stage had been set up inside the grounds of the shrine. We were there in late April on a national holiday—Green Day—plus, it was an auspicious day according to astrologists, so it was a good day for weddings. Several wedding ceremonies were taking place under the sunny skies, and there were also lots of visitors to the famous shrine. The crowds were making noise and having a fun time. We didn't mix with them but went directly to the statue of Hōichi the Earless and to the mounds commemorating the Taira samurai who had haunted him.

The shiny leaves on the trees were thick and dusky, filled with spiderwebs. The camellias looked shabby, but the flowers were blooming and falling to the ground. Seven memorial mounds stood in a row. One of them was dedicated to Taira no Tomonori, a historical figure I rather like. The mounds were off to the side, where there weren't any other visitors. The ground was slightly higher than the surrounding area, giving a good view of the Dannoura Strait where the naval battle had taken place. Standing there in the shade, the mounds did seem cursed or full of ghostly resentment somehow, just as my friend had said.

Right then, she let out a small shout and jumped back. Surprised, I turned around and heard her say, oh my god! That statue of Hōichi gives me the creeps!

Hōichi? What's the problem?

Look, he's staring at us even when we turn our backs.

Inside the little shrine building behind us, Hōichi gazed at us intently with dark eyes.

As we left, we realized we could see the shore of Kyushu beyond the strait.

That's probably where the naval battle took place all those centuries ago, said Oguri-san. I imagined the water red with blood.

As I looked at the water, I thought, so this is where it happened. As the naval battle of the Dannoura straits was coming to a close and the Taira boats were sinking in defeat, Taira no Tomonori said, "I've seen all the things I should have seen," and jumped into the sea. He had done everything he could do, and he chose to kill himself with dignity rather than be killed or captured.

My friend said, Kyushu looks so close, when I think about those samurai, I feel really, really sorry for them—they must have wanted to get over there so badly. The water is so rough and the current so strong that even if they'd tried to make it to shore, they would've been carried away or crushed in their armor.

Oguri-san took over the driving. We got on the Kyushu Expressway after Shimonoseki. I suppose young men are good drivers after all. He drove fast, pedal to the metal. At times, the tiny compact shook as the wind struck the side of the car.

New Moji. East Kokura. South Kokura. Yawata. The towns sped by.

The moment we got on the expressway, there were camphor trees everywhere. Their leaves were tinged with red and yellow. Wild wisterias were blooming with flowers that crawled down the hanging stems. The paulownia trees bloomed here and there, but their flowers, which were the same color as the wisterias, rose into the air.

I asked, you know the expression "mountains laughing" they use in haiku? When they use that word, what season are they describing?

This season right now, Oguri-san answered, keeping his hands on the wheel. It's used to describe the moment in spring when the hillsides develop their color and look nice and bright.

They sure seem to be laughing all right, my friend said as she started to laugh too. Do you suppose the camphor trees are the only ones who laugh? Don't the others do it too?

Wakamiya, Miyawaka. Both these similar-sounding names appeared on the signs as if the sign-makers had forgotten the town's name and were trying to remember. Koga. We had a bowl of champon noodles in the roadside stop there. Fukuoka. Sué. The names were becoming more and more historic. Lots of ancient history took place here.

Now we were getting into the region that used to be the main point of contact between the ancient Japanese nation and the Asian mainland. Dazaifu. Tofurōato. That's where the ruins of the ancient sea walls erected in the seventh century are. The site of the medieval Karukaya checkpoint was there too.

Oguri-san said, occasionally you can find bits of ancient rice by the ruins of the sea walls. I found a single grain, and I treasure it to this day.

Chikushino. Tosu. The highway parted there into the expressway that headed for Nagasaki and the one that headed toward Oita.

We reached Kurume. Then Hirokawa, literally "broad river," named after the river that flows through it. At Yame, which is famous for its tea, we stopped for a drink.

Nearby at Nankan, there used to be a biwa player named Yoshiyuki Yamashika, who like Hōichi the Earless, recited the stories of the decline and fall of the Taira clan. The last time I heard him play, he was over ninety years old. That was over a decade ago.

My friend, who had her cellphone to her ear, was speaking clearly so she could be easily understood: yes, darling, Mommy will be back in Kumamoto before long. It was a calm day. Outside the car, the spring landscape flowed by. The mountain trees looked so plump they seemed ready to burst. Spring was full on, and as twilight fell, the landscape felt full of erotic passion. *Somehow, the air is ever so slightly blue, as delicately pale as the root of a young spring onion.*

The delicate waters of the Kikusui River. The delicate town of Ueki. Then finally Kumamoto. *One roof tile has gone missing.* Starting now, *the spring twilight will silently march onward, into its own silent fetal duct.*

SOME TIME WENT BY. I returned to California, and although May is usually dry and sunny, it was so wet that year that it seemed like there were entire water droplets suspended in the air. There were no blue skies, only *overcast skies* in which *flags fluttered back and forth, back and forth.* It was one of those days when I received an email from Oguri-san.

Last night, someone invited me to go on a drive
with them in the middle of the night to the valley
south of Mt. Aso. The pale moonlight was like
out of some fantasy. The rice paddies filling
the valley were brimming with water, little frogs
were pleasantly peeping, and for a little while,
I felt refreshed. However, my friend only lets me
ride in the back seat so I sat back there sipping
some coffee, and thinking that this must be like
the pilgrimage that Oguri made.

OGURI-SAN WAS REFERRING to an old Japanese story about a fellow with the same surname. According to the story, a man called Oguri Hangan was unjustly murdered, but through a series of miraculous events, the Lord of Hell sent him back to life in the form of a *gakiami*—a deaf, blind, sick man who had a distended stomach and couldn't walk. Fate brought him to the lodgings of Terute, the woman he loved, who didn't recognize him but out of kindness dragged him along on a wagon for several days. After her, other generous people also pitched in and eventually took him all the way to the hot springs in Kumano. There, the miraculous hot springs healed him and restored his original form.

I wrote back, so you've just figured me out, eh, Oguri-san? What we did was exactly that—a *michiyuki,* a long journey in search of healing. I wrote about taking journeys—an important element in the classical literature we both like so much. I wrote about how plant, animal, and place names are so important to the old stories. I wrote about tenderness. About finding consolation. About other unimportant things. Soon I received the following response.

I realized something.
When you don't know what to do and
can't see any way out of a predicament,
when you can't simply sit still and
just want to bolt out and run away,
sometimes simply getting out and moving
can save you.

Some more time went by. Oguri-san wrote to me again, but this time his email seemed like a cry of surprise. The doctors were right. It wasn't cancer. It was the illness he'd mentioned named after the guy who discovered it. That meant it was treatable.

The substitute charm had worked. The spell had worked.

And I'd been Terute for him, taking Oguri on the journey that brought him back to health.

I'd just turned fifty years old.

I'm no longer young. I've gotten flabby, and my spots and wrinkles and gray hair are second to none. I may look old now, but when I was young, I was like the young maiden Terute in the story, pulling countless sick, wounded, and decrepit men along. I've pulled along lots of them, lots of sick and damaged men to the hot springs on the slopes of Kumano, where I dunked them into the rejuvenating baths. And it always worked. The power of pilgrimage hasn't lost its strength.

This time, however, instead of going to the hot springs on the Kumano slopes, we'd made our pilgrimage to Yuda Hot Springs where Chūya was born, and instead of a wagon, we took a compact car. He didn't just get pulled along passively. Sometimes Oguri also took the wheel, despite his sickness and wounds, but I suppose that's to be expected. We're modern people after all. There's one line in the story of Oguri Hangan that goes, *How kind of them, they are asking after the maiden.* I thought of the twittering of the skylarks, the calling of the black kites, and the high-pitched voices reading the poems of Chūya Nakahara that spoke to me so much... And to top it all off, the gray compact that had carried us along was a Daihatsu Move. 🐵

Note from the author: This is Chapter 6 from *The Thorn-Puller: New Tales of the Sugamo Jizō.* Throughout this chapter, I have borrowed the voice of the poet Chūya Nakahara. There are places where Chūya's words appear slightly differently than they originally did in his poetry, but this is a result of me uttering them in my own voice. If this bothers you, please forgive me.

In addition, I have borrowed the voices of the Buddhist narrative (*sekkyō-bushi*) *Oguri Hangan,* the epic *Kojiki* (*An Account of Ancient Matters*), the medieval classic *The Tale of the Heike,* as well as the voices of my friends Junji Baba, Yukiko Ono, and the poet Mikirō Sasaki.

Note from the translator: Most of the passages in italics are from Chūya's poetry. The onomatopoetic expression *yuya yuyon* (as well as its other variants with elongated vowels and slightly different spellings) comes from the poem "Circus," where it describes the movement of a trapeze artist swinging back and forth through the air. It is worth noting that this expression is distinctive and unusual even in the Japanese, so it stands out in Itō's text. For this reason, the translation puts it in an italicized transliteration rather than fashioning some English equivalent.

Barry Yourgrau

Toad

MY GIRLFRIEND SENDS ME OUT for a bottle of water. It's night, our first one, at a resort guest hut in a palm forest. I tramp along in the tropical moonlight on a pathway under the frond-topped trees. I yawn, still groggy from all the traveling to get here. The shadows of palm trunks cut across the way like dark sword blades.

The resort's modest store lies ten minutes on. The path seems deserted at this dreamy hour. Then I realize it isn't deserted. A small figure appears ahead in the moonlight and crisscrossing shadows. I slow. I blink. I stop. I exclaim in shock.

"What are you doing here?" I blurt, thunderstruck, as my girlfriend's elderly petite mother approaches.

She reaches me, giving one of her little self-conscious laughs. "I just came quickly to see if you two were okay," she says.

I stare at her in disbelief. "You came two thousand miles just to see if we were okay? You couldn't call?" I bend to kiss her cheek.

"It's not two thousand miles," she scoffs. "And the frog is very nimble."

"What *frog*?" I retort.

"The frog ferry," she says. She gestures back along the path behind her.

I gasp and shrink back. An enormous toad squats in the moonlight there, just off the path by the floral undergrowth. Its goitrous throat pulses slowly.

I gape at it, then at my girlfriend's mother, speechless.

"So how is she?" she says. "You're both okay?"

"Yes—fine," I mumble. "She's dozing. We're both tired. But fine. But—so you're staying here at the resort too?" I ask, bewildered, eyeing the hulking toad beyond her.

"No, no, no!" she replies. She's leaving now, she doesn't mean to intrude. She takes a step back. "Just tell her I wanted to check that everything's okay," she says maternally.

She turns to go.

"No—wait—" I protest lamely, as she starts tramping toward the toad, a chubby elfin figure in a natty ensemble with very long scarf.

The toad waddles out to meet her. It blinks its great hooded eyes as she struggles up onto its back. "Have a great time, you guys!" she calls. She gives a wave that makes her sway violently off-balance. I cry out in alarm and rush toward her. "I'm fine!" she exclaims, clutching hectically onto the toad's neck. The toad emits a thunderous croak. It leaps spectacularly, and soars off above the palm trees, into the night. The long scarf of its diminutive passenger trails like a banner across the moon.

I watch until they're out of sight. In a daze, I resume my errand.

Back at the hut I rouse my dozing girlfriend to give her the water. I relate to her the news of her mother's visit. She flaps her hand groggily, dismissive.

"She's always doing something like that," she says. "Like this *tonight*?"

"Whatever. Is this the only bottle you brought?" she complains.

"It's all they had till the delivery tomorrow," I tell her. I watch her guzzle more than half the bottle. "God, I could drink it all, but here," she pants, handing me what's left. "I'm so tired after all that travel," she murmurs, and she slumps back onto the pillows.

I finish the bottle slowly, lingering over each swallow to extract the maximum effect. Then I crawl in carefully beside her under the sheets. For a brief while I lie awake, thinking of the great toad and its little elderly rider. The palms clatter gently above our hut as I fall asleep. 🐵

Jun'ichi Konuma

Every Reading, Every Sound, Every Sight

translated by Sam Bett

IN THE CITY OF AHMEDABAD in Gujarat, between Mumbai and Delhi, there was once a private collection of works by Alexander Calder. Although I saw it only in a write-up published by Christie's, my eyes couldn't get enough, feasting on the sight of Calder's work and photos of his letters, the building where he stayed, all the tropical flowers and fruit. And as if the images were not enough, the short captions prompted me to undertake bursts of research that made me lose all sense of time.

One of the photographs showed Calder with his arms spread wide, standing before an elephant. At first glance, just your average travel photo. Then I saw another. This one didn't feature Calder. It was a bird's-eye view of a kite-flying festival. In fact, the kites were fighting, flying high in the sky on rugged lines, as Calder recounts in his autobiography.

Calder studied mechanical engineering. He was also fascinated by the circus and went whenever he could to sketch the animals. His sketches from the 1930s include casual studies of animals at rest as well as his various attempts to capture them in motion. It must have been his dissatisfaction with classical sculpture that led him to create works with wire, allowing him to render motion, and thus time and space and the transformations between, in three dimensions. With this in mind, I found myself imagining as best I could how the eye of this artist who had gone from sketching animals to making "mobiles"—a term coined by Duchamp, who also came up with "stabiles"— had perceived the elephants and kite fighting of India. Seeing those kites in action recalled Khaled Hosseini's novel *The Kite Runner*. Set in Afghanistan, it then got me thinking about the connections between that country and India.

In 1954 Calder received a letter from Gira Sarabhai of Ahmedabad. She wrote that Calder and his wife could be their guests if he would make some art for her family while he was there. A leading Ahmedabad family, the Sarabhais had built a fortune in the textile industry. Gira's father, Ambalal, an industrialist and advocate for Indian independence, had eight talented children who became politicians, industrialists, and artists. Gira, the youngest, was among other things an architect who had studied under Frank Lloyd Wright

in the United States. Calder and his wife, Louisa, stayed with them for three weeks in January 1955. He left behind seven larger works and a number of small pieces that fit in the palm of the hand.

I'd heard the name Sarabhai before. John Cage was introduced to Indian philosophy and the works of Ananda Coomaraswamy by a woman named Gita Sarabhai. (One might even say that Cage's exposure to Indian thought ultimately enabled him to sidestep a spiritual crisis. Indeed, the cyclical "seasons" found in works such as *Sonatas and Interludes* and *String Quartet in Four Parts* attest to Gita's influence.) Gita and Gira? At first I thought they were the same person. But I was wrong. The two were sisters, a musician and an architect.

The Sarabhais were patrons of the arts. Apart from Calder, over the years they extended invitations to other leading artists, architects, and musicians, including John Cage, Cartier-Bresson, Isamu Noguchi, Robert Rauschenberg, and Le Corbusier. The idea for the Calico Museum of Textiles, a popular institution to this day, came to Gautam Sarabhai, one of the brothers, in a conversation with none other than Coomaraswamy. These various connections come to light as we peer into the all too brief time the Calders spent in Ahmedabad.

I've been asked to write about journeys—does this story have anything to do with what a journey is? Shouldn't a journey be more dynamic? Unless it generates motion, as when Calder built his mobiles and stabiles based on animals, isn't something missing?

A JOURNEY IS A HARD THING TO DEFINE. What does a journey actually entail?

Journeys are something you do, not something you talk about—couldn't we just say it like that? But is there such a thing as a journey independent of the words used to describe it? I tend to think not, but perhaps we can use this idea to form a kind of working hypothesis.

The journey is what is gleaned from the verbal account or the written tale. The traveler writes the tale, or someone else writes about it. Well, then, is the journey in the teller of the tale? Inseparable from the person who experienced it? What about other mobile beings, like animals? Some creatures attach themselves to others, so that they can move around. I'm thinking of a plant or a microbe, or even something inanimate—like a coded message, I suppose.

Words allow us to retrace the journey's process, the experience, giving shape to what exists outside of language.

But must the sojourner be active, while the sojourned place accepts a passive role?

When people hear about a journey, what captures their attention—the sojourner or the sojourned?

ALAIN DANIÉLOU, perhaps best known in Japan for *Gods of Love and Ecstasy: The Traditions of Shiva and Dionysus,* is someone I thought of as a specialist in Indian music, but this is mostly an expression of the place his journey took him. In his youth, Daniélou studied voice under the baritone Charles Panzéra —who later became the subject of an essay by Roland Barthes—and composition under Max d'Ollone. For a time, he was a professional dancer. In 1932, he made the first of many trips to India, accompanied by the Swiss photographer Raymond Burnier, who would remain his lifelong companion.

Daniélou met Rabindranath Tagore and set Tagore's poetry to music, creating the "Song-Poems" we know today. He became the director of Tagore's music institute. For fifteen years, he devoted himself to the study of Indian languages, literature, religion, and culture. He became adept at playing the veena. After the war he and Burnier settled in India.

On his return to Europe in 1960, Daniélou worked at institutes in West Berlin and Venice, embarking on research in India and beyond that took him to Afghanistan, Cambodia, and Laos, and to Latin America. He was a prolific writer. His autobiography, *The Way to the Labyrinth: Memories of East and West,* in addition to serving as a travelogue, hints at why he chose to distance himself from Europe.

Although Daniélou's father was an anticlerical Breton politician, his mother was a devout Catholic and the founder of a religious order, and his older brother a Jesuit prelate and theologian. Rejecting his Christian upbringing, Daniélou eventually converted to Hinduism, taking the name Shiva Sharan. His

worldview and disposition tended toward the journey rather than settling down. How scandalous it must have been for the younger brother of a theologian to be the translator of the *Kama Sutra.* I admit it may be a gross exaggeration to read this as an expression of the mobile qualities of sound and music, or of sexuality. Flipping through Daniélou's substantial autobiography, it's impossible not to be a bit overwhelmed by the breadth of his circle of friends and acquaintances, however common this might be among the French.

The Way to the Labyrinth includes a photo taken in India by the adventurer and travel writer Ella Maillart, though the text does not mention Ella's name. Maillart was born in Geneva in 1903. After reporting on Soviet Turkestan in 1932, she nearly gave up writing when her style was criticized as unorthodox. But many readers, happening upon her work, found it delightful and encouraged her to continue; so once again, she set off to investigate the lives of non-Western peoples and record her observations. Her travels took her to the Caucasus; to Manchuria, then a puppet state of the Empire of Japan, and Beijing; to Srinagar under Indian rule; and to Afghanistan, Iran, and Turkey—resulting in a great many books, the first of which were written in French before she switched to English. Her travel writing from the 1930s through the 1940s, about regions that were still fairly unknown to Europe, holds up well today.

In her teens and early twenties, Maillart excelled at sports—sailing, skiing, and field hockey—and even competed in the Olympics, which I find rather intimidating. However, in her travels to India with her beloved kitty, Ti-Puss, and in her interest in finding commonalities between Eastern wisdom and the life of cats, I feel a sense of affinity, however groundless that may be. I wouldn't be surprised if this way of seeing animals derived at least in part from her exposure to the cultures of East Asia, and of India and its philosophies.

In 1939, as the Second World War was beginning, Swiss-born German writer and anti-Fascist Annemarie Schwarzenbach joined Maillart on a journey by car from Geneva to Kabul to escape Europe and overcome her morphine addiction. Maillart later wrote a book about their journey, which was published in English and aptly titled *The Cruel Way.* Perhaps these novel-istic, or better yet, adventuresome pleasures are why this kind of daredevilry makes me want to shout for joy.

THERE ARE THOSE, of course, who do not turn their jour-neys into words or writing. In fact, they make up the majority. Our journeys, once stored within the body, are often forgotten. But sometimes fragments show up in our lives.

THE CANADIAN COMPOSER Colin McPhee, during his third extended stay on the island of Bali, wrote *A House in Bali* (1947) and spent years laboring over his opus, *Music in Bali,* published two years after his death in 1964. Born in Montreal in 1900, McPhee lived in New York and later Paris, with stints in Bali in between, spending his final years in Los Angeles as a professor of musicology at UCLA. Drawn by the music of another land and its people, he took an objective and systematic approach as he plumbed and plied the waters of Balinese musical traditions, and the links between music and society. He made no trips to Bali after the Second World War. One wonders what form Bali, and all the faces of the islanders and their music, took in McPhee's memory.

Written for two pianos and an orchestra supple-mented by gamelan instruments, *Tabuh-Tabuhan: Toccata for Orchestra* (1936) not only has textures of the traditional gamelan, but also has a jazzy swing, while echoing, at least for today's listeners, orchestral works written much later, like Steve Reich's *Three Movements* and *The Four Sections* from the 1980s.

Arriving in Asia about forty years after McPhee, Claude Vivier, a fellow Montrealer, traveled first to Japan and gradually worked his way south toward Bali in 1977 when he was twenty-nine. He spent several months on the island, where he studied gamelan. On returning to the West, he began composing slightly different music—departing from the influence of Gilles Tremblay, his teacher in Montreal, and Karlheinz Stockhausen, his teacher in Cologne.

Five years before Vivier set off on his journey through Asia, Tōru Takemitsu joined French composers

Iannis Xenakis and Betsy Jolas on a trip to Bali. In 1975 he published *Ki no kagami, Sōgen no kagami* (*Mirror of Trees, Mirror of Grasses*), in which he interprets the music of Europe and the music of Asia through the dialectic of movable/immovable.

In terms of his use of ensemble, and of melody, and the layering of sounds—as found in works such as *Pulau Dewata, Lonely Child, Zipangu,* and *Bukhara*—there is nothing quite like the music Vivier wrote after spending time in Asia. Granted, if you take a step back, you can find overlaps in minimal music and in a wider musical context, but in terms of serious work written for performance in a concert hall, from where I stand, these pieces have no counterpart. *Pulau Dewata,* "island of the gods," does not specify the instruments with which it should be played, prompting the cre-ation of unique ensembles, which suggests an inclination to direct music away from the world of the concert hall.

Openly gay from an early age, Vivier relocated to Paris in 1982, and the next year, in March 1983, he was stabbed to death by a man he had met in a bar. He would have turned thirty-five that April. Vivier had been abandoned at birth, sent to an orphanage, and adopted at age three. From thirteen he attended Catholic boarding schools. Throughout his life, he was unable to sleep with the lights off.

McPhee had married the young anthropologist Jane Belo, a student of Margaret Mead, in 1931. Together, they went to Bali, where Belo was doing fieldwork, and McPhee pursued his interest in gamelan music. By the early 1940s, McPhee and Belo were divorced, and he was living as a gay man, sharing a brownstone in Brooklyn with W.H. Auden and Benjamin Britten, among others.

When it comes to those individuals who gravitate not toward Europe or America, but toward Asia or Africa, what must we take care not to overlook, beyond concerns of locality, culture, and civilization? But therein lies the problem, since the expression "overlook" is rendered suspect by "look" and its feigned objectivity, and yet I can't help wondering whether there might be some other way of accessing these figures, through a deeper sensitivity.

THEN IT OCCURS TO ME. Could a journey be a convergence of connections?

THERE ARE CASES WHERE no journal or travelogue was made, but the work, the music, tells the tale. I call it work, and know that there is nothing wrong with that, but what gives me pause is the existence of a process, during which the musician "works out" the composition in their head, or on the page, or in the back and forth that happens in the studio. It is a process influenced by the variables of timing, and of setting. I'm thinking of Don Cherry, the trumpeter who developed free jazz alongside Ornette Coleman.

The term "free jazz," just like it sounds, is applied liberally, covering a wide swath of music. Exponents of the genre, such as Ornette Coleman and Billy Higgins, or Eric Dolphy and Charlie Haden, may have a lot in common at the root, but the ways in which their buds, branches, and leaves extend themselves, or find expression, vary considerably. What makes Don Cherry "free" is the way he moves. He performed alongside a colorful array of musicians, from names like Albert Ayler, Archie Shepp, and Sun Ra, whose work embodied the term "free," to the likes of Sonny Rollins, Naná Vasconcelos, and Gato Barbieri, as well as Latif Kahn, Terry Riley, and Krzysztof Penderecki. Although born in the United States, Cherry spent much of his life based out of Paris and Scandinavia, and in his travels he performed with a great many musicians. Today, however, this mobile lifestyle is hardly an aberration. The thing to remember, though, is that back then, in the second half of the twentieth century, this mobility was meaningful, especially when it involved mixing with musicians from different traditions. Cherry learned to play the pocket trumpet and the conch, the kora (a stringed instrument from Africa), the mbira (thumb piano), and the electric keyboard, as well as a variety of percussion instruments, and he modified his voice, from sound to speech, in the service of a song. One might say that he journeyed through the possibilities of music. Among these is the concept of world music, at the core of which exists, it seems to me, the Indian idea of Nada Brahma, holding that the world is sound, consisting of vibration, and that the whole universe consists of sound vibrations.

From Cherry's study with the singer Pandit Pran Nath and sarodist Vasant Rai, who taught workshops in the United States, and later with the Dagar Brothers in India, we can get a sense of his fascination with Indian sensibilities. His music, or better yet the music toward which Don Cherry aspired, may have been a product of the same era as the civil rights movement and the Vietnam War, but it is also part of the African American musical tradition, while being placed in the more esoteric genre of "world fusion." This is not really a music you can pick apart to identify its influences, or its origins. Music visits—haunts—each person differently. A change of place leads to new collaboration: another way that music contains the journey.

AT TIMES THE JOURNEY IS indeed expressed through the work. The architect Itō Chūta and the artist Isamu Noguchi strike me as prime examples of this. The works Noguchi left behind all over the world are inseparable from their sites, or from their settings. Well, most of them. His works were born from the topography and local stone and sand, though he sometimes used contrasting materials brought in from elsewhere. The essence of art, as described by Tōru Takemitsu in *Mirror of Trees, Mirror of Grasses,* also applies to the works of Isamu Noguchi. To commemorate the passing of this artist whose bloodlines ran both East and West, Tōru Takemitsu wrote a piece for solo flute entitled *Itinerant.*

We have Hayden Herrera's *Listening to Stone: The Art and Life of Isamu Noguchi* and Ryū Niimi's *Isamu Noguchi: Journey to Garden Arts,* but I think we would benefit from a study that draws connections between setting, site, the spirits found therein (*genius loci*), culture and civilization, and the works of Isamu Noguchi, or at least attempts to pin and mount the journeys and projects undertaken by Noguchi, a man perpetually out of place—by his own account, and perhaps even by his own doing.

IF DON CHERRY TYPIFIES world fusion music, then Chūta Itō typifies world fusion architecture, long before the advent of postmodernism. In the early twentieth century, as Japan turned away from Asia to align itself with Europe, and professors at Tokyo Imperial University were sent abroad to European universities, Itō refused to start his journey in the West, instead beginning a three-year journey in Eurasia, moving through China and on to Burma, India, Ceylon, Turkey, Egypt, and Greece before touring Europe and the United States. The desire to group him among the explorers of other centuries, like Ibn Battuta, Marco Polo, or Xuanzang, imposes an outdated spirit of romance on his journey. The forms to be found in the illustrations in his field notes and on the postcards from his various destinations, as well as in the designs of such structures as Hitotsubashi University Kanematsu Hall, Great Kantō Earthquake Memorial Hall, Great Kantō Earthquake Memorial Museum, and Yushima Seidō, are peculiar and yet somehow irresistible (calling to mind *Tokyo: The Last Megalopolis,* Akio Jissoji's film adaptation of Hiroshi Aramata's historical fantasy novel *Teito monogatari*). Itō had been "seeing" these configurations, in the visionary sense, from an early age, but he was also clever enough to render them numerically, a combination of aptitudes that makes him fascinating. I'm dying to know how he engaged with people and animals and other things as he traversed the continents. It should come as no surprise that he brought international attention to the Yungang Grottoes, on the edge of the Gobi Desert in China. Something must have called him. That must have been it.

As a person prone to seeing, and with visionary power, Itō enjoyed a highly developed sense of sight, and his eyes and hands were so in tune with one another that he seems to have had no difficulty drawing whatever he saw. I can't help but imagine a comparably sensitive person, but one whose ears could hear as well as Itō's eyes saw. They might have found their calling as a composer, devoted to exploring the hitherto unheard.

In any case, there's something a bit jarring, yet nostalgic, about Itō's buildings, such as Tsukiji Honganji and Okura Museum of Art in Tokyo, and Honganji Dendōin in Kyoto. It is the part that goes untold in what we call a travelogue, the part that never turns up in the time-bound descriptive process known as

language, as if the countless images bottled up inside of their creator have finally come spilling from these buildings like phantasms. Itō may not intersect with Ernest Fenollosa, who described the East Pagoda at Yakushiji as "frozen music," but in the works left by this well-traveled architect, one would argue that oscillations born from words and music over time, just like in travel, are gradually transposed from East to West, creating something of a moiré pattern that appears frozen in place. Though admittedly it is going a bit too far to call these buildings an expression of his journeys.

WHAT THEN, or what kind of thing, is a journey? Whoever or whatever it entails, and however it transpires, a journey, or that which has the feel of a journey, must happen in another time and space, rather than being a mere extension of our day-to-day existence. Otherwise, the journey is doomed to the realm of the personal. For the journey to become a story, someone has to do the moving, and someone has to write it down. It might be the same person, or it might be another person acting in their stead, working from hearsay.

NOT LIMITED TO peripatetic travel, the story could take the form of an account of an extended stay, or of biography or memoir. Perhaps only a fraction of the most substantial works carry the language of the journey. The story might be nonfiction for the most part, but nothing says that travel writing, or nonfiction, can't be smuggled into works of fiction. All of this amounts to language, or the tapestry that language weaves, and to how we trace the movements of time and space we call a journey, in whatever we are reading.

THERE IS SOMETHING TO be said about firsthand accounts, but secondhand is fine as well. Having been there doesn't mean that you won't lie or make mistakes, and words need not be taken at face value.

WRITING THAT TAKES TRAVEL as its focus must go beyond the places visited and the people found there. And it can't be just a record of the props and the environs, or the culture of a place. What of the journey as a glimpse of place, of things that happen to travelers while there, and how they cope?

TWO PEOPLE MEET AT SUCH and such a place. Sure. Interesting. But more often than not, it's just a starting point. The journey is more like a cluster of such points, encompassing the lines connecting them.

WE DON'T NEED A DETAILED account of what a person did along the way, wherever they went. It could be any part, even the smallest fraction, if the fractional makes up a journey. Sometimes it's a one-off; other times, the same place is visited repeatedly, so often that it has the feel of daily life, and yet we can still call it a journey. But is it still a journey if you're visiting for work? If you're there on fieldwork, in a professional capacity, is journey still the proper term? If not, what's the issue? Is it the question of motivation? The end (point)? Or the points along the way?

HOW ABOUT RESEARCHERS—are they on journeys, of one kind or another? Sure they are, would be my first reaction, though I can't help scratching my head. Maybe not. There's nothing odd about a person visiting a place that captures their attention. Even scholars make journeys. That said, I have to wonder whether "journey" is the best term for them. Perhaps their sense of purpose is a bit too strong to call what they do a journey. To journey is to go somewhere and discover some aspect of the place. The discovery would seem to be an essential factor. But doesn't that sound like a treasure hunt? The egoism of making the unknown known. What we call fieldwork is often fueled by an affection for the journey that transcends the professional.

WHICH BEGS THE QUESTION of what is at the journey's core. Or is that notion an illusion? We feel compelled to disqualify a certain kind of foray from being a journey, even though it could be otherwise described as travel, or a voyage, tour, or trip.

BRIAN JONES, a founding member of the Rolling Stones, died a year after recording *The Pipes of Pan at Joujouka* in Morocco in 1968. Jones had been to Morocco

before. And he had made recordings. On his first visit to Tangier, he became transfixed by the performances of street musicians; and despite lacking a shared language, somehow managed to establish a mutual understanding, asking them about their instruments and how they were played. According to those in his party, if Jones saw an instrument he didn't recognize, he was unable to contain himself.

He played rhythm guitar in the band, but this was just the surface, or a fraction of who he was. Jones was an instrumentalist of boundless ability, who played guitar but also played harmonica, or the harpsichord, or the dulcimer, or the marimba, and a slew of other instruments, including percussion and wind. Rather than specialize in a single instrument, he opted to explore a broad variety of expression in his path as a musician, maintaining a playful relationship with sound and music.

It seems that Jones heard about Moroccan music from those who visited the country before him, in particular American writer Paul Bowles and the British painter and novelist Brion Gysin. But it was only in seeing the place for himself that he became truly entranced by its sounds and its music. The following year, Jones returned to the field with recording equipment. Taping as much as possible, he would return to London and go over the material, mixing it with the signature rhythms of soul music. At least that was the plan. *Death of a Rolling Stone: The Brian Jones Story,* a biography by Mandy Aftel, contains a testimony from George Chkiantz, the album's recording engineer. Jones had thought that the recording process would be easy, but he got more than he bargained for. In June 1968, he finally obtained a recording that met his standards. (This was around the same time that a newly married Jean-Luc Godard captured the "Sympathy for the Devil" recording sessions in London. Jones can be seen in the studio, but he looks so ghastly, it's almost like he isn't even there.)

At this point, however, by all accounts, Jones had mostly lost control of his drug use and his relationships with his bandmates—a far cry from the magnificent focus he exhibited while listening to the musicians of Joujouka and recording their performances, despite not knowing where he was or what he was doing the rest of the time. Perhaps, for Jones, Morocco was an alternate universe, cut off from the realities of London. True, even in Morocco, the decadence of London could come crashing in when he stepped away from the local music. But maybe in that music—both when these musicians were performing right in front of him, and when revisiting recordings in the studio—he occupied another time and space, created by a music that departed from his everyday experience.

Jones had seen through the production of the 1968 records, but in July 1969 he was found dead, at the age of twenty-seven, floating in his swimming pool. The album was released in 1971. The explosive acoustic pressure of the ghaita (pipes), whose richly layered nasal tones were a stark departure from Western sound and music, and the tebel (drum) reappeared within a decade's time on Ornette Coleman's 1977 release *Dancing in Your Head*. Taking a different tack from Don Cherry, this album captures a free jazz pioneer giving shape to his own musical journey.

ABOUT A HUNDRED YEARS before Brian Jones or Ornette Coleman visited North Africa, Gustave Flaubert, accompanied by Maxime Du Camp, undertook an ambitious journey through the region over the better part of two years, from 1849 into 1851. Not everything they saw and heard was wholly unfamiliar or alien to them. This was before what we now call the tourism industry, but hubs with strong European ties existed here and there. Du Camp took numerous photographs, creating what is now a valuable resource. Flaubert must have begun writing *Madame Bovary* soon after returning from his journey. The two were still in their late twenties. Just about the same age as Brian Jones.

Now considered a classic, *Flaubert in Egypt* is less a consistent account than an assortment of unfiltered jottings. Halfway through the book a rather lengthy passage details Flaubert's evening with the dancer Kuchuk Hanem. A child and an old man played the rebab, which produced what the author describes as tone-deaf noise. Thereafter, Kuchuk Hanem danced and played the tarabuka, a performance that gradually turns into a physical encounter.

Around the same time, the French painter Eugène Fromentin made three visits to North Africa, in 1846, 1848, and 1853. His third stay, notably longer than the rest, led to the writing of *Un été dans le Sahara* (*Summer in the Sahara*) and *Une année dans le Sahel* (*A Year in the Sahel*). Compared with Flaubert's fragmentary prose, which variously lends itself to moments of sheer clarity and moments of laconic dullness, Fromentin's work remains conscious of the reader, giving it a certain integrity. As a result, it is not without passages that could well come across as pedestrian, but what of the following account from *Summer in the Sahara,* which takes place in Aïn-Mahdi? Along the way from Algiers to Blida, the painter meets an organ grinder from Auvergne and is disturbed by what he hears. The man is playing *À la grâce de Dieu,* written by Loïsa Puget for the theater. The painter writes that hearing the song "ruined the entire day." Soon after, he elaborates as follows:

But upon parting ways with the Negro musicians, that memory came back to me, only this time it was much less bitter than before. It seemed to me that this new meeting gave an otherworldly meaning to the first. In comparing these two miserable rovers, one from Bernou, the other from Cantal or Savoie, I could not help admiring the ingenuity of chance even more, and mused that someday these two bards would cross paths, one with his tortoiseshell guitar, the other with his organ, and that they would play their Negro songs and Parisian songs together, in the middle of an Arab town that has now become French territory.

Let's not get distracted by the "miserable rovers" or the "Arab town that has now become French territory" and instead focus on the dizzying sensation we experience when this travelogue shape-shifts into a prophetic text or work of science fiction, as the author, who would go on to write only one novel, the masterful *Dominique,* envisions a scene that could be likened to world fusion music a hundred years into the future.

We are captivated not by Fromentin, who daydreams of the meeting, so much as by the organ grinder, by

the Negro musicians. Not the seers, but the seen—
those who live immersed in the everyday. It may just
be that traveling, insofar as it is a departure from the
everyday, offers a recess from life, a way of extricating
oneself from existence. One can be a storyteller only
after one returns from the journey, from adventure.

SINCE THE MID-TWENTIETH CENTURY, when transportation,
sightseeing, and information became vastly more
accessible, what we once called a journey has become
something more like getting around—more like,
but not quite. Those who think the journey is dead are
gravely mistaken. Lots of people move around. Artists,
musicians, and authors all rely on travel. Unless you
see it as a journey, it is simply movement, following
a pre-established harmony or plan, not much different
than a business trip. But is there really not a difference? Without this plan, no one could achieve what
is desired, or even create a schedule. Is there no way
out of this? An accident? Or getting sick? When we
fall ill, the items on our schedule are slashed out, one
day at a time. It is then that we realize that our plans,
our designs, like almost everything else, are established over a substrate of nothingness. And life goes
on, day by day.
    What was a journey again? 🐵

My First Trip

translated by Morgan Giles

Mikako Brady
THE OLD MAN IN THE RED CAP

I HAVE MANY MEMORIES of trips I took as a child with my parents—fragments of long car rides to visit my grandparents in the summer and the trips we took to see relatives who lived far away—but they're all jumbled up and thrown together.

When you put a child in a car for a few hours to take them on a trip, they're going to need the bathroom desperately at some point. I remember my father stopping the car at a small school in the countryside so I could run in to pee. Maybe it was the weekend or a holiday; the school was deserted and dead silent. I'm not sure how I was able to get inside—maybe the school was under construction or being renovated, because there were bulldozers and big trucks parked in the schoolyard, and concrete blocks and bags of cement everywhere.

My father, who was sitting in the driver's seat, and my mother, who was holding my baby sister, didn't get out of the car with me. I was going off on my own in a place far from home that I'd never been before, so even though it was a trip to the toilet, it was in the truest sense my very first trip on my own.

I was half-running down the hall when an old man peered out from the shadow of a stack of construction materials. He was wearing a red knit cap and grimy, oversized work clothes. I asked, "Where is the bathroom?" He took me all the way to the door of the girls' room and said, "Here," then disappeared with a smile on his face. I went in and did my business, but when I opened the door of the toilet stall, the old man was standing there in the girls' bathroom. I was surprised, but I wasn't scared. I thought maybe he'd been so worried about me that he came back. So I gave my hands a good wash, told the old man in the red hat goodbye, and ran out of the school back to where my parents were waiting in the car.

What happened that day is something that has always stuck with me. Though at the time I thought nothing of it, as I got older, I started to wonder exactly what he was doing there that day.

This old man, who could've been a construction worker putting in extra hours on his day off or

a homeless person, a pervert or a grown-up with a
real sense of responsibility, a protective spirit or
one that brings poverty and misery, has become the
prototype for me of what a man is.

Miwa Nishikawa
BAGWORM WALLETS

I TOOK ONLY ONE TRIP with my father. Just one.

I must've been five or six. I was wearing a yellow
dress with a belt around the waist, and my father
was taking my brother and me to the aquarium in
Shimonoseki. Shimonoseki is in Yamaguchi prefecture,
at the southernmost point of Honshū. I was born in
Hiroshima, and sometimes we'd go to visit my mother's
hometown, Iwakuni, in Yamaguchi, but other than
that, I had never been anywhere else. For as long as
I could remember, my father and mother had the kind
of relationship where the slightest word led to a fight.
My father never stayed in my mother's parents'
house, and my mother didn't come along on this trip
either. Kids grow up taking their cues from their
mother. So my brother and I were always slightly
distant from our father. If he'd never taken us out on
little adventures or whatever, that would've been
fine with us. It was the late 1970s, early '80s. That's
just what I thought fathers were like.

But getting all worked up when he occasionally
thinks about his family is also what a man does.

A sudden trip. Suddenly splashing cash around.
I don't know the particulars, whether the trip was
something my mother had suggested, or if my father
came up with it on his own. Anyway, for the first
time I rode a shinkansen and ate a bento bought at
the station. All these little things, done as if to say,
"This is what a dad can do," undeniably made me feel
indulged to the bottom of my heart.

"So what do you think, Your Royal Highnesses?
How's it feel to ride a shinkansen?"

I remember so clearly the look on my father's face
as he asked us this. We were sitting on those blue
seats with armrests, nervously picking at our bentos.

"Yeah. I like this."

Perhaps I said this partly because my father looked
so proud. But the shinkansen *was* really fast.

In front of our mother, my brother and I jostled and
scuffled with abandon, but alone with our father, we
were somehow out of our depth. We were truly on our
best behavior as we walked through the Shimonoseki
Aquarium. I saw my first soft-shelled turtle. Dad
told me that if it bites your hand, it won't let go until
the next time it thunders, and I wondered just what
kind of creature this was.

It was getting dark. We sat under the red sky, resting
a little under the maple trees planted around the
station until it was time for our shinkansen home. My
father plucked off a bagworm cocoon hanging from
a branch, split it open and skillfully flattened it
with his fingertips. The inside of the cocoon spun by
the little inhabitant, who had absconded somewhere,
was pale and smooth—completely different than
the outside, which looked like a dirty rag. A bagworm's
cocoon is very strong, my father said. During the war,
people would collect them to make wallets.

I seem to remember the maple trees we sat under
having their fall colors, so I thought it was late autumn
when this happened, but on reflection, that yellow
dress had short sleeves, so I suppose this trip must've
been during summer vacation. The way that my father
pulled off the cocoon without hesitation, too, I knew
he was convinced that its inhabitant wouldn't be
there at this time of year. I heard that later the station
in Shimonoseki was burned down by an old man who
had nowhere to go after being released from prison.
Maybe all the maple trees burned up with it, and

maybe all my memories are wrong: were they really maple trees, and was there a soft-shelled turtle at the Shimonoseki Aquarium? Starting to suspect that perhaps nobody ever made wallets from bagworm cocoons, I googled it and lots of images came up. So there really were bagworm wallets. My father is eighty-three now. I don't think we'll be traveling together much anymore, but nobody else, save for my father on that day, has ever told me that you can make wallets from bagworm cocoons.

Yui Tanizaki
THE MOUNTAIN AT NIGHT

THE DARK OUTLINES of the trees stood out against the blueish-gray spilled-ink sky. I had thought that the night sky was black, but now I realized that when something much darker was in front of you, it would look gray. The highway that cut through the mountain had the shape of that darkness. Though we passed them in a heartbeat, I could clearly make out the very tip of each branch in that instant. Things far away came closer, revealing their details for just one moment, then quickly moved into the distance. And then the next thing would come. The mountain at night was a giant, mysterious mass. The car went into the tunnel, then out of it. Many times, it went through and out. The inside of the tunnel was orange, further heightening my unease. It was the color of the tiny light bulb on the ceiling of my room, the one I stared at when I had a fever.

We must've been on the road for just short of two hours, but it felt far longer. From what my parents say, I cried the entire time. I would fuss whenever they put me in the car, and there was little they could do about it. And it wasn't just a half-hearted tantrum, I would cry and scream, yelling as though the end of the world was coming. "Oh, it was awful," my mother recalls. She says that when relatives followed us in their car, they could see me contorting my face, pressing my nose against the rear window, kicking my little legs. The adults were appalled.

I don't know why I cried that much. I'm sure I was scared. But despite that fear, I could not take my eyes off the sight of the mountain at night. We were going to my father's parents' house, which we always seemed to travel to at night. I was usually a shy kid, but once we got there I became even more reserved, sitting silently in the corner. Maybe I felt embarrassed from all the crying and screaming in the car. My father had joined my mother's family register and taken her surname. He was the youngest of five children, so my cousins were all older than me, and I had no one to play with.

My paternal grandfather died young, but my grandmother always doted on her son, my father, as if he were still a small boy. Surrounded by his brothers and sisters, called by his childish nickname, sharing a drink, my father always seemed a little more relaxed than he did at home. It was odd to me, so I watched, silently.

Hirokazu Koreeda
THE CRAB

THAT MARCH, with college graduation not far off, I went to Amami Ōshima. I went on my own.

I'd heard that Amami was where my father's mother was from. The trip wasn't about anything as ambitious as searching for my roots, but perhaps on some level I did want to experience the landscape of her childhood.

My grandfather started seeing my grandmother, who was the prettiest girl in the next village over, and soon they as good as eloped, leaving the island and going to Taiwan. There, they had my father. But the honeymoon didn't last long between this pampered son of a doctor and the daughter of a baptized Christian. Right from the start of their marriage, my grandparents couldn't stop fighting—so much so that their whirlwind romance feels like little more than a lie. Usually my grandfather lost, I'm told, and when he did, he would get a pair of scissors and take his anger out on the pictures in the photo album, cutting out my grandmother's face and throwing the tiny pieces in the trash. So most of the Koreeda family photos from when they were in Taiwan don't have my grandmother in them.

I boarded a small ferry in Kagoshima, and we were tossed about by awful waves before reaching the port in the early hours. Reeling, I got on a bus, which shook me around some more. At the youth hostel on a hill on the outskirts of the island, I set down my bag and slept until evening. I went out for a walk once my seasickness had subsided and while it was still daylight. I walked along the sandy beach for a while, taking care not to get my shoes wet. The sea was calm, with not a soul around. How much longer until din-ner? I wondered. I'd barely eaten since that morning, so naturally I started feeling hungry. Just when I was thinking it was almost time to head back to the hostel, I caught sight of a crab at the water's edge. For no particular reason I sped up to get closer to it. The crab held up its claws, threatening me, Hold it there! It seemed angry. Looking closer, I saw that its body was semitransparent and a strange color of red. I sensed a kind of humanity and sanctity in its actions. I gave up on getting any closer and returned to the hostel.

What had the crab been trying to tell me? After breakfast the next morning I went out again to the beach. At the water's edge, cast in a silver glow by the morning sun, lay the crab, dead. Its body was now an even paler red than the day before, even more transparent. And next to the crab was another, nestled close to it and dead, too. I wondered if they were a pair. Maybe beyond where the crab had blocked my way yesterday, his wife had already died.

It's been thirty years since that happened, but even now, each time I open my grandparents' photo album, I remember that crab.

Utamaru

THE SUMMER OF '74, FIREFLIES AND DOGS AND THE FIRST CRY OF HIP HOP

I FEEL THAT WITH THINGS LIKE THIS, the older the memory is the cooler it is, and my mother did take me all over the country from a pretty young age, it seems, but honestly, I don't remember a thing.

I guess the first trip that I can kind of almost remember happened in the summer of 1974, when I was five, and my parents took me to Princeton and New York.

Why Princeton? Well, an American woman my mother had become friends with through work was employed at Princeton University, and she let us stay at her house during summer vacation. The house, which was very close to campus, came with a dog. It had a pool and was surrounded by land with woods and a river, in a wonderful environment that was mysterious even for America.

Why I can pin this down to the summer of 1974 is because at that time, whenever a camera was pointed at me, I'd go into a Masked Rider transformation pose. I remember so clearly how the American kids my age in the neighborhood went wild for it, yelling, "Oh, karate!" Another thing is that I often played in the pool with them, but also, one night an unbelievable

number of lightning bugs started flying up from the river, and that sight—which even as a child made me think, "I'll probably never see something like this again"—is burned into my brain, so I'm certain that it was summer.

What's more, I can still, for some reason, remember all the events of those days in rich detail: how I loved playing around with the dog, Jeff, so much that the day before we left, I finally tried to ride him like a horse and of course he threw me off and I sobbed, more from the awkwardness of being rejected than any pain; how one of the kids I was especially close with had a big brother who was a police officer, and the way my heart pounded as he showed me the first real gun I ever saw.

After that we went to New York. When I think that I was right there, only a year after the birth in the Bronx in the summer of 1973 of the original form of what would later be called hip hop, I'm overwhelmed with emotion.

While we were there, we went to see *The Wiz,* the all-Black production of *The Wizard of Oz.* Five-year-old me couldn't have understood the English lyrics, so to be real with you, I probably slept through most of it. But five years later, in 1979, when the movie version came out in Japan, I saw in it a vivid reflection of the mood of those times and of the lawlessness of New York, and at ten years old I felt a strange sense of nostalgia for that place.

AS I REREAD THE SENTENCES ABOVE, which I wrote for the Japanese *MONKEY* magazine, a horrible doubt arose in my heart.

"Are those memories... true?"

So just to make sure, I went to the Wikipedia article for "The Wiz (musical)" (although I probably should have done at least that much fact-checking in the first place) and found that its first performance on Broadway took place on, oh my god, January 5, 1975. C'mon, that's the winter of the following year!

Later, when I checked with my mother, she said that we went to Princeton again a few years later, and that maybe I'd blended the stories about the pool and the fireflies with what happened before. Oh, right, well, that must be it! My bad!

So I'd like to take this opportunity to issue a correction. Of the descriptions in the original text, seeing *The Wiz* and falling off Jeff actually happened in early 1975, and the other summery anecdotes probably happened in 1978. It seems like, without me knowing it, all this was reorganized into a more dramatic series of events in my head. Memories are such a convenient thing for the storyteller; they're so easily twisted unconsciously, and this, you might say, is just another typical example. I wanted to take this opportunity of publication in the English *MONKEY* to apologize! 🐵

MIKAKO BRADY (b. 1965) lives in Brighton and writes about life in England. *I'm Yellow and White and a Little Bit Blue,* one of her nonfiction books, was a bestseller in Japan in 2020.

MIWA NISHIKAWA (b. 1974) is a filmmaker and an author. Her critically acclaimed films include *Dreams for Sale* (2012) and *Under the Open Sky* (2021) and her novels include *The Long Excuse* (2015), which she made into a film in 2016.

YUI TANIZAKI (b. 1978) is a novelist and translator. Her award-winning books include *Asia in the Looking-Glass* (2019) and her translations include *The Underground Railroad* by Colson Whitehead.

HIROKAZU KOREEDA (b. 1962) is an internationally acclaimed filmmaker. His feature-length films include *After Life* (1998) and *Shoplifters* (2018), for which he won the Palme d'Or at Cannes.

UTAMARU (b. 1969) is a rapper and a radio personality. His extremely popular program *After-Six Junction* runs every evening from Monday to Friday.

Brian Evenson

A Report on Travel

I.

It feels strange to be writing a report on travel when, like the majority of humans, I have spent the last year traveling hardly at all. The last time I got on a plane was exactly one year, one month, one week, and one day before I began writing this report on travel, a report that is rapidly becoming a report on whatever the opposite of travel is.

I did not purposefully begin writing this report on travel exactly one year, one month, one week, and one day after I took my last plane flight. But now that I have realized this to be the case, it feels significant to me. Admittedly, anyone who reads this is likely to read it well after the one year, one month, one week, and one day anniversary of the last time I flew on a plane has passed. Even if I somehow manage to finish and revise this piece before midnight and quickly email it to my editor, M., and even if he immediately opens the email and reads it—even then, since he lives in Japan and on the other side of the international dateline, he will not be able to read this exactly one year, one month, one week, and one day after my last plane flight. At the very earliest, he will read it one year, one month, one week, and *two* days after.

Indeed, since it is now slightly after midnight, unless I can immediately board a plane and fly rapidly westward, frantically writing all the while, even I myself will not manage to read this piece on the one year, one month, one week, and one day anniversary of my last plane flight.

I do not have a plane that I can immediately board. And even if I did, I do not believe I am ready yet to board one. Indeed, I do not know when I will again feel comfortable boarding a plane.

II.

My wife, K., did not want me to go on the last plane flight I went on. She encouraged me to cancel the ticket, and in retrospect she was entirely right about this, as she is about most things. But the ticket was non-refundable and my fear of becoming ill was slightly outweighed, in those early days of the pandemic, by my desire not to waste money. Before last year,

I traveled on planes frequently, twenty or thirty flights a year. There was a certain repetitive rhythm to this that punctuated my life. I would travel to a city—H., say, or B., or A.—I would read my work to people who seemed for the most part to desire me to read my stories to them, and then I would travel home. I would read the same stories in different cities, until the moment I became tired of reading the same stories, and then I would choose different stories to read. Sometimes I would convince myself I was going to read different stories, but by the time I stood up and took my place behind a podium that looked more or less like the podium I had stood behind a few days earlier in a different city, I would have convinced myself to read the same stories I usually read. At other times, I would see someone in the audience who I was sure I had seen in the audience of another city, and I would on the fly change what stories I was reading, only to find out, in speaking to them afterward, that I had ended up reading exactly the same stories that they had heard me read before.

III.

This year, instead of traveling by plane, I have, like most other people, been looking at and talking with people I know via a computer. Every two weeks I meet for one hour on Zoom with five Marxist thinkers to discuss a book we are all reading together. One person, B. (me), lives in the United States. Four others live in the United Kingdom. A sixth lives in Australia. Because of the difference in time zones, there is only one hour when it is comfortable to meet, when it is not too early or too late for one or another of us. And so, while my friends in England discuss our book just after dinner, I discuss it in place of lunch, and my friend in Australia sets her alarm clock an hour early to discuss it before breakfast.

The squares we occupy on the screen within the window of the program are lit by all different sorts of light or absences of light, depending on the time zones we are in. When we meet, I find myself resizing the window of the program, which adjusts how many people are in a row and how many columns there are. I arrange my window into a long strip. Ideally, if people enter the Zoom in just the right order, and if one of the three from the UK can't attend, I can arrange the position of the squares so that they roughly represent where we are on the globe: the Australian in the morning to the left, myself at lunch beside her, the UK friends in the evening to the right.

Whenever I manage to do this, it gives me a strange sense of satisfaction, almost as if I am in a plane, very high up, impossibly high up, seeing the globe spread before me. *There's Australia,* I say to myself, and *There's America,* and *There's England.*

But then the sixth friend joins and the strip is not long enough to hold all six people in a single line and everything rearranges.

There have been times when I have been tempted to tell my Marxist friends that I am doing this, that I am resizing the window and rearranging their placement to simulate their location in the world, but to do so would suggest I haven't been listening to the discussion of the book. In addition, I do not know the etiquette of manipulating people's squares within a Zoom, though suspect that if there is an etiquette I am breaking it.

Then again, for all I know they too are doing the same thing to the windows of their screens, attempting to achieve the same result. Perhaps we are, all of us, secretly rearranging the squares, trying to make the order just right, so our eyes can scan from left to right and in so doing travel across the world.

Though chances are it is just me, alone, doing this, as a way to pass the time until I can again bring myself to board a plane. 🐒

© Isabella Fassler

Hiroko Oyamada

Along the Embankment

translated by David Boyd

I WAS ON MY WALK, the only part of my routine that I've been able to keep up, when a tree caught my eye. It was along the embankment by the river, growing at the top of a fairly steep slope, close to the road. I took the same path yesterday, but there was no tree here, I'm pretty sure, and this one didn't look like it had just been planted. On the ground at the base of the tree, among the overgrown weeds, were pieces of trash: a red paper sleeve for fries, a couple of crushed plastic bottles that had yellowed, and some clean-looking tissues. On the trunk there were blotches: lichens, or some sort of stain, or maybe the bark was diseased. No sign it had been transplanted. This tree had already been here, it had to have been. Sometimes, things like this happen when I go out walking. In an age when it takes only weeks to build a house, it's no surprise when a vacant lot becomes a neat little block of homes. But sometimes a dilapidated shack appears out of nowhere, or maybe a worn and weathered Buddha or stone monument, or you come across a pretty little house with a blue roof, blue walls, and blue window frames that you notice only as it's being torn down, and it's unsettling. Whether there was something wrong with my eyes, or my mind, or something else, the tree wasn't large. It didn't look young, either. It was so much taller than me, but its trunk so much thinner than mine. While its branches were covered with some leaves, the whole tree seemed airy. The leaves couldn't have looked more leaflike: spindle-shaped, with both ends coming to pointy tips, green, with darker fronts, and backs that weren't exactly white. They were shaped like cherry tree leaves, but a little longer and without the jagged edges, and they actually had a similar thickness and similar veins, but the shape of the tree was different, with branches spilling out from a little lower on the trunk than a cherry tree, and that was why from a distance maybe it looked less like a head of broccoli than parsley gone to seed, but the more I write, the further away I get from the tree before me. It was basically a tree like any other, if a little malnourished. It had fruit: as green as the leaves, covered in tiny black spots. As big as . . . if I made an OK sign with my thumb and my pointer finger, it would just about fit inside the hole. They were hanging from the branches, dangling from very short stems. From what I could see, they looked pretty round. They didn't have the dimple of an apple, the calyx of a persimmon, or the cap of an acorn. There was no sign posted by the tree, either. So what kind of fruit was this? I looked around. At the bottom of the bank, beside the water, I saw a faded straw hat. It was an old man, and he was watering the rocks and weeds by the river.

No one waters rocks and weeds. The old man had to be watering something growing there. Sometimes people use public property and turn it into a vegetable garden, mostly old people who presumably live nearby, people who don't seem that well off but probably aren't destitute, either. Tomatoes, eggplants, and cucumbers crop up suddenly among the rocks and weeds. In some places, you can find old people, each with their own garden, no more than twenty or thirty meters apart: one garden looks like Versailles, laid out with an eye for geometric order; the next spreads out like a jungle, unruly weeds all over the place; the next surrounded by a lattice of garden stakes, laying claim over the land. The old man had to be one of these people, except I couldn't tell what he was watering. From where I stood, which wasn't far at all, they looked like ordinary green weeds, nothing but weeds. I thought about saying something, asking the old man if he could tell me what the tree was, if he knew. He was holding a large gray watering can, with a gray bucket on the ground beside him. I couldn't tell if it was tap water inside or river water. His gray outfit made me wonder if he really was a guerrilla gardener. I decided not to ask and looked back up at the tree. I had to have this fruit.

When something belongs to somebody, it's easy to steal, but it's hard to take something that belongs to no one. When I was in kindergarten, I ate all the Nanking cherries from a stranger's garden (they were deliciously tart); on a field trip in elementary school, I had a piece of tropical fruit from the greenhouse at a botanical garden (maybe it wasn't ripe yet, but it was dry and mealy and tasted sour); every morning in middle school, I helped myself to the gardening club's cherry tomatoes. I always knew that what I was doing was wrong, and I did what I did having thought through all the things that'd happen if somebody ever found out. I didn't think anyone was going to show up for me after all this time, but if they did, and they wanted me to take responsibility, I would. I would want to. But when it came to fruit growing in a place like this, well . . . Once it's on the ground, it's fair game. I once saw an old woman at a shrine, collecting nuts that had fallen from the gingkos. Another time at the same shrine, I saw children from the local nursery gathering acorns under the oaks. A heartwarming autumn scene, but only because what they were picking up had already fallen from the trees. If they had climbed up and stripped the trees, then the children would probably have been reprimanded, and who knows what would have happened to the old woman. I squinted at the ground. When my eyes adjusted, I could see some fruit among the plants and trash. I picked one up, but when I turned it over, it was blackened and bruised. The next one I saw was so rotten and falling apart that I didn't bother picking it up. And the next one I grabbed had a red stink bug on the bottom that buzzed as it flew toward me, so I shrieked and dropped it. The air from the bug's beating wings blew at my face like a herald of autumn. The fruit on the ground had fallen before their time: they were diseased, or worm-eaten. A young man I always saw on my walks sped by on his bicycle as fast as he could go. He wore the same thin white T-shirt (maybe an undershirt?) all year round, with beige shorts, leaning forward and pedaling with everything he had. I reached nervously for another fallen fruit. From what I could see, there was nothing wrong with this one. It felt light. It was smooth, with a waxy sheen. Kind of hard. I put my nose up to it, but I couldn't smell anything. When I gave it a shake, it felt as though it was packed with something light. No signs of rot. Looking closer, I could see a line running around it, some sort of seam holding the two halves together to form a whole. And that meant there had to be a seed inside. What if it was a walnut? It seemed to be around the right size. Walnuts yet to ripen— and if that's what they were, maybe in autumn I could collect the ones that drop, and then roast and eat them. I put the one that I'd picked up in my pocket and started walking home, pulling it out once in a while and holding it tightly in my hand. When I got back, I used my mom's computer to search for pictures of walnuts. At first, the only images that showed up were walnuts ready to eat, all dried and brown. Some were shelled, some not. Others had been turned into some kind of sweet. Not what I was looking for, so I typed in "on trees" and "Japan" to see what that would do. Nothing looked like what I'd found. The one I brought home was perfectly round, but all these walnuts had pointed tips. I guess walnut shells are a little pointy. Besides, the walnuts in the pictures were bunched together in clusters, but the ones on the tree were all growing separately. I'm sure there are different kinds of walnuts, so this could be another type, but it might also be something else, a different kind of plant altogether. I grabbed the fruit and took another good look at it, then I took a picture. I dug a nail into it, which left a little mark, but the skin didn't break. The mark darkened, and it seemed like it was going to get even darker with time. When I jammed my nail into the line in the middle to see if I could get it open, it wouldn't budge. I went to the kitchen and took out a knife, then ran it through the line. It split right open. Only the outermost layer was green. Beyond that, it was white and slightly transparent. In the middle was a cavity: oblong, uneven, and deep, in the shape you'd get if you sliced the lumpy, brainlike shape of a walnut in two. But why was it empty? Where did the fruit—or I guess it was the seed—go? The seed part, the part you'd eat if it were a walnut, was missing. No insect had made its way in and eaten it, either. Clearly, nothing had ever been there, but if that were true, what had made that complex shape? Was something going to fill it before autumn came, something that would become a seed? I traced the flesh with my finger. Still nothing there. Moisture seeped from the white opening, slightly sticky to the touch. I sniffed my wet finger. There was no smell. It had even less of a scent than water, and it was clearer, too. If anything, what I was smelling was me. I slipped the tip of my tongue into the space in the middle. Only the tip of the tip of my tongue fit, the sides touching the slick white flesh. A second later, I tasted an intense bitterness. I pulled my tongue back. It wasn't only my tongue—my whole mouth had gone numb. I rinsed my mouth out with a cup of water, and that got rid of some of the bitterness, or so I thought, but soon it gave way to a dull pain that spread over my whole tongue. Even my lips hurt. I went to the bathroom to see if my face looked crooked, but I looked the same as always. I went back to the kitchen and drank some milk. It felt like a layer of milk was forming over the bitterness already coating my tongue. Thinking it might help if I ate something, I had a piece of a rice cracker, then decided to fight fire with fire and opened one of the cans of beer that my mom kept in the kitchen, but the bitter layer had already dried hard like rubber and clung to my tongue. I had to wonder if the bitterness was going to stay with me until my taste buds regenerated. I gave up, brushed my teeth, and went to sleep. When I woke up, rain was falling outside, the wind was picking up, and I spent the next several days in bed. Shifts in air pressure always take it out of me. The bitterness faded eventually. From under my thin blanket, I listened to the window rattling, and wondered if the fruit was falling from the tree now.

The next time I passed by the embankment, to my surprise—or maybe it wasn't surprising at all— the tree was gone. Where it should have been I found only a tiny round stump. It was maybe a little bigger than the circle I could make with my thumbs and pointer fingers. The face of the stump was so white that the age rings were barely visible, but I could see faint wavelike patterns left behind by some blade. The stump was so close to the ground that weeds would probably cover it within days. I walked around. There were a few fruits on the ground that seemed to belong to the tree, but they were all visibly rotten. I was leaning down to look at the ground when I heard footsteps running up the embankment toward me. I looked up and saw the old man in the straw hat, holding something green in his arms. The thing was basically round but also a little long. From the way the old man held it, it had to be heavy. He was wearing work gloves. When I took a couple of steps back, he said, "It's a wax gourd." "A wax gourd," I repeated after him. "It's okay," he said, "I scrubbed it down." "Scrubbed it down?" I stared at him, but he didn't even flinch. He looked into my eyes and said, "These gourds, they're covered in tiny little prickles." "Prickles?"

"Like a layer of frost. They're pretty much invisible, but they sure sting like hell if you touch them. Just put some gloves on, rub the gourd down with an old cloth, and you're good to go. The prickles come right off. Here." The surface was a deep green, no pattern, no bumps, no dips. The old man held out the gourd, practically thrusting it at me, elbows first. "Here, here you go." From his words and the way he was holding the gourd, he wasn't even asking if I'd be willing to take it off his hands; it was more like it had already been decided: I was going to take it, and I'd better get on with it. Maybe this was something I'd already agreed to, at a time I couldn't remember. I felt like this sort of thing had happened to me before. I took the gourd, curling my palms over the top as it rested on my arms. It was as heavy as it looked. It was cool against my skin, almost clinging to me. I brought my arms in and held it against my chest like a baby. "Did you grow this?" "I planted some seeds once, a long time ago. I must have left some gourds behind, then they rotted and their seeds took care of the rest. They just keep coming back now, and I have more than I can eat. Every year, I figure the soil's got to be spent, but there they are, tons of them." "Wow." "Keep it somewhere cool and it'll hold until winter." I've heard that, I was about to say, and that's why they're also called winter gourds—but the old man had already turned away and walked down the embankment. The slope was so steep that he didn't walk down so much as slide down, keeping his body upright as he went. Did he really run up the slope carrying this massive gourd? Not many people could pull that off. The man didn't thank me for taking the gourd, and I didn't feel like I should thank him for giving it to me. Then I remembered about the tree. "Um! Excuse me?" The man looked up toward me. The bottom of the embankment seemed so far from the top. "Um, I'm pretty sure there was a tree here before! With fruit on it?" The man furrowed his brow and shook his head. It looked like he meant "I don't know," not "I can't hear you." I carried the gourd home. On the way back, the guy in the undershirt blew past me on his bike. He never used his bell or his voice to let me know he was coming, but I could tell —through some kind of force, some shift in the air—

so he never scared me. The ones you need to watch out for come walking up normally with everyone else. I kept worrying my arms would go numb and I'd drop the gourd. It was almost like it was breathing softly through its skin. I couldn't imagine that it had ever been covered in a layer of invisible prickles. Then the weather took another sudden turn, and so did my health. For a while, I had to stay home. The next time I walked to the embankment, it was already under construction. They were covering the whole area in concrete and stone that they'd brought in from somewhere, burying the stump, the weeds, and everything else. The old man's gourds were all under concrete, and where there had been only wild weeds and scraps of trash, dog walkers and children appeared on the graduated steps installed along the riverside. Benches and more lampposts were set up, and teens from the neighborhood came on dates while young people gathered to set off fireworks, even though they weren't supposed to. I never saw the old man or the guy in the undershirt again. The glare from the ash-colored pavement was too much for me, so I stopped walking to the embankment, too. After a while, the fruit I'd brought home turned brown where I'd cut it, collapsed inward, and dried out. I felt like it had to mean something special, so I put it in a small handmade pouch my mom had given me, and then when I was carrying it around I won 100,000 yen in the lottery, so my mom and I went out for sushi and shared three small bottles of sake. 🐵

© Nicole Xu

Yasunari Kawabata

———

From the Northern Sea

translated by Michael Emmerich

I HAVE DECIDED, Mr. S, to mail you this letter.

Given how busy you must be, I know it is rude to send something so long, and yet....

AS A CHILD, I sometimes thought I would like to write fiction.

This was, I suspect, a consequence in part of my being a creature of the northern regions, whose climate, though it may encourage an affinity for literature, was far removed from the sense of color that characterizes modern painting.

As one might expect, given the harshness of the land, an unshakable Buddhist resignation took root in the hearts of its inhabitants. One had the impression, too, that people here saw only intangible traditions—family lineages, bloodlines, and so on—as legitimate sources of pride. To live out one's life in the same small village or town, palms joined in prayer, clinging to one's faith in Amida's vow of salvation, seemed to be the fate shared by not just the elderly, but also of the young, even young children. More often than not, those who attempt to break free of such crushing feudalistic pressures fell into an even deeper isolation.

All of nature and all things human, too, were a monotonous gray: nothing but the roaring of winter winds, snow skittering through the air, the thunder of the ocean. When you lived amidst all this, even if you did feel, stirring in your heart, the urge to fill a canvas with vibrant colors, your body was too frozen, your hands too numb. This was no world for a visual art like painting.

When I was twenty-one or twenty-two, still living in the town where I was born, I wrote two pieces that might be described as fiction.

A young couple sits on the grass at the edge of Yoyogi Parade Ground amidst the bobbing carrier pigeons, enjoying a secret rendezvous. But they break up, and the man settles into an unremarkable marriage with one of the woman's friends. Years later, the lovers run into each other again. It was a childish plot, but that didn't matter: all I wanted was to write the landscape of Tokyo. When the woman meets her former lover, she finds him disappointing. *Can it be?* she thinks. *Was he always this hopeless?* Gradually, though, it starts to feel right again. I suppose, at my young age, I could not bring myself to let the story end with her feeling disillusioned by her lover. On the way home, however, after their meeting, the woman begins to doubt herself—perhaps, she thinks, the only reason she had started thinking better of him again was that she was jealous. There must have been something worthwhile in my treatment of the psychology of that reunion, because the piece was chosen for publication when I submitted it to a magazine.

Something disagreeable happened, though, when it appeared in print. A woman friend who I did not particularly like announced that I had based the male character on her husband. She went around telling everyone, as if it made her proud. What an extraordinary example of feminine vanity! The entire thing made me feel sick to my stomach, and so I made up my mind to never again, until I died, take up human affairs in my writing. So, the next story I wrote was a sort of fairy tale about a human masseuse who, wandering the streets late at night, ends up going off to massage a frog's stomach—something like that. While it was true no one would ever claim to be the model for such a story, it was also the case that no magazine would ever want to publish it.

Truth be told, though, since I was little, I have always been fascinated by monsters and shapeshifters and the like. And I don't mean stories of the Western type—the alluring metamorphoses that populate the Greek myths, or great tragedies like that of Hamlet's ghost. No, I was partial to those Japanese tales that leave you feeling as if you are listening to a mournful song coming from a distance—the story of the tree spirit at Sanjūsangendō, for instance, or stories about the spirits of insects, rivers, and clothes.

Come to think of it, these stories, too, are rooted in Buddhism, like all those tales in *Record of Miraculous Events in Japan* that teach the law of karmic causality.

I stopped writing fiction after those two silly stunts.

TWENTY OR SO YEARS LATER, though, the sense of relief brought by the end of the war, and the feeling of liberation that came with the defeat, led me to write two or three more works of fiction, more or less. I was spurred to do this, I suppose, by the joy I felt, however superficial it may have been, knowing that I would no longer be looked at askance if I dissented from the morality into which I had been born, and because I had come to believe that a middle-aged woman ought to be able to live at least a little bit as she pleased.

For example, I had always counted myself fortunate to have grown up, from as far back as I can recall, without my mother. Even as a woman, I place little stock in motherhood. To this day, I am secretly convinced that my greatest blessing has been the fact that my mother did not bring me up. The thought of wallowing in blood relationships repels me; I will not be bound by the rapacious loves of family. I am more free than that, more pure. And yet in the context of a prewar morality, I could never have talked openly to others of this rebellion I am living. Even now, in these postwar times, I don't enjoy talking of these things.

I didn't want to speak about them directly, out loud, but I also didn't blame myself as much as I had in the past for thinking in this way; perhaps that is why, a little more than twenty years on, I tried writing fiction once again.

I thought, as I wrote, that I would show it to you. But on reflection, I am no longer so young; I cannot goad myself into the sort of thoughtlessness it would take to trouble you, busy as you are, with one of my capricious stories. After all, look at me—two decades since I first submitted a painting to a public competition, and I have not progressed one bit as a painter, or exhibited any growth. For a woman like me to share a story with you would be outrageous.

And yet painting has become my karma, an inescapable burden I carry from a previous life that torments me even as I pour myself into it, day in and day out. If only I were not a painter, I tell myself each time a flower or a bird catches my attention; doubtless, I would have been a more ordinary woman—more retiring, charming. I would not have harbored this spiteful look in my eyes. . . . I know this, and yet I have come to terms with the fact that there is nothing else for me to do but carry on painting in my own inartful way. Trying my hand at fiction that does not quite live up to the name has made this clearer to me than ever before.

So I gave up, ripped up the story I had written, and determined to write this letter instead. I cannot imagine it would ever be of any use to you in your own writing, but as someone who once dreamed of composing fiction myself, I would be gratified if even a single line gave you the makings of an idea.

It strikes me that writers rarely turn to women's life stories, or confessions, for material. The episode (if that is the word) I will recount to you, Mr. S, is little more than a fairy tale.

I WAS SELECTED AS THE winner in an open competition that was, I think you could say, the single most important in launching new painters' careers.

Despite the ongoing recession, the unemployment, and the poverty, the city's shops were overflowing with a virtual mandala of goods. I was working at a company called K Confections, where I designed chocolate boxes shaped like dolls or animals that took their places among the many colorful items in display windows.

I would scatter small silver and gold beads that glittered like Jintan Pearls over the arabesques adorning the boxes filled with chocolates that were wrapped in gold or silver foil or colorful papers with Russian designs. Those shiny beads are called *argent*.

I came up with the idea of putting little gold circles on the animals, and ribbons, too. When those boxes went on the market, I used to feel so excited walking around town, checking the candy store windows.

I started work at seven with the other women at the factory, and in the afternoons I would take the samples I had created to the design department at headquarters and begin preparing new sketches. My monthly salary equaled the men's, but I was unaccustomed to the work and often made mistakes, and I got the sense everyone disliked me. In those days, it was not yet accepted that women could work, and since I was paid as much as the men and intruded on their territory, people were jealous—my being a woman certainly never won me any sympathy, nor led anyone to try and help. I was plagued by all sorts of troubles. Entering into romantic entanglements like a typical young woman was not an option.

I can't tell you how much I suffered, though, having come to Tokyo from the North at a time when so many were unemployed, before I finally managed to find that job. In an age when women had to rely on others to support them, to try to work as a single woman, and to make my way as a painter all on my own, was the definition of recklessness. Even now, whenever I look up at the dull grayish-white sky that descends over Tokyo at dusk, I cannot help recalling how miserable I felt back then, standing on some rooftop or waiting outside a wide crossing in some back alley for a train to pass, wondering with tears welling in my eyes whether I would ever manage to find a patch of empty land, anywhere in this vast metropolis, where I could stand firmly on my own two feet, if having a place where I could lie down and get a good sleep was too much to ask.

I had no time after I landed that job, so I would work on my own paintings as the sky grew lighter, and then set out for work in time to arrive by seven. You could say I lived out my entire youth—those days when both my heart and my body were blazing, sending sparks flying every which way—between the crack of dawn and when I departed for the factory, and then again each night from dusk to a little past midnight. That was what my life was like when, for the first time, one of my paintings took the prize in that competition.

In those days, it really was the case that once you passed through that door, as it were, for two or three years you would have no trouble selling your work, guaranteeing you enough of an income to keep yourself fed. There was an added glamour when the winning painter was a woman. The newspapers covered the story in a big way, and all the department stores in town would display her photograph. But while it was easy enough for people with connections or who came from a certain background to open that door, it was very hard indeed for those like myself who possessed neither of those things.

I lived in a rented room on the second story of a house owned by a warm-hearted woman in a grubby area on the outskirts of town, near the factory where I worked. I spent all my time either painting there in the early morning hours or going to the factory during the day, so I never had time to go out and socialize. I had no friends or older peers in the art world to come tell me the news when the prize was announced, and no chance to gather with other students in our teacher's house to wait together for the announcement. I returned home from work too late to make the trip to Ueno Hill, shrouded by then in darkness, to check the results. I went to bed that night knowing I would have to wait and read the notice in the morning paper, but I was so nervous and felt such despair at my own feebleness that I began to cry. My chest heaved with the stupid sadness of knowing I had to make my way through life alone.

It must have been past midnight when I heard a car driving along the narrow street, and then the honk of a horn. Automobiles were still uncommon in those days. And it turned out to be more than one. I had won the prize.

"How're we supposed to find this place, so late at night?" one of the reporters asked. "Took some doing, lady, let me tell you."

The flashes of the various newspapers' cameras filled my little room with white smoke.

Three men from B Newspaper waited until last. One came up to me.

"Don't you think you might like to change?" he asked quietly.

"Change?" I replied, confused. "Oh—thank you. Yes, I'll do that."

I was so flustered by the unexpected joy of having won the competition that I had presented myself to the cameramen just as I was, still dressed in my nightclothes, my hair hanging around my shoulders. The newspapermen were partly to blame, as well— it seemed almost like a race, each of them rushing, as soon as they saw me, to be the first to ignite their flashes. Though to be fair, it was summer, and I was poor and lived alone: perhaps there was little difference between my nightclothes and a light cotton kimono.

I blushed when that man suggested that I change, realizing too late how I was dressed, and went to the closet and took out the dress I wore for special occasions. It was rose-colored, since that color was in fashion at the time, with a heavily gathered bust.

I had only that one room, so I had to change in front of the reporters.

"Ah, now you look beautiful," he said kindly.

While I was at it, I wiped my face. I worried, somehow, that the tears I had shed as I fell asleep might have hardened there, leaving trails on my cheeks.

Then I looked at him. What a nice, thoughtful man he was.

"Don't you think you might like to change?"

To this day, I can hear the compassion, the love overflowing in those words.

How long had it been since anyone had spoken so kindly to me?

Amidst that frenetic scene, utterly typical of city desk reporting, I saw in that man's behavior an act of genuine solicitousness. A droplet quietly trickled into my heart.

He too was quiet and composed. When he spoke, he sounded, to me, like someone who lived in a peaceful household, surrounded by a pleasant family. He struck me as a very different breed from those young reporters who are constantly getting themselves riled up, fighting to cover themselves in glory.

He was just another reporter who gave me his business card and left, and when he finished his article for the next morning's paper that would be it, we would never meet again—and yet, quite unexpectedly, two or three days later he sent me a blown-up print of the photograph taken by the cameraman who came with him, along with a brief note. After a formulaic bit about how he would be praying for my success, he had written: "I hope you will live a pure, virtuous life. If ever I can be of any assistance, please do not hesitate to make use of me." That "make use of me" struck me as startlingly pragmatic, but also indicative of a certain humility.

I was grateful for his warmth and thoughtfulness, but I had no intention of imposing upon a man I had met only in passing. Perhaps I had learned not to put too much stock in people's kindness, but it was not really that: I wanted, instead, to treasure the gentle words he had spoken, to take comfort in them. It would have seemed odd for me to respond to his letter, so I simply put the photograph in a frame and sat for a while gazing at it. Needless to say, none of the other newspapers sent prints of the photographs they had taken. Unexpectedly, the nightclothes I had been wearing looked, in the pictures, like a pretty floral kimono.

"Don't you think you might like to change?"

Those words could come in handy in all sorts of situations in life, don't you think?

Not long after that, I quit my job. I chose a path that would allow me more time to paint. I organized a show and used what I earned from the sales to support myself for the foreseeable future. And I visited the offices of various magazines and newspapers to try and interest them in buying my illustrations.

By the time a year had passed, I found myself still walking after sunset, nothing to show for my effort but that one prize, grasping at straws to make it from one day to the next. The fickleness of people's hearts, and the depth of their greed, did me no favors.

I took out that old letter the man had sent me, and, well . . . I never really intended to "use" him, nothing so clear-cut as that, but I guess this was, in a sense, what I did. The thought occurred to me that there might be some advantage to talking with a reporter at a major newspaper, and I decided to visit him. He lived in a large, imposing house. I had not anticipated that. I should have known, though, from how he spoke, and from his attitude. I felt as if I had run up against a solid wall. Unable to bring myself to open the splendid gate, I left and wandered the streets of Tokyo for a while before heading home. To this day, I have never told him about that visit I made to his house.

Ten years passed.

I became a regular presence at the major exhibitions, and some years I would receive a prize, so that I was able somehow to make my way as a painter. In the tenth year, when I was doing paintings of the Seto Inland Sea, I held a solo exhibition centered on those landscapes.

I doubted the man would remember me, but I decided to send him an invitation anyway to thank him for the thoughtfulness he had shown me in my youth, when I had won that first prize. I inquired at the newspaper's headquarters, but they said he was stationed far away.

Though I knew there was no way he could come to the show, I sent a letter anyway, and enclosed the announcement. Please allow me, I wrote, to take advantage of this occasion, as I prepare to hold my first solo exhibition, to express my hope that one day I might have a chance to see you and convey my gratitude in person. I wrote, too, that while I was now married and enjoyed a peaceful home life, every so often I still said to myself: "Don't you think you might like to change?" I mean this, I wrote, quite literally. Sometimes those words startle me from the stagnation of daily life into a new awareness, and give me the strength to carry on anew.

I received a thick envelope in reply. I am touched by your kindness in sending this invitation, despite my being so far away and thus incapable of being of any assistance—indeed, the fact that distance makes it impossible for me to attend only increases my pleasure. Over the years, many people have reached out to me, treated me as a friend, knowing that I am a reporter. These relationships come into being, and then drift away. For me, too, this forgetfulness has become second nature. The same thing has happened with the painters I know. No one writes me letters, now that I am no longer in Tokyo. Your letter was a stream of clear water. And indeed, like you, I have never once forgotten my interview with you a decade ago.

At the end of the letter, he wrote: As you say, I too would very much like to have a chance to meet some-time in person, but at present I lack the confidence to do so. Perhaps in another decade, I will have gained the confidence in myself that I require.

Reading that letter, I started crying and could not stop.

It seems he looks at my paintings at the exhibitions each year.

But what was this "confidence" of which he had written? What did it mean? I was left with a sense of unease. Or perhaps, instead, he had given me an opportunity to dream?

I did not write a reply. I felt it was unnecessary for either of us that I do so.

And then another decade passed.

"Don't you think you might like to change?"

I am no longer the young woman I was twenty years ago. The war happened.

I felt unsettled after the defeat—that I needed to "change" once again, though this time it was the nature of my studies that was at issue. I doubted whether, in my current state, "startled by the sound of the wind," it would even be possible for me to paint in oils. I have never been able to keep pace with current trends among painters, and the group to which I belonged had split up, so for two or three years I had been uncertain how to go forward and had not submitted my work to any exhibitions. Then, finally, a new group was established, within which I took a somewhat peripheral place, and we held our first exhibition.

A letter arrived.

I was stranded abroad as a member of the press corps, he wrote, and when at last I made my way back to Japan I went immediately to see the exhibitions—but none of your paintings were on display. I assumed you must have disappeared forever, like the burned-out city of Tokyo itself. But it turns out you are alive. Perhaps, though, those words ought to be addressed to me—you, not I, should be saying them.

I realize now that a decade has passed since I told you we could meet in a decade. Still I lack the confidence in myself to meet you. Please share more of your work with me.

Once again, reading that letter, I could not restrain my tears, just as had been the case ten years earlier, and twenty years earlier. I wrote him a long letter in reply. I was desperate to have him understand everything about my life—about my husband, our children, how I lived my life. At the same time, I felt he already understood me very well. Perhaps he had been watching me as I stepped out to sweep the street before our house, to play with our dog in the yard.

Odd as it may seem, I had all but forgotten his face by then. I knew nothing of him. I had no interest in asking others, and I have never spoken about him to anyone.

What did he mean, though, when he wrote of *confidence*? What sort of confidence did he need in himself before he could meet me? Am I the sort of woman it takes confidence to meet? I had no idea what he meant.

I doubt we will ever see each other again. When we exchanged letters in the twentieth year, neither of us expressed a desire to meet if the occasion should present itself.

ONE OF MY WOMEN FRIENDS is divorced and lives alone, and is now in a relationship with a reporter. The reporter is the son of a prominent family; he has a wife and children. He goes to her place on the way back from work, late at night, and drinks a large bottle of sake. They get drunk together, and then he catches the last train back to his own home. When the woman is drunk, she sings "Meeting Is the First Step toward Saying Goodbye." From her perspective, you would think it must be terrible to have nothing but a bank account rapidly being depleted and an arrogant man who could leave her at any moment, but I suppose that is the only way she can keep going—she has to drown herself in something. Her husband left her for a younger woman, and her only daughter died.

Once, when the reporter borrowed a large sum of money from her, he wrote a promissory note on a business card, in English, with the name of the newspaper where he worked and his position. The woman laughed at his use of the language. He probably learned English just for this, she said, showing me the card—for when he needed a loan. I found the whole thing rather scary.

The badge the reporter wore on his chest, affixed to his high-quality homespun jacket, was from the newspaper where the man I had corresponded with worked.

Perhaps in reality, that man, too, was getting drunk at some woman's house, on sake she had paid for; or maybe, given how self-effacing he had been interacting even with a woman painter only just awarded her first prize, he never managed to achieve anything and had ended up stuck at the bottom of the company hierarchy. As for me, perhaps I had attained that state of mind typical of the elderly, in which one passes the whole day gazing out at the trees in the garden, thinking that it might be best to prune a certain branch on the persimmon tree to bring out some fruit on another branch.

"Don't you think you might like to change?"

I no longer feel any desire to meet him. But even if he were to present himself before me out of the blue one day as a dissipated ex-reporter with a brazen attitude, or if I were to appear before him unexpectedly as a woman coarsened and worn down by family life, I know neither of us would be the slightest bit disillusioned.

To live is not to cast aside all that one has gathered up in the stream of months and years, and it does not mean trampling down everything one carries in one's heart. If two people never see each other, does that necessarily mean they are distant?

If we are reaching for the moon in the water, if he and I are two monkeys hanging from a thin branch, one dangling from the other's arm, reaching, like the monkeys in the paintings on that theme, to scoop up the moon reflected on the water's surface, then even if the moonlight is bound to spill away through my fingers, still I want to dip my hand into that cold water and hold the moon here, if only here, cupped in my palm. Do not see in me the form of a person, or the heart of a person. I am the moonlight on the water.

"Don't you think you might like to change?"

Just once in my life, I would like to offer someone words like these.

Perhaps I will keep saying them to myself until I grow old, and my life ends.

"Don't you think you might like to change?"

I feel I would like to say these words to this world we now live in.

Mr. S, do you feel pity for this woman painter? 🐒

Kyōhei Sakaguchi

———

The Lake

translated by Sam Malissa

NEAR MY HOUSE THERE'S A LAKE, with water that bubbles up from a spring, so you can drink it. It's not like I drink it every day. There's no sign or anything that says this water is suitable for drinking.

I put tap water in a dish for the black cat, but it goes straight for the brownish rainwater instead. Even when I put food out, the cat doesn't notice, just keeps drinking the rainwater, so I tap between its shoulders, and it turns to look at me, takes a single bite of the food, then goes right back to drinking rainwater. I've opened my mouth to catch raindrops as they fall, but I've never tried to drink from a puddle.

I'm feeling anxious, and have no idea why. I must be anxious about something. No one is telling me to get something done by a certain time. I'm no good with that kind of thing anyway, so I don't even try. I can't relax, my legs are fidgeting. People always tell me I'm fidgeting, but this is different. I'm not shaking the piggy bank to try to get at what's inside. Something's bearing down on me. The fuse is lit. I can't see the fuse. But that doesn't mean there isn't one. And I don't know what's going to explode.

Aaah, someone cried out, cowering by the side of the road. This frightened people, and they kept their distance.

I couldn't ignore it, and went closer. Are you okay, I asked, and she said, it hurts. When it's this bad I'd rather die, she said. It's weird, wanting to die rather than feel pain. It makes more sense to try to feel less pain. I thought maybe I would sleep, but I get into bed and can't sleep at all. I can't relax. I can't calm down enough to do anything. I try to read and can't make out the letters, and when I turn on the TV, it only gets worse. When I'm working, I feel like I'm losing my mind, so I take some medicine and somehow I can go to work. Then as soon as work is over, I feel like this.

Hey, I thought. Could it be that you're anxious? I asked, and she looked at me. Yes, I'm anxious, said the woman. Do you feel like you just can't stand to be anywhere and you pace around the house in circles? I asked, and she said, it's always like that. Her breathing had been ragged, but now she seemed a little calmer. She eyed me warily. I feel the same way right now, I told her. I thought it was just me, she said. I told her about how I was feeling, and she said it sounded pretty much the same as what she was going through. She asked me what she could do, but I don't know how to escape it either. I can't sleep it off, and pacing around the house never feels like it'll help.

Times like this, I go to the lake to drink the water. Drinking it doesn't really settle my nerves, so I didn't tell the woman about it. I call it a lake, but you can see the bottom. It's only about ankle deep. Banana trees grow all around it. I took off my shoes, stepped into the lake, found a flat rock to sit on, then drank the water trickling through the cracks in the rock. The island in the middle of the lake has a boathouse and a sweet shop, and it overflows with people on weekends and holidays, but where I was sitting way on the far side of the lake, no one comes. The water was clear and little bubbles floated up from the green-colored sand on the bottom. Water was bubbling up all over. The leaves of the banana trees were reflected on the surface of the lake. I could see only a tiny bit of sky, but it was dazzling.

Usually I have the place all to myself, but for a change someone else appeared. I didn't notice when he first arrived. Then I spotted him through the tall grasses that grow in the water. An old man, snow-white hair tied back, under a large camphor tree. He was sniffing around the brownish-red rockface by the exposed camphor roots. I looked more closely at the old man. He was licking at the dirt.

In front of the rockface was a large gray heron, standing straight on its spindly legs. It looked like a person standing there.

All the while, my palm was touching the water. It was cold.

The heron watched the old man walk back toward the flat rocks where I was. The man looked more like an animal in the wild than the bird did. He sat down on the edge of the rock and lit a cigarette. Then he introduced himself as Fuku. This rock used to be the entrance to a shop, he told me.

The whole area used to be full of restaurants, and most of them were expensive. There was one cheap place though, a Chinese restaurant called Three Smile House, run by a Mr. Yo, and they served all kinds of things—curry and hotpot and grilled chicken. Smoke was always billowing from the kitchen. Why was I

there that one time? Shoes and sandals were always strewn on this rock. Rows of restaurants stood along the water's edge. They were packed so tightly, I often got lost. It was always nighttime here. Lots of the signs were in Chinese, and it felt like I was actually in China. The menus and the staff spoke a jumble of Chinese and Japanese. It was in the middle of the lake, so there were no paths, just rocks scattered about that we could walk on.

The water is nice and clean, so let's open some restaurants here, is what everyone said. No one owned property, so opening a place in town was tough. But they were in a brand-new place that they knew nothing about, so they had to do something. It was easy to become someone entirely new, and it didn't matter much whether you had a name or not. No one had a name on the boat over, no one even had any sense of self. Someone died, we dropped them over the side of the boat, then another person appeared, jumped right out of the water, completely naked, but since no one else was surprised, I felt that I shouldn't be surprised either. I was afraid, but the four other people I was with just kept rowing calmly. Looks like you're shorthanded, said the person from the sea, and started rowing. Thanks to him we were able to get to port much sooner than we expected. Nobody gave another thought to the one who'd died. The naked person looked completely different from the one who'd died, so no one thought he was a reincarnation. But then the name he gave was the same name as the person who died. He probably knew about the dead one.

We floated on and on. No one ever turned around to ask where we were. Now and then the man's body would disappear in the waves. He was naked. Cold. His body was dead, but he still felt the cold. I was used to it. The man would die, but I would still be there. Because this was my place, had always been my place. The man would be walking, and I would overtake his body with no qualms, relying on the connecting air, passing between tree after tree, flattening the grass, going down to the unseen dust, entering into it, and look, there's a cave, a cave that goes on and on forever, where no one else was walking. I had no legs, but I could walk there. The man died, but it had nothing to do with me. Every time I touched the ground, I recalled the sound of someone's footsteps.

"It was kind of a splash-splash. Every day, come nightfall, and though I called it footsteps, it was really the sound of water. Because there were a lot of people there," said Mr. Fuku. Even walking through the town, he could hear the sound of water. Nowadays there's not a single restaurant on the lake. Mr. Fuku pointed at some rocks in the distance, telling me that there used to be pillars standing on this one and that one.

The sound of water was everywhere. From far off came people and animals and birds and insects, gathering together. Even the scent of the roads the animals came by joined in. There's only ever now, always. I can't even imagine the past. There's no knowing what I would have done if I knew then what I know now, no way of knowing what anyone else was doing. It's always the me of this moment, in this body, here for my use.

I heard the sound of water. My hands were getting cold. Brown moss clung to the damp rockface. I thought it was mud, but looking closer, I saw that it was moss, stringy like strands of hair. How long has moss been growing here? I couldn't tell where the water was coming from. The moss moved like a living thing. The water flowed without stopping. There were a few small holes in the rock. Must have been eaten away by the water. One hole the size of my thumb was at knee level, with a rusty iron rod jammed into it. The water running down the wall traveled the length of the rod and dripped into a large earthen jar. The jar was always full. When I looked inside, it was pitch black. Beyond the rockface is the sea. Drinking the spring water always makes me forget about the sea. I can't hear the waves. And yet the jar was full of water, which struck me as odd. I had forgotten all about it.

I heard a splash and turned around to find people there. People I didn't know. It seemed I had been with them for a while, but then suddenly I realized they'd vanished. A bird flew through the sky, looking down at me. From above I appeared very small. Lost among the riot of trees.

I had walked a while to get here. Here there were no trees, not even one. The river had dried up, and there were no more animals. But it didn't feel like I was alone. I tried tapping on something nearby, then picked up a stone and threw it. I observed my body as I did this. I was conversing with someone who was not there. Doing so came naturally to me. This was because I wasn't actually doing any of this. I must be somewhere else altogether. I thought I must be dreaming.

I was able to stand, but I wasn't sure how I had managed it. Everything that happened a bit earlier I could remember quite clearly. I was hungry, I wanted to eat something, but there was nothing to eat. Every step I took, I heard water splashing. There were apes, five of them. They were talking, their fingers gesturing nimbly. A different kind of ape than me. I was an ape as well. I'm remembering all sorts of different things. The memories were not the apes' nor were they mine. When I think about the things I'm remembering, I feel like I might be losing my mind. I tried my best not to think too much, but I didn't know how else to pass the time.

The apes standing in front of me looked off into the distance every so often. When one of them looked in one direction, the one next to it looked in an entirely different direction. I had no idea what they were doing. I fidgeted my legs, I was anxious, but I just stared at them, silent. Everything came to me as a shock. Each time I heard a splash, the scene changed, always with people there. They were looking off into the distance too. What are you looking at? I wanted to ask them, but I didn't know the words. I tried to say something to them, but no words came out. Even though I had the words.

I'm putting everything that's happening here into words. I only drank the water because I was thirsty. Then the sound of the water entered my mind. The sound wasn't alive inside my mind. It was dead, but it didn't notice. The sound took a few things that I know, gave them shape, and showed them to me. It looked like someone. I tried to remember who, but the only faces that welled up were those of people I don't know. I'm not making any of this up. I'm trying my best to express what was happening inside of me as faithfully as I can. I know where this is. The ground is covered in water. It wasn't the same place I am now.

When I looked closely, I saw that their faces were different. I decided to give them names. Ay was the tallest ape, and it stayed silent the whole time. It never made a sound. Ay carried what looked like a club, entirely stripped of bark, possibly polished since the surface caught the light and gleamed. Ay kept to the back of the group, now and then stopping to poke something with the club. Rather than observing the objects it found, Ay appeared to be receiving a kind of stimulation from poking them. Sometimes it got overstimulated and passed out. Just lay there on the ground, eyes closed. Then it would get back up as if nothing had happened and run to catch up with the others. They never stopped to wait, they just kept going.

In the lead was Bee. Bee kept them moving, paying no mind to Ay collapsing. Bee seemed to have a very short memory and led them past the same places again and again. The others adjusted their route each time, following behind Bee. Sometimes they even trampled on Ay. Every time they stepped on Ay, Bee was surprised. Bee seemed to know that the one on the ground was Ay but never tried to help. Bee appeared to tense up, as if the ape on the ground might be an enemy. Bee could never stop, just kept circling around Ay.

Ay was sleeping on a boulder, which was surrounded by a weave of roots. The tree trunks stood in a tangle. The other apes somehow made it over the boulder, hugging the trunks and hanging from the thick branches. Not a single branch broke. One of the apes even stepped right on Ay to avoid breaking any branches. It was Cee's job to find the path. Right arm wrapped around a tree, Cee spotted the trail, then told the others. Before Bee could start them up again, they gathered together and seemed to be checking on how everyone was feeling. Every time this happened, they switched around. When I looked closely, I could see that their faces had changed. A different face for each different role.

They noticed me and signaled in my direction. We hadn't looked at each other before. I had thought they didn't know I was there. That's why I was able to remain calm, able to think. The trees were looking at me too, though it wasn't me who knew that. I can't

speak with beings that aren't human. It was the apes who could do that. They didn't have any words, but they could speak to the trees. I started to think that I was the creature that couldn't speak. I have words. I can use them to describe the five. But the way they were moving was different. I'm not sure I can communicate their subtle transformations. I don't have the words for it.

I looked for somewhere to hide. I hid in their memories, which were easy for me to get to. Because they weren't yet aware of their memories. Once they realized that they wouldn't find me by looking with their eyes, they decided to sleep. Lying down didn't get them to sleep. Walking made their bodies tired. But they could walk on and on. They could hear the sound of water, but it wasn't water. Nor did they think it was water. When they spoke, they made no sound. Far away a voice cried out. This wasn't the lake. It was a stand of charred trees, thick with the smell of soot. The sound of a tree cracking reverberated. It wasn't loud, but it kept going. They walked on, undying. They were able to pursue. Rain started to fall. Once it started, it didn't stop. Next thing I noticed, buds were sprouting.

It rained for days. My wet body felt cold. I searched for a place where the fires still burned. There was a spot where the flames continued despite being rained on. The sky stayed dark. As I walked, my skin could sense where the warmth was coming from. Then I started to learn things one by one. There were plenty of things I forgot as well, but for each of those, some part of my body changed. The parts that changed also knew how to walk.

I can't recall how much time passed. The things that are now gone appeared before me as things I didn't recognize. They weren't silent. No, they were loud. Sounds I had never heard before rang in the distance, and a separate time flowed, apart from the raining present. How long could the walking go on? I couldn't ask anyone. Even if I tried to speak, there were no vibrations, so no one could hear. The sound of the rain became my voice. I forgot my own voice. When I remembered it, the rain only grew louder. I was swallowed by the flood. All I could see was sound. It didn't hurt. I flowed on like I was breathing. I shrank, then expanded. Outside my body the trees were burning with withering light. The ground was cracked and dry. The five had nothing to eat, and it looked like they were weakening. Nonetheless, the water was nearly overflowing. The water began to ignore its own essence, taking on any and all shapes. Forgot the sun. Here, it has always been night.

I FOUND A PLACE WHERE the water flowed softly. It was very quiet. When I hid it was even quieter. I heard a person's voice. Someone was singing a song. Words that I knew, becoming a voice. I was just imagining all of it. Everything I ever thought I was just imagining was there. The five apes set off again. They had no destination. But I knew where they were going. This is in my head. Not what was actually happening. Always split in two that way. It was night, but I could see the sunrise. Birds were resting in the water. I saw them with my own eyes. When I spotted a creature, I tried to imitate its movements. I was swallowed up by the water and lost sight of the creatures. I died and once more encountered the apes. Each time they had different faces, but something was the same. I kept thinking about what that something was. The one who kept saying they could never figure it out was me. My voice became their faces. Looking at their faces, I could hear a keening sound nearby. They were hard of hearing and couldn't make out my voice, but they didn't miss a single movement from the tiniest insect. To them, a hidden insect looked like one of the movements in my mind. From time to time they pulled something out from the inside. Their fingers were deft, they could pull out anything. The things born that way were all things that were not already there. They had never seen these things before, but they were not surprised. The only one surprised was the one doing the pulling.

Amazingly, I wasn't surprised either. Because these were things I had known but forgotten, appearing once again before me. Only then did the rain stop. They became the rain, and I along with them. All at once they multiplied, increasing in countless numbers. I became a part of it. No need to hide anymore. I looked at my new rainy shape. I traveled far, falling on places that did not know rain. Falling didn't hurt.

Rainwater flowed everywhere. Footsteps sounded on the ground. I was approaching some creatures. The five were walking. The trees drank me up. It wasn't up to me where I was going. I knew nothing, but I walked straight on. I learned all manner of skills. Without even realizing it, I grew, and I stopped thinking about what form I would take next.

I was at the tips of the branches and below the roots. I lived away from the tree, evaporating, becoming lightning, striking. Several people died. I was walking through the forest. The creatures were startled. There were no nutrients in me. So no one tried to eat me. The animals all fled. Uncaring, I flowed on. Again and again I formed into a spirit and floated up into the sky. I was sturdy, never breaking. Each time I fell in a different place. Sometimes I lingered. Years have gone by. I've forgotten how to keep track of time. They looked upward, trying to find themselves. I waved my hand. Not that they could see it. I no longer have hands. I only felt like I was waving my hand. No one noticed. I knew how they were feeling, as if it were me feeling it. I looked upward. At long last the five came to a halt.

Inside a cave, endlessly wide, my self-as-rain flowed into a narrow crack. I was one of the stars, glittering far away. My light was always nearby, shining in their eyes. Eyes floating in space. Then pitch black, and I couldn't see a thing. I could no longer see them. The inside of the cave had dips and protrusions. A single drop of light hung in each eye. Underfoot, I spread out from end to end. Each time they ran around I was kicked up, blown away. Each time my sound rang out, I was born again. Each time I fell on the drenched ground, I was born once more. I still did not know any words. In a daze. I watched this beginning again and again.

The light of the sun enveloped my body. My legs were moving. The damp earth danced upward. The water was muddy. The grasses springing from the surface were vivid. Creatures walked along the branches. When they rubbed against the leaves, they found me. I could see everything, far into the distance. My voice came out. All I did was hear it. I had been born again, so my ears were still fresh. I came from somewhere I didn't know at all to this place, the

same place as always. Not the lake. Just a place with flowing water.

I know where I flowed from. I can tell a long story. I may not know anything about the long ago, but I can keep on talking and talking. My fingers move, and I am born again. I crush the grass underfoot, and though I cannot breathe, I still laugh. I enter their mouths between their bared teeth as the clouds ripple on the surface of the water. Legs streaked with mud. I swarm beneath toenails. A woman with reaching fingers appears out of the water. Her wet hair reaches down to her knees, her body brown, she swims away from the ring of five, alone. The fish pay her no mind.

I'm in the water, in the trees. The five take turns being the woman. I illuminate the place over and over. When I open my eyes, it's dawn. The water is clear straight through, and each hiding place has a different flow of time. It was night, but I could see the far-off mountains. In a place lit by no lamps, the sound of feet splashing in water. I crouched in the grass. There's a banquet in a tatami room. A group of hairy men. A woman, silent, staring out. On the veranda, Mr. Fuku, pointing at me. Fish swim under the restaurant. In the pitch black beneath the floor, I flow. I stare endlessly into the blue water.

The woman drank her liquor, watching the moon. The sound of a breaking plate. I'm born from the earth, spring to the surface of the water. I can breathe. They look in my direction. They notice me. I've been in the earth all along, breathing. Startled, I escape into the water and forget everything. The night disappears.

Near my house is a lake. I took the trolley there. It was a hot summer day. I sat in the back of a truck, alone. I looked at the puddles. I spoke with the insects. I heard far-off voices. Long, long ago, I was born, and I walked to this place. There were no trains. It was all covered with grass. Boggy, difficult to traverse. Many people sank into the marsh. They are still living their lives in this town. A factory was built. I don't know what they make there. The sky was blue as far as I could see. Pure white smoke billowed from the factory. Before I knew it, there were many factories. I opened my eyes and saw vines climbing. The sounds of cutting through metal rang out from the factories. The whole area trembled. They watched carefully. Atop the felled trees, they began to cause a ruckus. They drank the water from the leaves. The roof was covered in vines. The branches grew into a tangle.

The truck came to a stop in front of a large rock. When the tide is high, the ocean comes up this far. Now the ground is dry. Fish swim in the puddles. The ground at the bottom of the puddles is cracked. Many boats have come here. Come from far away. This was a long time ago. I was thirsty. The child next to me had vanished. I had come this far on my own two feet. Aboard the boat they lifted my body. I opened my eyes. No one is around. The fish come close, the birds cry among the clouds. Over and over I'm swallowed by the waves. Pebbles and sand accumulate. The rain falls. In my stomach, it's still falling. The stones become rounded. The rain becomes a drizzle. I can't tell if it's morning or night. The water spilled out. It was a quiet day. I did it all over again from the start. Before humans were born, I did it over and over again, just like this. Next thing I noticed, I had been swept away by the waters. Washed to a place where no one can get to on foot. I forgot completely. That's why I did it all over again. It's always a different place. Different humans appear. They remember everything. My eyes are open. Pitch black. The water trembles and my face distorts. Beyond my reflection, I can see roads unknown. 🐵

Taki Monma

Cardboard Boxes and Their Uses

translated by Ted Goossen

I ALWAYS HAVE A NIGHTCAP before I go to bed. I spread out my futon, plop down, and have a drink. When the weather turns cold, I drink under the covers, feeling all snug and comfy. I fill a largish glass to the brim with cold sake, place it on whatever plate is lying around, and carry it to my bed. Then I sit down, heave a deep sigh, and take a sip. As the liquor slides down my throat and courses through my body, I start to feel good again. I take a second sip, then a third, and eventually the glass is empty. At that point, I may fall asleep or, perhaps, get a burst of energy and head to the kitchen for another glass, which may be followed by a third and so on and so forth, until I find myself sitting cross-legged on my futon, primed for battle. You could say that's my "Bring it on—give me your best shot!" moment. At other times, though, I wake up the next morning with the full glass untouched at the head of my futon. That usually means that I set my drink down, stretched out and then drifted off while imagining the unbroken sleep I was about to enjoy.

Yet the truth is that I never get to sleep until morning. I may drink my glass of sake all cozy under the covers, or cross-legged on my futon, swearing up and down that nothing will rouse me—my "No way am I waking up tonight!" mindset—but then that damned beeping starts in. There used to be a ceramic bell beside Granny's bed, but one time when she rang and rang and I still didn't come, she hurled it against the door, shattering it. After that, I picked up a child's toy that beeps when she presses the button. It's soft plastic, so she can throw it as hard as she wants and it won't break.

Once again, those beeps managed to work their way into my brain. The liquor had wrestled me to sleep, but that damned sound still woke me up. I couldn't respond right away—the booze was holding my body down too. Still the beeping continued. At that point I was so angry, I was ready to explode. I sprang out of bed and marched to Granny's room. On the way, I whacked my face on the corner of the kitchen shelf, knocking my glasses crooked.

What the . . . ? I fell asleep with my glasses on?

I took them off and cooled down for a moment. Then I opened Granny's door.

"What is it?"

"I need to pee."

"You don't need me for that. That's why you've got this chamber pot," I said tapping the lid.

I reached down and flicked on her bedside lamp. In the circle of yellow light, Granny's cheeks had the pouty, bashful look of a small child. She tucked in her chin a bit and gave what looked like a faint nod. Grabbing the railing of her bed with hands as scrawny as chicken's feet, she was able to raise her upper body. Then she swiveled around so that her legs hung over the side. She had reached a sitting position, but that was as far as she could go. Before, she had been able to twist and turn to reach the pot from there, but she had gradually lost that ability. Now she was stuck, unable to figure out her next move. I watched her in silence. She was no heavier than a baby, so I could have lifted her up and placed her on the portable commode with no problem. *You're a mean bitch, you know. Tormenting an old woman.... That's a lie. If you don't move, you become completely bedridden.... Like hell. You enjoy it.*

THE FIRST THING I DO in the morning is empty Granny's commode and wash it. First, though, I check its contents carefully. They say that the color and shape of the stool are a barometer of a person's health, so I probe it for any sign of hidden problems. The slightest bit of red sets my heart fluttering, for it can indicate internal bleeding. In most cases, though, it turns out to be a piece of tomato skin or some such thing. Feeling vaguely disappointed, I dump the contents in the toilet, rinse the pot at the outdoor sink, and return it to her room.

Granny's breakfast is toast and a mug of milk. She eats it sitting on her bed using the table that once held her TV. We used to eat our meals together at the kitchen table. When we had finished, she would make her way to the living room sofa, where she would spend most of the rest of the day in front of the TV. Sometimes, though, she would doze off stretched out on the sofa. I would use that time to straighten up her bedroom and, if it was sunny, hang her bedding outside to air. One day, though, she called to me from the living room, where she had been watching one of her programs. "Can you make my bed?" she asked.

I had been bustling around, putting out the bedding, drying her pajamas, and letting fresh air into the bedroom. "Why? What's the problem?" I called as I returned the vacuum to the closet. "I need you to make my bed now," she said more forcefully. I went in and found her lying on the sofa. "Please, I need to go back to bed," she repeated. "Why don't you sleep where you are?" I asked.

"My side hurts."

"So why don't you sit up?"

"When I do my backside hurts." She was almost sobbing.

"I just busted my backside hanging out your futon," I muttered as I set about preparing the room for her. She managed to make it back under her own steam, clinging to the walls and furniture until, finally, she leaned over and tumbled into bed with a thunk. In a moment, she was fast asleep. What was causing her pain?

Granny's room was a tatami room directly connected to the kitchen, but I had moved in a bed for her. I figured that would make things easier for both of us. I purchased a small TV set and stuck it in the corner. During the day, she was still able to reach the toilet on her own by holding on to the furniture, and for nighttime I placed the portable commode next to her bed. We started eating our meals separately, me in the kitchen and Granny on the edge of her bed facing the old TV table. Yet the rooms were connected, so we could communicate if we left the door open. I could keep an eye on her, while she could tell me if she wanted something, like a cup of tea or more of a dish she liked or another bowl of rice, stuff like that. That rarely happened, though. More often she would say, "I hate this," and leave most of her food uneaten. Still, since we ate facing each other three times a day, we always ended up talking about something, though our topics were limited. Naturally, we liked to gossip about the people in our lives, but since we were so isolated, the stories we told each other were largely about the past. Granny tended to grumble a lot about things that had bothered her, things she couldn't seem to let go of. I chided her for this.

"Why do you always bring up those old stories? Try looking to the future for a change."

"I have no future," she said.

"Oh dear, please forgive me. I'm so sorry," I answered. To tell someone in their nineties to "look to the future" was unconscionably cruel, I realized, like urging someone standing on the edge of a cliff to press ahead. Yet at the same time the exchange struck me as funny somehow, and I couldn't help but laugh.

After meals, I always clean up the dishes and then bring her a full glass of water and a washbasin and place them before her on the table. "Now your false teeth," I say, extending my hand. She removes her upper and lower plates and hands them to me. Then she takes a big swig of water, swishes it around in her mouth, and spits it in the basin. I take back the basin and dump the water, then carefully clean her false teeth with a toothbrush. When I finish, I hand them to her. Once they are back in her mouth, her crumpled face returns to normal. We do this three times a day.

I had taken advantage of one of those breaks to sit on the sofa and watch TV when the beeping started. Beep-beep, beep-beep, beep—whump! The last sound was the beeper hitting the door. Leaving the set on, I went to check her room.

"What is it?"

"My back hurts. I need a compress."

That's par for the course. I checked her back and, sure enough, there's one already stuck there.

"There's a compress there."

"That's yesterday's. I want a new one."

"It's an important program I'm watching," I said, pulling off the old compress.

"Ouch!"

I bet it hurt, having it yanked off that way. The skin underneath was a bit red, so I moved the new compress to a different spot. "Since you're up, could you bring me some tea?" she asked. I went and brewed enough for the two of us. Then I sat for a moment in the kitchen, sipping my tea and listening to the TV blaring in the living room. Since Granny could see me, she wouldn't raise a fuss. There were times, though, when I had to leave her alone to run my errands. I would shop for food, or visit the hospital to pick up her medications. On my return, I would sometimes glimpse her near the kitchen cupboard hustling back to her

room. I had told her exactly where I was going when I left. Had she forgotten? Did she think I had abandoned her? Whichever the case, it appeared she used the time to wander about the house, looking out the window at the yard, making sure that the car was indeed parked in the garage.

"Don't walk around when I'm gone! If you need to walk, do it when I'm here!" I shouted at her.

"I wasn't walking around!" she said nonchalantly.

"Don't fib. What if you fell and couldn't get up? If you break something, it's all over."

All over. I said it again. How cruel can I be?

ONE DAY, when I came home from an errand, an unfamiliar bicycle was parked outside, and the front door of the house was wide open. As if that wasn't alarming enough, a whole bunch of shoes—one pair an adult's, the rest children's running shoes—were scattered about the vestibule. "What the . . . ?" For a second, I couldn't believe my eyes. When I looked back to the street, I saw a number of kids walking past. School had just let out. I went to Granny's room where I found a woman and a group of children. "I'm terribly sorry," the woman said. She went on to explain the sequence of events that had brought her there.

She had been riding by on her bike when she came across Granny crouching on all fours with her head down in the middle of the street. She had managed to reach the street from the house, but once she got there she found herself unable to crawl either forward or backward, so she was looking for some kind of help. "I didn't feel comfortable entering a stranger's house alone, but school had just let out. So, I asked some children who were passing by to come with me." The woman was terribly apologetic; yet I was the one who should have been apologizing. I thanked her again and again, my head bobbing up and down as I spoke. The children doffed their baseball caps and said their goodbyes. I couldn't tell how many there were. Granny was looking pretty happy there in her bed: a complete stranger had helped her back to her room, and she had been surrounded by children, even if only for a few moments. "My back hurts," she said, as if nothing out of the ordinary had happened. "Please give me a compress." "Get it yourself," I shouted back. "After all, you're well enough to go out alone!" I heard the beeper hit the door.

"I could wring your neck," I said, though not loud enough for her to hear.

AFTER THAT, it became harder and harder for me to leave the house. Of course, there were a few things I had to go out for. On those occasions, I always worried: had I left the door unlocked that one time, or had she managed to let herself out? I couldn't stop obsessing about the lock situation. At the same time, however, I felt as though I were shutting her in a cage. Around the middle of autumn, an instructor from the nursing school came to pay a call. She brought with her a letter of introduction from the head of the hospital where Granny was a regular patient. I invited her into the living room. Before graduation, as part of their training, nursing students are sent out by hospitals to get some hands-on experience in home care by looking after the elderly. So it was that over the next month two nursing students came to tend to Granny once a week.

The first day, they arrived with their teacher. Together, the three of them changed into shorts and maneuvered her into the bath. That's because I had said during the interview that it was getting more and more difficult to bathe her. The following week just the two students came. "We'll be here until 3 pm," they told me, "so feel free to go out and run your errands." I figured it was a good time to stock up on food, so I drove the car to the supermarket and went on to the post office. There was still time left, so I spent it cruising country roads with no particular purpose in mind.

The following week, as soon as the students arrived, I gave them a boxed lunch for Granny and took off. I hopped on my bike, rode to the station, and boarded a train for Tokyo. Tokyo was full of people. Although it wasn't rush hour, the train was crowded: when we stopped, passengers spilled out the doors while others piled in. At some stations, though, only a few got on or off. When a seat opened up in front of me, I sat down. Now I could sit back, relax, and look around. It was the train that circles downtown Tokyo, the Yamanote Line, so I didn't have to be worried about being whisked off to some godforsaken place. A young man in a suit was standing not far away, holding on to a strap. He looked comfortable in the suit, so I doubt he was a new hire. Unsurprisingly, his hair was a mass of black, while the nape of his neck had been shaved so close it gleamed blue. I imagined how upset the mother of a young man like that would be when he told her he was getting married. Would she try to knock him down? As my fantasy became more elaborate, I found myself glancing in his direction more and more frequently. *What was I, some kind of female lech?*

THE LEAVES WERE FALLING from the trees by the time the two students' month-long internship ended. On their final day, they brought along a photograph of Granny set inside a stand they had made and placed it at the head of her bed. "Next year we may ask your permission for the same arrangement again," their teacher said. "Would you be willing?" "Of course, I would be delighted," I replied. I was going to add, "Though hopefully there'll be no need," but wasn't sure if she'd get the joke.

With colder weather, washing the commode in the outside sink became more of a pain. I had to attend to the pipes to keep them from freezing. The winter before, I had gone out to rinse the pot during a cold snap only to find the pipes blocked, which was no fun at all. In situations like that you have to grope around for solutions, one step at a time. After all, it's stuff you don't know, and you have no experience.

The biggest problem was the bath. It was growing more and more difficult for Granny to reach the bathroom on her own. On top of that, she preferred to bathe in the tub, even in the heat of summer. If I said that showers in summer were enough, she replied that she wanted to soak, even if the water was only up to her hips. I had to use every trick in the book to convince her to let me give her a long shower. Granny's back was beautiful. How was that possible when her hands and face were so shriveled up? I contemplated this every time I washed her. Nevertheless, when it got cold, I knew she would insist that she be given baths come hell or high water, and I would have to come up with something. It was already a major effort just to get her as far as the bathroom. Instead, I would heat up her room and wipe her down with a moist towel. It refreshed me too. *Ah, this is great,* I told myself, and the feeling would carry me through dinner and cleaning up until, finally, I could take my own bath.

"Granny, I'm taking a bath now. I'll be in the bathroom," I called to her.

"I want to go too," she whimpered pathetically. "I want to take a bath."

I walked away without a word, cursing her in my heart. *Sometimes you ask for too much,* I thought as I kicked open the door to the bath and lowered myself into the water. While I lay soaking in the warmth, I tried to come up with a method that would make it possible for me to move Granny to the bath.

The next morning, I was tying up some empty cardboard boxes to put out with the recyclables when it hit me. As in, *Hey, these are stronger than they look!* We had received a number of things that had come packed in boxes: the TV in Granny's room, the yearly gift of apples from her friend in Aomori, the oil heater we bought to warm her room at night. In every case, the box was much larger than the object inside, thanks to the styrofoam used to protect it. Once removed from its packaging, the contents were surprisingly small—my reaction was always, *Is that all there is*? I picked up the cardboard boxes I had already folded and returned them to their original shape. Then I lined up several in the living room to gauge their sizes. *Maybe this one will do,* I was thinking when the beeper sounded. So I picked it up and entered Granny's room.

"What's that?" she asked. Her attention was so absorbed by the box I was carrying, she seemed to have forgotten why she had summoned me. She was transfixed by the box.

"Could you try to get in?" I asked, setting the box down in front of her.

"Was wood too expensive?" Granny asked, calmly.

"Huh?" I blurted, taken aback by her question.

Was wood too expensive? To her, the box was not a box but her casket. Nor was the mighty cardboard box fazed—it fit Granny inside and carried her all the way to the bathroom without complaint. It was, however, a one-time experiment. 🐒

Yūko Tsushima

———————

Flying Squirrels

translated by Rose Bundy

ONE NIGHT, I took my two children to see flying squirrels in a forest. It was a hot day in midsummer. Someone had told me that if we visited this forest at night we could see flying squirrels gliding from tree to tree in search of food. We decided right away to make the two-hour trip from our home in Tokyo. That was four years ago, my son's last summer.

For a long time, I had wanted to see flying squirrels in the wild. I had seen some in a zoo, but they were curled up asleep, so I couldn't really say I had experienced them. For a lifelong city dweller like me, the idea of flying squirrels gliding among the trees struck me as almost mystical. Still, if it hadn't been for my son, I wonder if I would have made a special trip just to see them. From the time he was old enough to take an interest in the world around him, my son had been fascinated by earthworms, caterpillars, and spiders, as well as aquatic life forms like loaches, goldfish, diving beetles, and water scorpions. He also liked reptiles that few others did—frogs, newts, lizards, and snakes—and his fondness for them grew year by year. His offbeat tastes extended to bizarre forms of plants like cacti, *marimo,* and carnivorous plants. He would, without fail, become totally engrossed in stories about anything strange or astonishing: outer space, the inner workings of animal or human bodies, or the atom.

I knew all this about my son, so the sorts of things that would interest him naturally caught my eye, while watching television or walking down a street. I wanted to share what I saw with him, or, if I spotted something for sale and it was not too expensive, I might buy it for him. And I was never disappointed by his reaction, as he excitedly snatched up the object. The sight of flying squirrels gliding from tree to tree would, I was sure, fill him with delight, and from the moment I heard about the forest, I wanted to take him there, anticipating his happiness.

My son had turned eight. He was steadily maturing, and I was doing my best to provide him with opportunities to have as wide a range of experiences as possible. It had been a rather busy summer—we had gone camping as well as taking a trip of about ten days—but when I brought up the flying squirrels, my son, without a moment's hesitation, said he wanted to go see them. My daughter declared that if my son were going, she wanted to go too. Four years older than he, she was less interested in the squirrels than in making sure her brother didn't gain an advantage over her.

If we left Tokyo by express bus at three o'clock, we would arrive at our destination by around six at the latest. We would eat dinner there, while waiting for darkness to fall. As I understood it, the flying squirrels emerged from their nests and became active around seven thirty and continued for about an hour. I was surprised to learn that the squirrels did not live hidden deep in the forest. Flying squirrels make their homes in the hollows of ancient trees. But these days, forests are managed for timber, and so ancient trees can no longer be found there. The squirrels have discovered trees that are hundreds of years old, growing near shrines, not far from human habitation, and it is in these trees that the squirrels now live. They travel each night to the forest, their original domain.

The flight of flying squirrels is analogous to a descent with a parachute; the ground they can cover with each flight is limited. From a high perch on one tree, they will glide down to a lower point on another tree. They then climb to a high perch on that tree and glide down to yet another tree. If all goes well, the squirrels can reach the forest by repeating this process, but there are fields and major roads between the shrine and the forest, and they are forced to contend with this unfamiliar terrain, waddling across like moles. They also are in danger of being attacked by dogs or hit by cars. All this, I learned after my arrival at the site.

Based in the local school, a group had organized to protect the flying squirrels. One of their goals was to have as many people as possible experience the flying squirrels, and in the process, provide information about their present situation and raise funds. It was a member of this grassroots organization who, on an appointed day and time, took my children and me to the grove of trees at the shrine.

As the bus approached our destination, I saw from the bus window how the sun in the western sky was beginning to slash the hillside forest in two, one band of brilliant light and another of darkness. I felt uneasy, my feelings drawn deep into the gloom, as it occurred to me that my children and I had not even reached our destination. What terrifying misadventure had I blundered into? The bus drove on through flat farmland that offered nothing of visual interest, with sad-looking fields pressed up against the low, gently rounded hills. Fortunately, I had given medication to my son, who was prone to motion sickness, and he was asleep.

Disembarking from the bus, we took a taxi to a school near the shrine, where we joined a group of about a dozen people who had also come to see the flying squirrels. We were handed the packed dinners I had preordered, having been informed that there were no restaurants or hotels close to the school. After eating, we looked at the preserved models of moles and field mice—animals that lived in the area—and, in a tiered classroom, heard a presentation, accompanied by slides and maps, about flying squirrels. The audience, comprising groups of middle-school students, families with children, and old people with an abundance of time on their hands, was surprisingly attentive, some members even taking notes. Perhaps finding the atmosphere of a nighttime classroom novel, my children sat up straight and listened intently.

After the presentation, we were given the opportunity to purchase such things as T-shirts, books, postcards, and bookmarks, the proceeds of the sales going to support the preservation of the flying squirrels. My children felt we obviously had to buy something, and so I bought my daughter a T-shirt and my son, a book about frogs, which had nothing to do with flying squirrels.

At seven thirty, we finally started out for the forest where we would see the squirrels. We were instructed that we could use flashlights for part of our walk, but once a signal was given, they had to be turned off. The squirrels were very alert to any signs of danger, we were told, and, if they sensed human presence, they would not emerge from their tree hollows. However, the guide had brought along a hand-held searchlight that shone red, since the squirrels are insensitive to that color. We were also warned not to make any loud noises and to keep conversations to a minimum.

Even with our flashlights on, the darkness around us felt impenetrable; I was terrified. With no trace of fear, my daughter walked on ahead alone, and I did not call her back. But my son was only in the second grade, and I gripped his hand more firmly than really necessary and urgently whispered to him again and again, "You can't wander off by yourself. If you do, it's so dark you won't be able to find your way back to me. You might even fall into a river."

I WAS NEVER FREE OF THE FEAR that my children might wander off and I would never see them again. Around the time my son was born, I had lost sight of the person who had been my husband, and I had to work, often leaving my children in the care of others. That experience probably had something to do with my fear. What if I was involved in some sort of accident? What if I was supposed to pick up the children and didn't arrive on time? What if something unexpected happened to the person minding my children, and she disappeared, taking them with her? What if we were on a busy downtown street, or on our way to an acquaintance's house, or again, surrounded by a mass of strangers in an unfamiliar land, and we were to become separated and the children were forced to wander lost forever, as though in a maze with no exit? I could not escape these fears.

It's bound to happen someday. There is no way you can keep them safe. Since I became a mother, I have heard that voice whispering to me from somewhere deep in my being. More than three years have passed since my son died of unknown causes on the eve of his graduation from second grade. My immediate reaction was that what I feared had finally happened, and yet, I wasn't confronting the incomprehensible reality of death. Instead, I grieved for my son as though he were missing. And even now, as I approach the fourth anniversary of his death, which I acknowledge during my waking hours, at night I still have fearful dreams in which I am terrified that someday, somewhere, my children will vanish from my sight.

THE GUIDE GAVE THE SIGNAL to turn off our flashlights and then he turned on his red light. From this point, we were reminded, we should be as quiet as possible.

"I wonder where your sister is. If she wanders off, I won't be able to find her." Alarmed by the deep darkness, I whispered to my son, as I drew him close.

Stifling his voice as much as he could, my son replied, "Shh. We're not supposed to talk. Sis is right over there. Don't worry."

Quietly, our group gathered in a grove behind the shrine where, we were told, we could easily see the hollows that were the nests of the flying squirrels. Two telescopes and some binoculars had been prepared for us.

The guide aimed the red searchlight toward the grove. Apparently, there were multiple nests, and he directed the red beam here and there, gesturing to us where to look, whispering, "You can see the squirrels' eyes reflecting the red light. If you look carefully, you can see two points of light close together. Those are the eyes." The guide's words were relayed from person to person to those at the back of our group.

"Where are they?"

"I think in that tree in the middle. There are two of them."

"Two of them? Oh, I see them now."

"There's one over there too. Wait, it's gone back into its nest."

The moment we had been looking forward to had arrived. Excited, we jostled against each other, tried to find the points of red light in the darkness. Anxious that I not miss out, I asked some people standing nearby, "Where are they? Which lights should I look at?" They pointed out where I should look, and finally having found the lights, I quickly assisted my son. I saw that my daughter was also being helped by someone nearby.

"Awesome! Their eyes are shining!" Amazed by what he was seeing, my son raised his voice, but quickly remembered and, looking embarrassed, shrugged his shoulders. Then, carefully in a whisper he asked me, "How come they have such incredible eyes?"

"I think the eyes reflect the light we're shining at them. The brighter the light we shine at them, the brighter the eyes seem to us."

"But why do their eyes look like they're shining?"

"I'm not sure. Maybe because they're nocturnal animals? But it really is extraordinary, isn't it, the way their eyes shine so brightly. I wonder why."

The points of red light from the squirrels' eyes were literally the size of the eye of a needle; without binoculars, it was impossible to see that there were two dots of light close together. In the darkness, it was difficult to tell how far we were standing from the squirrels, but most likely we were some distance away. Under normal circumstances, I wouldn't notice such tiny dots of light, but once I did, I was amazed by their intensity. I knew that what I was seeing was merely reflected light. Still, I could only gaze in wonder at the dazzling red points—too dazzling to approach us humans.

We were told that the squirrels were beginning to emerge from their nests, and once more we pushed and jostled against each other as we peered through the binoculars or telescopes, trying to catch sight of the squirrels as they climbed up the trees. Those who spotted the squirrels showed the others where to look, and my children and I were successful in locating some. The guide told us that some thirty-four flying squirrels lived in the grove, and unless it was a night of heavy rain and strong winds, about half of them left en masse for the forest once the night was fully dark.

Now that the squirrels had left their nests, our group rushed to the other side of the shrine. We were told that the squirrels would begin their gliding after climbing to the tops of the ancient trees. The bank of the stream that flowed along the far side of the grove, the guide continued, was the most promising spot to see the squirrels doing that, and he pointed out where we should be looking. He walked about our group, earnestly whispering to us, "Look in that area. It happens so quickly, you really have to pay attention." His young assistant aimed a red light toward the tree-tops the squirrels were expected to take off from.

I repeated the guide's words to my son and waited in suspense for the squirrels to begin their gliding. My daughter, I noticed, had at some point returned to my side. We were now farther from the ancient trees than before, and they formed a black wall that reached high into the sky. Somewhere in that darkness, though I had no idea how or exactly where, small, living bodies would glide through the air. Gazing at the spot illuminated by the red light, I was growing drowsy and childishly apprehensive. I felt somehow weightless.

"There, it's gliding, it's gliding!" someone's voice rang out. Then, though they kept their voices down, everyone grew excited, and whispers of "There's one," "I saw one," rose one after another. I could hear cries of wonderment and laughter and again jubilant voices saying, "It's gliding! Over this way now."

It seemed that there were quite a number of squirrels gliding, but so far I had been unable to spot one. Whenever I noticed a commotion in the group, I would turn in the direction everyone was looking, but—whether I just couldn't sense any motion or I was too slow—I couldn't catch sight of any squirrels gliding. If I'd had some idea of what sort of movement I was supposed to be looking for, some sort of concrete guidance, then it might have been easier to focus on the gliding motion of the squirrels, but I couldn't even imagine what it was that I was trying to see. Instead, all I could do was let my eyes sweep vaguely across the forest's darkness.

"Wow! A huge jump. It was huge."

Just then my vision seemed to blur for an instant. Was that it, I thought, and focused my eyes, but I saw nothing.

"That one glided a long way."

"I saw it. I saw it really clearly."

Hearing these excited voices right near me, I asked my son, whose hand I was still tightly holding: "Did you see it?"

"Sure, I saw it. It jumped right across. Did you see it too, Mom?"

"I'm not sure."

"There's been a whole bunch. You didn't see them? I've seen lots already."

"Really?"

My son nodded, confident in what he had seen.

Why was it that other people could see the squirrels gliding? It was so strange. I wondered if they were really seeing what they claimed to see, or were they just saying what was expected of them? I thought the latter might be the case. But the fact remained that I hadn't seen any motion for sure, and so I was reluctant to say that I had. I didn't know where I was supposed to be looking or what sort of motion I was supposed to track. I couldn't see a thing. My vision had blurred for an instant, but when I tried to refocus my eyes, I failed to see anything clearly.

In the same way, four years now after our excursion, I am unable to catch sight of my son. I think my son is right beside me, but when I look, he isn't. I think, I've found him now, but he's not quite the way he should be. It's only natural that he should be beside me, but I can only sense his presence and can't call him into my arms.

ONE DAY WHILE I WAS WALKING about looking for my son, I remembered the person who had cared for him when he was still an infant and decided to visit the apartment where we were living back then. Just as I expected, I discovered that my son had been left behind there. He had reverted to an infant who couldn't even crawl. Not only that, but when I tried to pick him up, he started crying—he had forgotten my face.

Our new house was finally completed, and I was busy putting things in order. Wondering what the children were up to, I peeked into their room. I had designed the room to be big enough for my daughter and son to share, but at that point their belongings were scattered about the room, even piled up on the built-in beds that I had chosen for them. I told them to stop playing and get to work, and started helping them tidy up, but a few minutes later, deciding it was more important that I finish the kitchen first, I returned there, after warning them that I would be back soon and that they should continue on their own. I didn't hear them answer, and I had no idea what my son was doing. During the time my son had been away from me, he nearly lost his ability to speak. That broke my heart, but I also felt that I should be content that he was with me once more.

I entered a building on a corner, recalling that I had on occasion left my son at the house that once stood there. It had been quite a few years ago, and the house was gone. It would be impossible to find the people who had once lived there; those working in the building now would have no idea what had happened to them. I wondered how my son was being brought up. Even if we were to meet sometime in the future, would he still feel affection for me as his mother? Would I recognize him in an instant? It was difficult for me to imagine what he would look like as an adult; he was so young when I lost him.

Walking along a road, I came across a frog. It was small, but on closer inspection it seemed to be an unusual species. Like a turban shell, the posterior half of its body was enclosed in a triangular tube. Under the tube was curled a pale green snake, smaller than an earthworm. Although I found it creepy, I felt it vital that I show it to my son, and so I rushed to capture it in some tissue paper. I imagined just how delighted my son would be, but I couldn't recall for the world where I should take the frog so that I could show it to him.

I knew my son was somewhere—I just didn't know where. Nor could I figure out why I didn't know. It was only natural that my son should be near me, but when I turn to look at him, he vanishes.

We took a trip once to a hot spring, where we visited an area set up with about a dozen greenhouses, large and small, built along a slope. Signs indicated how we should proceed, but the pathway seemed so circuitous that it was difficult to keep track of exactly where we were among the structures. The children ran on ahead, and I lost sight of them. There was room after room of cacti, of water lilies, of varieties of ferns, and of bougainvillea, and I passed from one to the next as though in a dream—enchanted by the beauty of each glass-enclosed room, but also anxious about where my children were. 🐵

Note from the translator: This is an excerpt from *Hikari kagayaku itten o* (A Single Point of Brilliant Light), published in 1987.

Aoko Matsuda

The Most Boring Red on Earth

translated by Polly Barton

The most boring shade of red on earth is period red.

How old was Rika when she first came to feel that way? Hard to say. She doesn't even remember how old she was when she got her first period. She remembers being there, in the toilet stall, feeling surprised, feeling embarrassed. But the memory wasn't the kind that kept its grip on her forever. When she saw a scene in a TV series written by a man showing a girl getting her first period, saw the same scriptwriter saying things in an interview like, "I want the women in my work to be fully fleshed out as characters, so when I'm writing my scripts I make sure to decide what age they got their first period," it made her smirk. *This guy thinks women = periods.*

Over ten years had passed since the surprising, embarrassing moment in the toilet, and Rika had grown thoroughly used to the red of her period. *Oh right, I get you*—that was about the size of her reaction when it came. Once most of it had been absorbed by the pad, the red seemed at a distance, so that she wasn't convinced it had ever really been red in the first place. It was no longer any color at all.

Which is why, the first time she noticed the thing happening, Rika couldn't be sure, and decided not to pay it any mind. *A trick of the eye, that's all. A simple trick of the eye.* When going about her life, going to school, going to work, more often than not she felt as if her body was not her own, and actually, it seemed to her that she got more praise for not paying attention to her body than for attending to it. Of course, paying attention to her appearance was a different thing altogether. There were many things in the world Rika didn't know, particularly when it came to bodies; the furthest that everyday conversation strayed into the topic was more or less the *I've got a headache, I've got backache* level—nobody around her would talk about bodies in any depth. And so, Rika had no way of knowing if this phenomenon was, in fact, totally natural to other people.

Her blood was orange. There she was in the bathroom, rinsing the conditioner from her hair, when out of the corner of her eyes that were opened just a crack, Rika saw a streak of orange go gliding past.

Huh?

She squeezed her eyes shut, holding the showerhead up to her face to splash it clean. In her consternation, she brought the showerhead too close, so it was less of a splash and more of an assault. When her vision cleared, she could see a new streak of orange, this time undeniable. The streak originated between her thighs.

It's orange juice.

Rika stared down at the streak, disbelieving. On closer inspection, there were fibrous strands in it, making her think of freshly squeezed orange juice. Her period blood had become pulpy orange juice. She had to find some way of dealing with this situation, and so *It's just a trick of the eye* made its entrance. Rika stepped out of the bathroom, dried herself, stepped into a fresh pair of underwear, stuck a new pad in place, pulled the underwear up, and declared the matter done and dusted.

The next evening, Rika was lying exhausted in the bathtub. She had fully imbibed society's maxim that it was more important to not cause those around you any bother than it was to take care of your own body, and so, heartless as it might seem, the fact that her period had become orange juice was already consigned to a far corner of her mind. Working on her feet all day was hard, doing so when she was on her period was harder; even taking painkillers didn't rid her entirely of the discomfort, and she had no spare energy to be checking the color of her blood every time she took a toilet break. The job was the most important thing. Rika's body silently endured.

Her bathtub was too small for her to fully extend her legs. Sitting with them bent up in front of her, Rika rested her right cheek on her right knee, which was sticking out just above the water, and let out a sigh.

Out swam a school of small fish from between her thighs. A few pointed leaves drifted out too, as if caught up in their flow. At the bottom were strewn some pebbles. It seemed that a small stream had sprung up all of a sudden, right in the center of the bathtub. The water of the stream was colorless and perfectly clear.

Ahh, it's my period.

She'd been forgetting it, but now Rika somehow understood.

Her period-that-had-become-a-small-stream looked cool and refreshing, even amid the warm bathwater, and the pebbles glinted. One of the fish leapt out of the water, sending sparkles of light flying in all directions.

It's sort of beautiful, my period.

Rika was captivated by the sight of it. Maybe all this time her period had been playing around like this, and she just hadn't noticed. Maybe it had made the most of the fact that she hadn't noticed it change color and do exactly as it wanted. Thinking this, she came to feel she'd missed out a bit, not paying attention to it.

The flow of the stream grew faster. The little fish swam quicker, as if escaping, and an egret that had come to perch on a rock in the middle of the river took flight. Something was happening. Rika opened her eyes wide, and stared down at her period. 🐵

I can't translate this!
Remarks from twelve translators

———

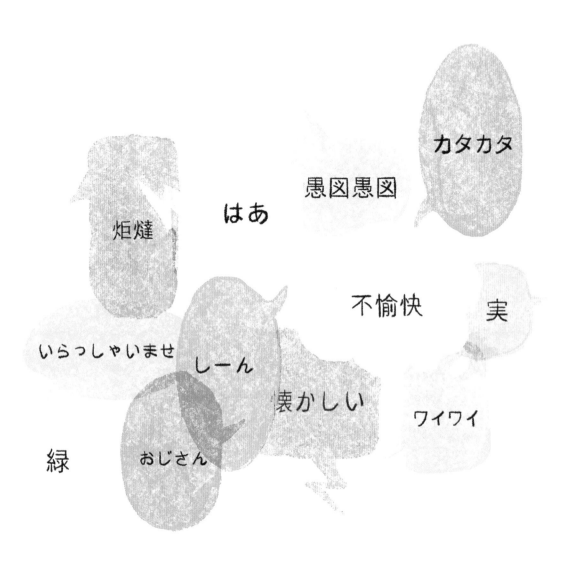

According to translation theorists, nothing can be translated—or, everything can be translated. But we translators have to work between everything and nothing, sometimes happy when we hit on what we believe to be a perfect solution, sometimes despairing, thinking, *There's no way to say this in my language!* We asked a dozen translators of Japanese literature to tell us about their moments of despair.

Jeffrey Angles
on *natsukashii*

In Japanese, one uses the adjective *natsukashii* (懐かしい) just about every time someone is reminded of something they recall fondly. Dictionaries give "nostalgic," "longed for," or "dear" as equivalents, but none of these options is used in quite the same way as the Japanese. For instance, when looking at an old photograph, one may use the commonplace expression, *"Aa, natsukashii!"* but a near word-for-word English translation—"Ah, how nostalgic I feel!"—is not something one would say nowadays. Instead, a modern English speaker in the same situation is more likely to say something more explanatory, such as "Wow, this brings back memories!" or "Ah, reminds me of the good old days!" *Natsukashii* also implies longing. Someone living outside of Japan might say, *"Washoku ga natsukashii,"* literally, "I'm nostalgic for Japanese food," but again, the most natural way to render this is simply, "I miss Japanese food."

In a 1993 review of Banana Yoshimoto's novel *Kitchen,* translator Lucy North pointed out that overly literal translations of phrases using *natsukashii* tend to sound histrionic, but she reminds us that for at least a millennium, Japanese aesthetics have prized nostalgia, and wistful longing for the past is common throughout Japanese literature and culture. Perhaps then it is natural that Japanese has such a precise word to express this feeling. As Proust might remind us, remembrance of things past isn't a feeling alien to Western society, but unfortunately for us translators, we don't have a single word like *natsukashii* to express it. While we were working on this text, Motoyuki Shibata mentioned that American author Stuart Dybek once remarked, "If there were a French equivalent for *natsukashii,* Proust could have taken a bite of the famous madeleine and just said, 'Ah, *natsukashii*!' But then he might never have written *A la recherche du temps perdu*!"

Polly Barton
on *obasan* and *ojisan*

In Japan, as in many other Asian cultures, it is common practice to refer to people according to the place that someone their age and gender would occupy within the family structure: a middle-aged woman is an *obasan* (an aunt), a young man an *oniisan* (an elder brother), and so on. This is not unheard of in English—*come on, Grandma, what're you playing at!* and the like—but it remains the exception rather than the rule. Often these terms are used in place of a name in addressing a person, which can bring up translational issues when we don't have a name to work with. But of late, what I struggle with most is when such words are used as descriptors—particularly *obasan* (aunt) and *ojisan* (uncle). In my formative stages as a translator, I had an equivalence in my head: *obasan* and *ojisan* "meant" *middle-aged man* and *middle-aged woman,* and I didn't deviate from that when translating. As time has passed, though, I've come to feel how woefully inadequate that is as a translation in most cases. For a start, such terms hardly trip off the tongue, and in English have a more formal and distanced register than the Japanese. But more specifically, they miss out on all the baggage that can accompany these words—the associated behaviors of people this age, which can in this case imply a modicum of eyeroll on the part of the person using them. Aoko Matsuda's latest novel, *The Sustainable Use of Our Souls,* is based on the problematic figure of the *ojisan* in Japanese society. But how to render this? "Middle-aged men"? It feels way off, tonally. But "uncles"? It just doesn't do the work. One part of me is tempted to lean into the rhetoric potential of "old guys" while knowing that it's more informal (and arguably, explicitly derogatory) than I'd like. Another part of me wonders if we just need to start normalizing the use of "aunts" and "uncles" in our translations, until the terms begin to assume the expressive possibility they have in Japanese.

Sam Bett
on *midori*

Michael K. Bourdaghs
on everyday words

Thanks to Midori, the muskmelon-flavored liqueur made by Suntory, this is one of those Japanese words that even those who don't know the language will associate with the color green. *Kenkyusha's New Japanese-English Dictionary,* incidentally nicknamed "the Green Goddess" for the color of its binding, gives "green" (noun) as the primary definition of *midori* (緑), but also suggests "verdure" or, when used as an adjective, "verdant." What both these definitions fail to capture is the elementary nature of the word, which any child would understand.

While an English speaker, fed up with the city, might express a desire to "go somewhere green," a Japanese speaker might say they want to "go see green." *Midori* is not a place, though, but a collective noun for what you see when plant life fills a natural setting. As a signifier for nature—a translation I've resorted to more than once—*midori* is tangled in cultural context, since Japan remains thickly forested. Leave the city behind in Japan, and chances are wherever you wind up will be *midori*.

In practice, what makes this word so hard to translate is its focus on "greenness" as a thing, whereas the English language conceives of the color as an adjective ("green boughs") or implies the color by describing texture ("lush foliage") or vibrancy ("bright leaves") or abundance ("carpet of moss"). Further complicating matters are the associations green has in English, where it can suggest envy, paper currency, inexperience, mold, or unripe fruit. This is one of those words that impel translators to say a little more than the original would need to say. In the past, I've gone with "leaves" or "trees" and even once "the mountains." In the future, I can imagine circumstances where I might brace myself and translate it as "fresh air" or "the great outdoors." In both springs of the pandemic, I was inclined to think of this most vital noun as "life."

Sometimes the simplest words present the biggest challenges. I have in mind quotidian objects that signal everyday life in a Japanese story or poem—the *hanten* (padded jacket) that a character wears, the *kotatsu* (low heated table) that he sits at, the *mikan* (satsuma oranges) he snacks on for lunch. These words not only signal a traditional Japanese setting, but also indicate that it's late fall or winter. Do we keep them in Japanese and overload the translation with glosses or even add footnotes? Or do we render them into (often awkward) English counterparts? In translating Sōseki's "Ten Nights of Dreams," for example, I turned *tenugui* into "*tenugui,* a long, narrow cloth," and *tokonoma* into "tokonoma alcove." (Note that although tokonoma is in the English dictionary and no longer needs the italic, many readers would not know what it is.)

This problem shifts over time, too: twenty years ago we would have needed to translate *edamame,* but thanks to their newfound popularity in the frozen food section of North American and European grocery stores, perhaps we can now simply let them be edamame—no gloss, no italic. Every year, English dictionaries add more Japanese words, granting us license to use them as is: manga, anime, aikido, and so forth.

The difficulty of these words revolves around an irresolvable contradiction that haunts the art of translation. On the one hand, a good translation will reproduce something like the experience a Japanese speaker has reading the original. On the other hand, a good translation from Japanese should say something that hitherto has been impossible to say in English—it should expand and subtly alter the English language by expressing something that previously could be said only in Japanese. And so we compromise, betray, and bend words into new shapes as we labor to make the exotic into the everyday and reveal the uncanny within the mundane.

David Boyd
on *mi*

Mi (実) isn't especially difficult to translate, but any word can trip you up. It all depends on what the word is being made to do. "Fruit" usually works in the place of *mi,* but I found it unsatisfying when translating Hiroko Oyamada's short story "Along the Embankment" (*Dote no mi*土手の実). In this story, the narrator discovers a strange *mi,* then tries to figure out what it is. It's not exactly like an apple, or a persimmon, or an acorn, we're told. It isn't a walnut, either. The unknowability of the *mi* is an essential part of the story.

"Fruit" seems to pull the reader in a particular direction. While Kenkyusha's *New Japanese-English Dictionary* defines *kudamono* simply as "fruit," it gives "fruit," "nut," and "berry" as the main options for *mi.* In other words, *mi* occupies all of these areas at once. It's "fruit" in the biological sense. Does English have a word that can do something similar? Not that I could find.

So, where do you go from there?

Accept "fruit." While it isn't a perfect solution, it's probably the best option. I did what I could to recover some of the lost energy of *mi.* For example, I limited the number of times that I used the word "fruit" in the translation. Wherever possible, I used words like "it" instead. That helped to restore some of the missing openness. I also cut *mi* from the English title; a more literal translation of the title could be "The Fruit along the Embankment." I did that to preserve a little mystery—even if the mystery takes a different form than it had in the original.

Anna Elliott
on *haa*

Interjections like *hee, fuun, fun, aa,* and so on often give me trouble when I'm translating. I'm currently struggling with the word *haa* in the Polish translation of Minae Mizumura's *Honkaku shōsetsu* (published in English as *A True Novel*). A number of characters use it, but Yūsuke, a socially awkward young man, defaults to it especially often as a one-word response to all kinds of questions and statements.

This short word *haa* carries quite a few different meanings. *Nihongo daijiten* gives three: a polite answer, an *aizuchi* (a phatic interjection), or (with a rising intonation) a questioning response or expression of surprise. The problem for the translator is that there is no single word that corresponds to all of these meanings—and while one could come up with a range of appropriate expressions to translate these various senses of *haa,* doing so would mean the reader wouldn't know that Yūsuke uses the same word repeatedly, in a sort of verbal tic. What to do?

Here are some examples from the novel:

1. "Okega wa mō yoroshii no."
   (Has your injury healed?)
   "Haa."
2. "Mezurashii tsukiyo desu."
   (The moon is so clear tonight.)
   "Haa."
3. "Dōzo osuwari ni natte."
   (Please take a seat.)
   "Haa."

In the first example, *haa* means "Yes"; in the second, it is an *aizuchi* ("Yes!" or "Indeed!"); while in the last example, it serves as "thank you." For now, I am thinking that perhaps he could precede whatever he says with something like "Ah," which would make him sound suitably awkward. For instance: "Ah. Yes." and "Ah. I see."

Haa and "Ah" even sound a bit similar. But "Ah. Really?" or "Ah. Thank you." don't seem to work as well, so the jury is still out.

Michael Emmerich
on homophonic names

Recently I read a novel in which the main character, a young man named Kaoru, has an awkward, not-quite-romantic encounter with a young woman named Kaoru. And a story about two women named Yuki who live in apartments across the hall from each other. And another story whose narrator, frustrated that the protagonist refuses to go along with conventional plotlines, keeps changing the protagonist's name and going on with the story as planned. At first the woman is called Kazama Yukiko; then she becomes Kazama Yukiko; and then, switching genders three times in a row, Kazama Yukio, Kazama Yukiko, and Kazama Yukio. In Japanese, the pairs or groups of names in each work are pronounced the same, but they are written with different *kanji*. In English, the names become identical. I would not say it is impossible to translate the names, or the sentences or works in which they appear, from Japanese into English. Indeed, I would not even say it is *impossible* to translate the non-identicalness of the names: Yukiko, **Yukiko**, and *Yukiko* are different in *something like* the way 行子, 由希子, and 雪子 are different. But *something like* is not the same as *identical*. I can translate words and sentences, but I cannot translate the *way* in which they mean.

Ted Goossen
on *fuyukai*

"Translation is fundamentally an act of kindness," Haruki Murakami once wrote. "It is not enough to find words that match: if images in the translated text are unclear, then the thoughts and feelings of the author are lost."

When I started out, I was satisfied just to find those "words that match." As I was translating Naoya Shiga's short novel *Reconciliation* (和解, 1918) for my PhD thesis, though, I hit a wall—the word *fuyukai* (不愉快, "unpleasant," unhappy" or "uncomfortable" in the dictionaries). *Fuyukai* clearly sits at the center of the story: it appears thirty-eight times in the 105 pages, clustering around key moments at the beginning and end. Yet, try as I might, I could come up with no word that "matched" the varied situations where it appears, which range from the trivial (being forced to wait in a bank) to the potentially catastrophic (an imagined patricide).

It took me a long time to realize that I had to reverse my usual approach: instead of counting on the word to describe the context, I had to count on the context to tell me what the English equivalent should be. Some of you will recall the many lists (Squalid Things, Adorable Things, Things That Give a Clean Feeling, etc.) in Sei Shōnagon's *Pillow Book,* written a millennium ago. Well, this was somewhat similar. I had been given a series of "*fuyukai* things," which together traced the evolution of the hero's psyche, from dark and inward-turning to bright and outwardly focused. Instead of possessing a hard semantic core, *fuyukai* turned out to be a chameleon, a shape-shifter that changed with its surroundings.

Needless to say, there were times when this made me extremely *fuyukai*!

Note: Haruki's quote is taken from "As Translator, as Novelist: The Translator's Afterword," from the book *In Translation: Translators on Their Work and What It Means,* ed. Esther Allen and Susan Bernofsky (Columbia University Press, 2013), 171.

Sam Malissa
on mimetic words

Whenever I see a *guzuguzu,* a *poroporo,* a *zotto,* or one of a million other mimetic words, my heart sinks a little. Not because I can't translate them— the three I mentioned might be "dawdling," "raining down in heavy droplets," and "a chill down your spine," depending on the context—but because I know something key is missing.

Most of the time when I translate them, I feel I'm losing the auditory element. Mimetic words both show and tell. We have onomatopoeia that do this in English, but they tend to sound like they belong in a comic book—zap, vroom, kaboom—and they are fewer in number and poorer in nuance than mimetic words in Japanese. Japanese mimetic words apply to a far broader range of ideas than actual noises, including appearances, feelings, and ways of moving.

Words with sound effects that make no sound leave me feeling vaguely unsettled. *Kirakira* for something sparkling, *musutto* for a sullen attitude, or the one that language learners love to trot out to impress and confound their friends: *shiin,* the sound of silence. I offer myself a halfhearted reassurance that these are just rich "sense units" that I can convey in English with the right word choice, and not an actual sound (even though after working with the Japanese language for so long, I swear I can hear them).

Then there are the definite sonic experiences, like *zaa* for pouring rain, *guuguu* for someone snoring loudly, or *waiwai* for a clamor of excited voices. In these cases I feel I'm letting readers down because they're not hearing what a reader in Japanese is hearing.

At least there are some times where the English vocabulary of onomatopoeia can handle the job to reproduce the sound itself. I suppose I'll just have to be satisfied with words like *katakata, dokan,* and *gashan*—clickety-clack, boom, and crash!

Jay Rubin
on *kokoro*

A major problem in retranslating Haruki Murakami's *Sekai no owari to hādoboirudo wandārando* was what to do with the word *kokoro* (心). Several commentators have pointed out that the map of the town in the book's frontispiece looks rather like a picture of a brain and noted that, more than anything else, the novel is an imaginative exploration of the brain as the seat of the psyche. The key term in this context is *kokoro,* most often translated by Alfred Birnbaum in his 1991 *Hard-Boiled Wonderland and the End of the World* as "mind," and by me in my forthcoming *End of the World and Hard-Boiled Wonderland* as "heart." If my translation seems more emotional in tone, that difference will probably have a lot to do with how I render this particular word. Unfortunately, "mind" is too exclusively cerebral and "heart" too tipped toward the emotional for *kokoro,* which straddles the full territory, including the moral, as in Sōseki Natsume's 1911 classic novel, *Kokoro.* In some contexts, where *kokoro* refers not so much to the psyche but to its contents, I have tried to bridge the gap by referring to both thoughts and feelings. Meredith McKinney had the right idea when she glossed *kokoro* as "the thinking and feeling heart," but like Ineko Kondō and Edwin McClellan before her, the best she could do for the novel's title was to keep the Japanese word.

Ginny Tapley Takemori
on *irasshaimase*

It's hard to translate *sekkyaku yōgo* (接客用語), the formulaic language that we hear in stores, hotels, and essentially everywhere that deals with customers. Most of these can be dealt with using appropriate sounding phrases: *kashikomarimashita,* for example, can be "Certainly, sir," and *arigatō gozaimashita* can be "Thank you for your custom" (as in my translation of Sayaka Murata's *Convenience Store Woman*), or "Thank you for shopping with us," or even just "Thank you." But one word that simply has no equivalent is *irasshaimase,* the word all employees call out whenever a customer enters the premises, effectively acknowledging their presence. You could perhaps say, literally, "Welcome," but that often just sounds weird in an English context. Usually when I've come across it, it has only appeared once and had no particular importance, so I could easily fudge it with "Good morning," or something of the sort. But in *Convenience Store Woman* it was repeated regularly throughout the book, and even became a kind of special word in its own right. In the end I decided to leave it in Japanese. It is the one word that anyone who visits Japan will hear wherever they go, and it seemed like the obvious solution since it worked so well in the translation as a whole. Fortunately the editor agreed with me, and I recall some reviewers commenting on it being a good decision, which was gratifying.

Hitomi Yoshio
on sentence endings

Japanese sentence endings convey different levels of politeness and gendered expressions, and they give texture and nuance to the narrative voice, often serving to establish the tone of the entire work, but they are one of the most challenging aspects of the language to translate. Using the polite form of "desu" or "masu" in sentence endings can sound soft and gentle, and even colloquial depending on how they are used, whereas the neutral form of "da" or "de aru" can give a succinct and formal impression. Most works of fiction, with the exception of children's stories, are written in the latter form, but sometimes authors use the polite form to create a unique tone, especially in first-person narrative. A famous example of how this polite form is used to dramatic effect is Osamu Dazai's "Villon's Wife," which is narrated in the voice of a young woman. This short story has been elegantly translated by Donald Keene, but the rich texture of the narrative proved impossible to convey.

When it comes to dialogue, an author writing in Japanese must choose whether to use masculine (often thought of as "neutral") or feminine sentence endings. Japanese voiceovers for old movies and TV shows from the West tend to overly use what is imagined as "feminine" speech, adopting anachronistic sentence endings such as "da wa" or "kashira." Contemporary authors who are more attuned to gendered speech may choose not to use exaggerated forms, or in contrast consciously play with gendered language. In any case, the sentence endings are key in establishing the voice of the characters, whether the gender is clearly marked, noticeably absent, or used in a performative way. Mieko Kawakami is a master at this, often combining gendered speech with dialect. English is a much more neutral language, so translators have to be creative in finding alternative ways to convey this essential information, relying on such things as word choice and qualifiers to indicate the subtleties of gendered expressions. 🐵

Contributors

JEFFREY ANGLES (b. 1971) is a professor of Japanese language and literature at Western Michigan University. His translation of Hiromi Itō's novel *The Thorn Puller* will be published under the new Monkey imprint with Stone Bridge Press in 2022. He has also translated two poetry collections by Hiromi Itō: *Killing Kanoko* and *Wild Grass on the Riverbank* (Tilted Axis, 2020). His translation of the modernist classic *The Book of the Dead* by Shinobu Orikuchi (University of Minnesota Press, 2017) won both the Miyoshi Prize and the Scaglione Prize for translation. He is the author of *Writing the Love of Boys: Origins of Bishōnen Culture in Modernist Japanese Literature.* Angles is also a poet; his book of Japanese-language poems *Watashi no hizukehenkōsen* (My International Date Line) won the 68th Yomiuri Prize for Literature. His essay "Finding Mother" appeared in vol. 1 of *MONKEY.*

POLLY BARTON (b. 1984) is a translator of Japanese literature and nonfiction, based in the UK. Recent translations include *Spring Garden* by Tomoka Shibasaki (Pushkin Press), *Where the Wild Ladies Are* by Aoko Matsuda (Tilted Axis / Soft Skull Press), and *There's No Such Thing as an Easy Job* by Kikuko Tsumura (Bloomsbury). After being awarded the 2019 Fitzcarraldo Editions Essay Prize, in 2021 she published *Fifty Sounds,* her reflections on the Japanese language. Her translations of Aoko Matsuda's "Dissecting Misogyny" and Tomoka Shibasaki's "Dinner at Mine" appeared in vol. 1 of *MONKEY.*

SAM BETT (b. 1986) writes and translates fiction. In 2016 he was awarded Grand Prize by the Japanese government in the 2nd JLPP International Translation Competition for his translation of "A Peddler of Tears" by Yōko Ogawa, which appeared in vol. 7 of *Monkey Business.* He is also a founder and host of Us&Them, the quarterly Brooklyn-based reading series devoted to showcasing the work of writers who also translate. His translation of Yukio Mishima's *Star* (New Directions) won the 2019 Japan-U.S. Friendship Commission Prize for the Translation of Japanese Literature. With David Boyd, he is co-translating the novels of Mieko Kawakami for Europa Editions.

MICHAEL K. BOURDAGHS (b. 1961) is a professor of Japanese literature and culture at the University of Chicago. His book *Sayonara Amerika, Sayonara Nippon: A Geopolitical Prehistory of J-Pop* was published by Columbia University Press in 2012 and has been translated into Japanese. *The Dawn That Never Comes: Shimazaki Tōson and Japanese Nationalism* was published by Columbia in 2003.

DAVID BOYD (b. 1981) is an assistant professor of Japanese at the University of North Carolina at Charlotte. His translation, with Sam Bett, of Mieko Kawakami's *Breasts and Eggs* was published to great acclaim in 2020, and their translation of her novel *Heaven* appeared in spring 2021; they are currently working on a third novel. His work has appeared in *Monkey Business, Words Without Borders,* and *Granta,* among other literary journals. His translation of Hideo Furukawa's *Slow Boat* (Pushkin Press, 2017) won the 2017–18 Japan-U.S. Friendship Commission Prize for the Translation of Japanese Literature. He has translated two short novels by Hiroko Oyamada —*The Factory* (2019) and *The Hole* (2020)—for New Directions. His translations of Kuniko Mukōda's "Nori and Eggs for Breakfast," Hiroko Oyamada's "Something Sweet," and Kanoko Okamoto's "Sushi" appeared in vol. 1 of *MONKEY.*

ROSE BUNDY (1951–2021) was Professor Emerita of East Asian Studies, Kalamazoo College, at the time of her death on March 17, 2021. Her scholarly work primarily focused on *waka,* and she published on the poetry of Japan's medieval court as well as on the issue of gender in poetry contests of the same period. She also published a number of translations of the poetry of Fujiwara Shunzei and Shikishi Naishinnō in the journal *Transference* and a study and translation of Izumi Shikibu's "Gojusshu waka" (Fifty-Poem Sequence), in which the poet mourns the death of her lover Prince Atsumichi (*Japanese Language and Literature,* 2020). She translated a number of works by Yūko Tsushima; an excerpt from her 1987 novella *Hikari kagayaku itten o* (A Single Point of Brilliant Light) appears in this issue of *MONKEY.*

ANDREW CAMPANA (b. 1989) is an assistant professor of Japanese literature at Cornell University. He has been published widely as a translator and as a poet in both English and Japanese, and is currently working on a manuscript on Japanese poetry from the twentieth and twenty-first centuries, exploring how poets have engaged with new technologies, such as cinema, tape recording, the internet, and augmented reality. His collection "Seven Modern Poets on Food" was published in vol. 1 of *MONKEY.*

ANNA ELLIOTT (b. 1963) is the director of the MFA in Literary Translation at Boston University. She is a translator of modern Japanese literature into Polish. Best known for her translations of Haruki Murakami, she has also translated Yukio Mishima, Banana Yoshimoto, and Junichirō Tanizaki. She is the author of a Polish-language monograph on gender in Murakami's writing, a literary guidebook to Murakami's Tokyo, and several articles on Murakami and European translation practices relating to contemporary Japanese fiction.

MICHAEL EMMERICH (b. 1975) teaches Japanese literature at the University of California, Los Angeles. An award-winning translator, he has translated books by Gen'ichirō Takahashi, Hiromi Kawakami, and Hideo Furukawa, among others. He is the author of *The Tale of Genji: Translation, Canonization, and World Literature* (Columbia University Press, 2013) and *Tentekomai: bungaku wa hi kurete michi tōshi* (Goryū Shoin, 2018) and the editor of *Read Real Japanese Fiction* (Kodansha) and *Short Stories in Japanese: New Penguin Parallel Text.* His translations of Masatsugu Ono, Makoto Takayanagi, and others have appeared in *Monkey Business* and *MONKEY.*

BRIAN EVENSON (b. 1966) is the author of more than a dozen books of fiction. His most recent work includes two story collections, *Song for the Unraveling of the World* and *The Glassy, Burning Floor of Hell.* "A Report on Hands," "A Report on Squares," and "A Report on Chimney Sweeps" appeared in vol. 7 of *Monkey Business.*

HIDEO FURUKAWA (b. 1966) is one of the most innovative writers in Japan today. His novel *Belka, Why Don't You Bark?* was translated by Michael Emmerich; his partly fictional reportage *Horses, Horses, in the End the Light Remains Pure: A Tale That Begins with Fukushima* was translated by Doug Slaymaker with Akiko Takenaka; and his short novel *Slow Boat* was translated by David Boyd. His stories have appeared in every issue of *Monkey Business* and now *MONKEY*; vol. 1 of *Monkey Business* features an interview with Haruki Murakami by Hideo Furukawa.

MORGAN GILES (b. 1987) is a literary translator and critic based in London. Her translation of Yu Miri's *Tokyo Ueno Station* (Tilted Axis / Riverhead) won the National Book Award for Translated Literature in 2020, and she is currently at work on Yu Miri's *The End of August,* forthcoming from Tilted Axis. She has also translated short fiction by authors including Hideo Furukawa, Hitomi Kanehara, and Nao-cola Yamazaki, with work appearing in *Granta, Wasafiri,* and *Words Without Borders,* among other literary journals. Her criticism regularly appears in the *Times Literary Supplement.*

TED GOOSSEN (b. 1948) teaches Japanese literature and film at York University in Toronto. He is the editor of *The Oxford Book of Japanese Short Stories.* He translated Haruki Murakami's *Wind/Pinball* and *The Strange Library,* and co-translated (with Philip Gabriel) *Men Without Women* and *Killing Commendatore.* His translations of Hiromi Kawakami's *People from My Neighbourhood* (Granta Books) and Naoya Shiga's *Reconciliation* (Canongate) were published in 2020. His translations of Sachiko Kishimoto, Kawakami, Shiga, and others are featured in vols. 1–7 of *Monkey Business* and in *MONKEY,* vol. 1.

LAIRD HUNT (b. 1968) has written eight novels, including, most recently, *Zorrie,* as well as *Indiana, Indiana* and *Kind One,* which was a finalist for the 2013 PEN/Faulkner Award for Fiction. *Neverhome* was published in 2014 to great acclaim. "Star Date" appeared in vol. 5 of *Monkey Business.*

HIROMI ITŌ (b. 1955) is one of the most important voices in contemporary Japanese poetry. English translations of her poetry collections include *Killing Kanoko* and *Wild Grass on the Riverbank,* both translated by Jeffrey Angles. *Monkey Business* vols. 5, 6, and 7 and vol. 1 of *MONKEY* featured excerpts from her novel *The Thorn Puller,* which will be published in 2022 by Stone Bridge Press.

SEIKŌ ITŌ (b. 1961) is a writer, performer, and one of the pioneers of Japanese rap. His novel *Imagination Radio* (2013) reflects on the March 2011 earthquake and nuclear disaster through the eyes of a deejay. He also writes nonfiction, including a 2017 book on Doctors Without Borders. Itō has long been interested in Noh, and he and Jay Rubin have collaborated with Grand Master Kazufusa Hōshō in a contemporary performance of the traditional Noh play *Hagoromo*; Rubin's translation appeared in vol. 1 of *MONKEY.*

YASUNARI KAWABATA (1899–1972) won the Nobel Prize for Literature in 1968 for his strikingly visual and lyrical novels, among them *Snow Country, The Sound of the Mountain,* and *Beauty and Sadness.* He was first published in the *Atlantic Monthly* in 1955, with "The Izu Dancer." As president of PEN Japan from 1948 to 1965, he encouraged the translation of Japanese literature.

HIROMI KAWAKAMI (b. 1958) is one of Japan's leading novelists. Many of her books have been published in English, including *Manazuru,* translated by Michael Emmerich; *Record of a Night Too Brief,* translated by Lucy North; and *The Nakano Thrift Shop, Parade: A Folktale, Strange Weather in Tokyo* (aka *The Briefcase*), and *The Ten Loves of Nishino,* translated by Allison Markin Powell. "The Dragon Palace" appeared in vol. 3 of *Monkey Business* and "Hazuki and Me" in vol. 5. "Banana" appeared in vol. 4 and was included in *The Best Small Fictions 2015* (Queen's Ferry Press). *People from My Neighbourhood,* translated by Ted Goossen, was published by Granta Books in 2020. The series continues to be featured in both the Japanese and English editions of *MONKEY.*

MIEKO KAWAKAMI (b. 1976) is an award-winning novelist, poet, singer, and actress. Her novel *Breasts and Eggs,* translated by Sam Bett and David Boyd, was published by Europa Editions in 2020 to great acclaim. *Heaven,* also co-translated by Bett and Boyd, was published in 2021, and a third novel will be released in 2022. Her short novel *Ms Ice Sandwich* (Pushkin Press, 2020) was translated by Louise Heal Kawai. Her short stories and prose poems, translated by Hitomi Yoshio, appeared in vols. 1–7 of *Monkey Business.* "Good Stories Originate in the Caves of Antiquity," a conversation with Haruki Murakami, was published in *MONKEY,* vol. 1.

SATOSHI KITAMURA (b. 1956) is an award-winning picture-book author and illustrator. His own books include *Stone Age Boy, Millie's Marvellous Hat,* and *The Smile Shop.* He has worked with numerous authors and poets. His graphic narratives appeared in vols. 5–7 of *Monkey Business:* "Mr. Quote" in vol. 7, "Igor Nocturnov" in vol. 6, and "Variation and Theme," inspired by a Charles Simic poem, in vol. 5. In vol. 1 of *MONKEY,* he published "The Heart of the Lunchbox."

JUN'ICHI KONUMA (b. 1959) is a well-known music and literary critic and a professor of music culture at Waseda University. He has written extensively on both popular culture and high culture; among his most important subjects are Tōru Takemitsu, Bach, and Colin McPhee. He was awarded the Idemitsu Music Prize in 1998 for his critical writing. He has published numerous books, including a recent collection of his own poetry, *Sotto.*

SAM MALISSA (b. 1981) holds a PhD in Japanese literature from Yale University. His translations include *Bullet Train* by Kōtaro Isaka (Harvill Secker, 2021), *The End of the Moment We Had* by Toshiki Okada (Pushkin Press, 2018), and short fiction by Shun Medoruma, Hideo Furukawa, and Masatsugu Ono. His translation of Kyōhei Sakaguchi's "Forest of the Ronpa" appeared in vol. 1 of *MONKEY.*

AOKO MATSUDA (b. 1979) is a writer and translator. In 2013 her debut *Stackable* was nominated for the Mishima Yukio Prize and the Noma Literary New Face Prize. In 2019 her short story "The Woman Dies" (from the collection *The Year of No Wild Flowers*), translated by Polly Barton and published by Granta online, was shortlisted for a Shirley Jackson Award. Her short novel *The Girl Who Is Getting Married* was published by Strangers Press in 2016. She has translated work by Karen Russell, Amelia Gray, and Carmen Maria Machado into Japanese. Her stories appeared in vols. 5–7 of *Monkey Business,* translated by Jeffrey Angles. "Dissecting Misogyny," translated by Polly Barton, appeared in vol. 1 of *MONKEY.*

ERIC McCORMACK (b. 1938) is a Scottish-born Canadian writer who skillfully blends elements of gothic fiction, black humor, metafiction, magic realism, and straightforward good storytelling. He has published a collection of stories and five novels, including *The Paradise Motel, First Blast of the Trumpet Against the Monstrous Regiment of Women,* and *The Dutch Wife.* His most recent novel, *Cloud* (Penguin, 2014), was translated by Motoyuki Shibata and published in Japan.

TAKI MONMA (b. 1933) is a novelist and short story writer who lives in Saitama, near Tokyo. Four of her stories, translated by Ted Goossen, appeared in vols. 3–5 and 7 of *Monkey Business.* Her work has been published in the Japanese editions of *Monkey Business* and *MONKEY.*

HARUKI MURAKAMI (b. 1949) is one of the world's best-known and best-loved novelists. All his major novels—including *Hardboiled Wonderland and the End of the World, The Wind-Up Bird Chronicle,* and *1Q84*—have been translated into dozens of languages. "On Writing Short Stories" in vol. 7 of *Monkey Business* is the second half of his conversation with Motoyuki Shibata, published in vol. 9 (Summer/Fall 2016) of the Japanese *MONKEY.* An interview by Hideo Furukawa appeared in vol. 1 of *Monkey Business.* His essays "The Great Cycle of Storytelling" and

"So What Shall I Write About?" appeared in vol. 2 and vol. 5 of *Monkey Business.* Vol. 4 of *Monkey Business* includes an essay by Richard Powers on Murakami's fiction.

HIROKO OYAMADA (b. 1983) is one of Japan's most promising young writers. Her short novels *The Factory* and *The Hole* were translated by David Boyd and published by New Directions. Her story "Spider Lily" was translated by Juliet Winters Carpenter and published in the Japan issue of *Granta* (Spring 2014). "Lost in the Zoo" and "Extra Innings," translated by David Boyd, appeared in vols. 6 and 7 of *Monkey Business.* "Something Sweet," also translated by David Boyd, was published in vol. 1 of *MONKEY.*

JAY RUBIN (b. 1941) is professor emeritus of Japanese literature at Harvard University. One of the principal translators of Haruki Murakami, he translated *The Wind-Up Bird Chronicle, Norwegian Wood, After Dark, 1Q84* (co-translated with Philip Gabriel), *After the Quake: Stories,* and *Absolutely on Music: Conversations with Seiji Ozawa.* Among his many other translations are *Rashōmon and Seventeen Other Stories* by Ryūnosuke Akutagawa and *The Miner* and *Sanshirō* by Sōseki Natsume. He is the author of *Haruki Murakami and the Music of Words* and the editor of *The Penguin Book of Japanese Short Stories.* His translations into English of Itō Seikō's modern Japanese translations of Noh plays appear in *MONKEY.*

KYŌHEI SAKAGUCHI (b. 1978) is a writer, artist, and architect. His work explores alternative ways of being, as in his books *Zero Yen House* and *Build Your Own Independent Nation.* His novel *Haikai Taxi* was nominated for the Yukio Mishima Prize in 2014. "Forest of the Ronpa," translated by Sam Malissa, was published in vol. 1 of *MONKEY.*

TOMOKA SHIBASAKI (b. 1973) is a novelist, short story writer and essayist. Her books include *Awake or Asleep, Viridian,* and *In the City Where I Wasn't.* She won the Akutagawa Prize in 2014 with *Spring Garden,* which has been translated by Polly Barton

(Pushkin Press). "The Seaside Road" appeared in vol. 2 of *Monkey Business,* "The Glasses Thief" in vol. 3, "Background Music" in vol. 6, translated by Ted Goossen, and "Peter and Janis" in vol. 7, translated by Christopher Lowy. "Dinner at Mine," translated by Polly Barton, appeared in vol. 1 of *MONKEY.*

MOTOYUKI SHIBATA (b. 1954) translates American literature and runs the Japanese literary journal *MONKEY*. He has translated Paul Auster, Rebecca Brown, Stuart Dybek, Steve Erickson, Brian Evenson, Laird Hunt, Kelly Link, Steven Millhauser, and Richard Powers, among others. His translation of Mark Twain's *Adventures of Huckleberry Finn* was a bestseller in Japan in 2018. Among his recent translations is Eric McCormack's *Cloud*.

TATSUHIKO SHIBUSAWA (1928–1987) was a prolific translator of French literature, known for his translations of the Marquis de Sade and the French surrealists. He wrote several collections of short stories, but *Takaoka's Travels* was his only novel. Shibusawa is also known for his essays, which deal with topics from dreams to the occult. He was a friend of Yukio Mishima, who based the character Yasushi Imanishi in *The Temple of Dawn* on Shibusawa.

JORDAN A.Y. SMITH (b. 1976) is an associate professor at Josai International University, where he teaches literary translation, Japanese culture, and comparative literature. He has translated poetry by Gōzō Yoshimasu (published in *Alice Iris Red Horse,* New Directions, 2016), Noriko Mizuta (*The Road Home,* 2015; *Sea of Blue Algae,* 2016), Tahi Saihate, and other contemporary poets in Japan. He is editor-in-chief of *Tokyo Poetry Journal* and co-creator of *The New Japanese Poetry,* a BBC Radio 4 series. As a poet, he has co-authored two volumes and published one collection, *Syzygy* (Awai Books, 2020). His translation of Hideo Furukawa's "Counterfeiting García Márquez" appeared in vol. 1 of *MONKEY.*

GINNY TAPLEY TAKEMORI (b. 1962) has translated fiction by more than a dozen early modern and contemporary Japanese writers. Her translations of Sayaka Murata's *Convenience Store Woman* (2018) and *Earthlings* (2020) were published to great acclaim. Her translation of Kyōko Nakajima 's Naoki Prize–winning *The Little House* was published in 2019. With Ian MacDonald, she translated Nakajima's *Things Remembered and Things Forgotten* (2021). Together with translators Lucy North and Allison Markin Powell, she is one of the cofounders of the collective Strong Women, Soft Power, which promotes Japanese women writers and their translators.

KIKUKO TSUMURA (b. 1978) is a writer from Osaka, and she often uses Osaka dialect in work. She has won numerous Japanese literary awards, including the Akutagawa Prize and the Noma Literary New Face Prize. Her first short story translated into English, "The Water Tower and the Turtle," won a PEN/Robert J. Dau Short Story Prize for Emerging Writers. Her novel *There's No Such Thing as an Easy Job,* translated by Polly Barton, was published by Bloomsbury in 2020.

YŪKO TSUSHIMA (1947–2016) was a prolific Japanese fiction writer, essayist, and critic. Called "an archeologist of the female psyche" (*Village Voice*) and "one of the most important Japanese writers of her generation" (*New York Times*), Tsushima won numerous awards for her writing. Three of her novels, *Child of Fortune, Woman Running in the Mountains,* and *Territory of Light,* and one of her story collections, *The Shooting Gallery,* were translated by Geraldine Harcourt. Her novel *Laughing Wolf* won the Jirō Osaragi Prize in 2001, and was translated by Dennis Washburn. Tsushima was the daughter of the celebrated Japanese novelist Osamu Dazai (1909–1948).

HITOMI YOSHIO (b. 1979) is an associate professor at Waseda University. She specializes in modern and contemporary Japanese literature, with a focus on women's writing. Her translations of Mieko Kawakami's works have appeared in *Denver Quarterly, Freeman's, Granta, Monkey Business, Words Without Borders,* and *The Penguin Book of Japanese Short Stories.*

BARRY YOURGRAU (b. 1949) is a writer of very short stories. His collection *Wearing Dad's Head* was reissued in 2016, and *A Man Jumps Out of an Airplane* in 2017. His memoir *Mess: One Man's Struggle to Clean Up His House and His Act* was published in 2015. His stories appeared in vols. 1–3 of *Monkey Business.* "Private Tour," a companion piece to *Mess,* appeared in vol. 7, and "Goose" appeared in vol. 1 of *MONKEY.* His work regularly appears in the Japanese *MONKEY,* translated by Motoyuki Shibata.

Credits

Page 5: *Amabie,* acrylic on papier-mâché, 2020 © Asako Tabata.

Page 6: *Amabie,* oil on canvas, 2020 © Asako Tabata.

Pages 14–15: *Contrails,* oil on canvas, 2012 © Scott Waters.

Pages 19–33: Graphic narrative © Satoshi Kitamura.

Pages 34–45: Illustrations © Johnny Wales.

Page 46: *La Paintine 35,* acrylic and oil pastel, 2021 © Matt Currie.

Page 48: Artwork © Akiko and Masako Takada.

Pages 54–55: Illustration © Taiyō Matsumoto.

Page 56: Detail from the cover illustration © Taiyō Matsumoto.

Page 68: Illustration © Alina Skyson and Sara Wong / TOOGL.

Page 74: Illustration © Johnny Wales.

Page 76: Photograph © Yoshiaki Kanda.

Page 83: Illustration © Diana Thorneycroft.

Page 98: Illustration © Lauren Tamaki.

Page 108: Artwork © Hiroaki Kuwabara.

Pages 110–11: *Guava* (1955), Gira Sarabhai's home, Ahmedabad, India, 1955 © 2021 Calder Foundation, New York / Artists Rights Society (ARS), New York

Pages 120–24: Illustrations © Justine Wong.

Page 126: Illustration © Sara Wong / TOOGL.

Page 129: *Mount Rokkō,* woodcut, 1916 © Rinsaku Akamatsu

Pages 130–31: Illustration © Isabella Fassler.

Page 136: Illustration © Nicole Xu.

Page 144: *The Surface of Lake Ezu,* pastel on paper, 2021 © Kyōhei Sakaguchi.

Page 150: *Entering the Lake,* pastel on paper, 2021 © Kyōhei Sakaguchi.

Page 156: Illustration © Lis Xu.

Page 162: Illustration © Sara Wong / TOOGL.

Page 165: Illustration © Alina Skyson / TOOGL.

ETEL ADNAN · ADONIS · CÉSAR AIRA · FADHIL AL-AZZAWI · SVETLANA ALEXIEVICH · IBRAHIM AL-KONI · OSAMA ALOMAR · TAHAR BEN JELLOUN · ROBERTO BOLAÑO · JAVIER CERCAS · MAHMOUD DARWISH · ANANDA DEVI · ALFRED DÖBLIN · ÁLVARO ENRIGUE · JENNY ERPENBECK · ELENA FERRANTE · GEORGI GOSPODINOV · JOÃO GUIMARÃES ROSA · RODRIGO HASBÚN · YURI HERRERA · PAWEL HUELLE · ISMAIL KADARE · HAN KANG · MIEKO KAWAKAMI · ETGAR KERET · YOUNG-HA KIM · J. M. G. ... YAN LIANKE · VALERIA LUISE... ...IN MABANCKOU · NAGUIB MAHFO... ...HERTA MÜLLER MUXIN · NAIVO ... ...BLO NERUDA · ANDRES NEUMA... ...ER PETTERSON RICARDO PIGLI... ...KE SCHMITTER SAMANTA SCHW... ...URHAN SÖNMEZ DOMENICO STA... ...HIROMI ITO · GOLI TARAGHI ... ...AVKA UGREŠIĆ KO UN · MARLE... ...VERHAEGHEN · SUSY DELGADO · CAN XUE · A.B. YEHOSHUA · NEGAR DJAVADI · ARMÉNIO VIEIRA · ENRIQUE VILA-MATAS · TRIFONIA MELIBEA OBONO · JOHANNES ANYURU · OLGA TOKARCZUK · WANG WEI · NORAH LANGE · NONA FERNÁNDEZ · IGIABA SCEGO · SERGIO CHEJFEC · ALIA TRABUCCO ZERÁN · MAAZA MENGISTE · ANDRÉS NEUMAN · JUAN JOSÉ SAER · W. G. SEBALD · ÉVELYNE TROUILLOT · JUAN VILLORO · LIU XIA · RABINDRANATH TAGORE · YOKO TAWADA · LÁSZLÓ KRASZNAHORKAI

WORDS WITHOUT BORDERS

THE ONLINE MAGAZINE FOR INTERNATIONAL LITERATURE

2,600 writers · 139 countries · 125 languages
A world of literature awaits.

Sign up for a free subscription:
wordswithoutborders.org/subscribe

The best literary publication in North America.
— Annie Proulx

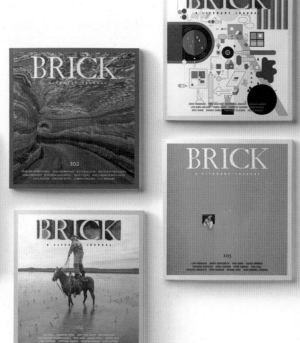

BRICKMAG.COM
🐦 📘 📷 @brickliterary

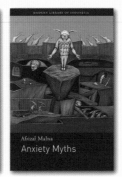

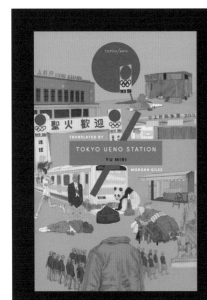
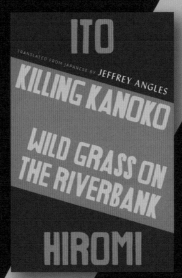
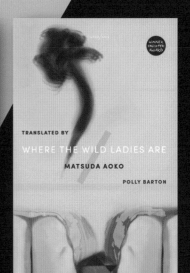

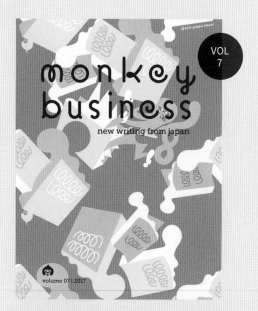
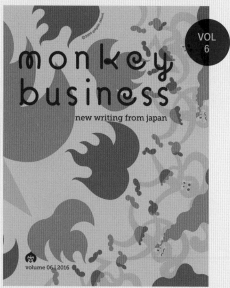

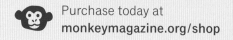

The FOOD issue

VOLUME 1 | 2020

MONKEY
NEW WRITING FROM JAPAN

GRAB YOUR OWN COPY TODAY

MONKEY

MONKEY CELEBRATES
MONKEY New Writing from Japan

SWITCH PUBLISHING   *www.switch-store.net*